M000313212

THE ARRANGEMENT

MIRANDA RIJKS

INKUBATOR
BOOKS

PROLOGUE

She's looking pretty this evening.

I watch as she skips down to Kalk Bay's main road, her silken blonde hair bouncing, dressed in skinny jeans, a pale-pink chiffon blouse and ankle boots that clip-clop on the tarmac. Excitement and anticipation are etched into her young face. And who wouldn't be exhilarated, holidaying here in South Africa for the very first time? The fiery red sun has just set, and darkness is descending rapidly. Even so, the slow traffic is incessant on this busy coastal road, and she has to dart between cars to make it across to the other side. She is brave. I'll give her that.

The Kaleida Bar is wedged between the road and the railway line, but when you're seated on the veranda, you don't notice the train tracks. You get the impression that the sea is within touching distance. It's only when the occasional train clatters past, just metres away from the edge of the ocean, you realise the waves are a little further away than you thought. It's a busy establishment that attracts South African locals and tourists in equal numbers. But not tonight. It's winter here on the Cape, the quiet season.

By 7 p.m., the air is chilly, and soon she'll need to wear that parka she's carrying, clutched in front of the cross-body bag that flaps against her stomach. She walks briskly along the pavement, as if she's a fly attracted to the strong beat of the electronic dance music pulsing through the Kaleida Bar. She turns to look in my direction and I slip backwards, into the shadows of the closed antiques shop. A second later she has disappeared into the bar, but that's ok; I lick my lips and savour the salted air.

There is a veranda outside, barely used during these winter months. The occasional smoker comes out for a few hasty puffs, but they won't be interested in me. I take my place and watch her inside. She's at the bar now, speaking eagerly with the young man who spends a little too long serving her. She takes her drink, a Coke by the looks of it, to a table for two right near the window, with a great view of the waves smashing the rocks below. Let's hope she savours her last ever drink.

She waits.

And she waits.

She glances at her watch. Her phone.

And she waits.

She makes a call, but talks to no one.

She flicks through social media, or perhaps she is playing a game on her phone. I can't see from here.

Two whole hours she waits, nursing just the one drink. I send her a text then, apologizing for the delay, saying I've picked up a local SIM card, and telling her I'll meet her by the tidal pool, suggesting if it's warm enough, perhaps we could take a skinny-dip.

It's the moment I've been waiting for.

Her face lights up, a peachy blush on her cheeks, visible even from this distance. She hops up and asks the barman something. Directions to the tidal pool and the beach, perhaps, as it's not obvious how to get there from here.

And then I follow her. Along the pavement. She hesitates as she looks at the concrete steps and the dark underpass. She glances over her shoulder, but she sees no one, so she hurries briskly down the stairs and into the dark and threatening subway that goes underneath the railway line and back up the other side. It's poorly lit here. Not a place to be after dark where the ocean crashes up and over the slippery rocks, pulling and pushing fresh water into the tidal pool. Not a place to be when all you can hear is the roar of the waves and all you can see are the shadows thrown from a faded moon.

She is standing adjacent to the pool, jiggling up and down to ward off the cold and turning her back to the ocean to prevent herself from being soaked by the icy spray from the sea. Stupid, stupid girl. No one should be alone out here at this time of night. Has she seen the sign that says 'Beware of the sharks'? Hasn't she realised that humans are her most likely predators?

As she swivels to look at the steps and the underpass, staring in vain for her lover, I creep up behind her, my feet silent on the sand. When she turns, I plunge the knife into her heart and she gasps, crumpling onto the sand in a concertina movement. A look of terror and dismay contorts her pretty face. She tries to say something to me, but it comes out as an indistinguishable gurgle.

'Too late,' I murmur. 'Every action has a consequence.'

I turn and walk away, sliding back into the shadows, ready to dispose of the knife and ready to make my way home.

1

The mundane becomes so significant in the instant that your life changes for ever.

I am putting a load of washing in the machine. Whites. I spot one of Ella's black socks just before I close the door. I growl. At seventeen, Ella is still so careless. Is it really that difficult to separate your darks from your lights?

I think of Abi and wonder where she is getting her washing done. Cape Town has had a series of droughts. Will the lady in her Airbnb do it for her, or will she have to wash her smalls in the sink? Or perhaps the water situation is so bad, she won't be able to wash her clothes at all.

And then the front doorbell chimes. Sighing, I walk through our small kitchen into the hall and peer through the spyhole in the front door. It's a couple. A man and a woman, smartly dressed.

In that instant, I know.

I fumble with the lock.

'Grace Woods?' the man asks.

I nod, but I'm already gripping the doorframe.

'I am Detective Inspector Pete Fairisle, and this is my

colleague, Sergeant Linda Hornby. May we come in?' They show me their badges, but I can't look. I just nod again and stand to one side so they can pass me. They wait for me to step in front of them, their backs up against the whitewashed wall, their heads against the framed watercolours of flowers painted by Ella and given to me for Christmas. I want this couple to walk straight back out of the house, but as they stare at me expectantly, I realise I have no choice. I lead them into my small living room.

They sit next to each other on my teal sofa, both of them leaning forwards, their hands on their knees. They're dressed as if they're about to sell me life insurance. I know they're not. I hover in front of my comfy armchair covered with the peacock-coloured throw that Mum knitted before she died.

'Please sit down, Mrs Woods.'

I do as I'm told. It's strange how they have instantly taken control, even though they're the strangers in my home.

'I'm afraid we have very bad news. Your daughter Abigail has been found dead in Cape Town.'

It feels as if my head is going to explode, as if all the blood has rushed up to my skull and my brain is being turned into mush.

'No!' I whisper. 'It's not possible. I only spoke to her yesterday. You must have the wrong person.'

The policewoman – I've already forgotten her name – leans forwards. She's near enough to touch me, but she doesn't. 'I'm sorry, Mrs Woods, but her body has been positively identified. She was wearing a small crossover bag. Her passport along with a prepaid foreign currency card was in a money belt she wore around her waist, under her T-shirt.' She takes out her phone and shows me a photograph of Abi's brown leather bag, the one that Ella gave her last Christmas. There is a spot of red on it. I stand up.

I hear a scream then. So loud, it is ear-piercing. My knees

and feet can no longer support me and I collapse in a puddle onto the floor. The scream goes on and on.

'Mrs Woods. Grace.' The policewoman crouches down on the rug in front of the fireplace, right next to me. The policeman appears with a cup of tea. Where did he get it from? How did he make that so quickly? I notice that he's holding one of my blue-and-white polka-dot mugs. He passes it to his colleague.

'Try to drink this,' she says, holding the mug out towards me, but my hands are shaking too much to grasp it.

'My baby.' I shake my head from side to side. It can't be true. Abi is twenty-one years old, with a dazzling future ahead of her. I knew she shouldn't have gone to Cape Town. I had a bad feeling about it and I didn't listen to my gut.

'What happened?' My voice sounds hoarse, foreign to me. I am sitting on an armchair now, but I don't recall moving from the floor to the chair.

'I'm afraid she was stabbed to death.'

'No!' I wail, my body rocking backwards and forwards. Some of the tea has spilled on the floor. The policewoman is dabbing it with a tea towel embroidered with daisies, my tea towel. I am glad it has spilled on the fake wood lino and not the rug; it won't stain.

Why the hell am I thinking about the floor when they have just told me that my baby girl is dead? What is wrong with me?

'Is there someone we can call?' the policeman asks.

'Bob. Oh God, and Ella!'

'Who are Bob and Ella?' the policewoman asks kindly. Only now do I notice she has the clearest pale blue eyes I have ever seen. What a horrible job these two have, breaking devastating news. She asks again, 'Bob? Ella?'

'Bob is my ex-husband and Ella is my daughter. She'll be on her way home from college soon. How am I going to tell her?' I wring my hands as the tears pour down my cheeks like rivers. I don't think I'll ever stop crying. Do my eyes have an infinite quantity of tears? I hope so.

'We will call your ex-husband and ask him to come over. Is there anyone else you would like us to call?'

I shake my head.

Time stops then. It is impossible for Bob to get to my house in less than half an hour, but it seems as if he arrives within a couple of minutes. He walks into my house for the first time in five years, his green tie lopsided, his face grey. He knows. They have already told him. I throw myself into his arms, and after a moment's hesitation, he hugs me so tightly, it feels as if all the air is being squeezed from my lungs. I am grateful. I am surprised by his stomach, which is large and solid. The new wife must be feeding him well. My tears soak the right shoulder of his white shirt. I can feel him trembling, or perhaps it is me. Eventually Bob pulls away and I feel doubly bereft. Bob is no longer mine. The last time we touched each other was nearly ten years ago.

'Ella. Where is she?' Bob asks with a croaky voice.

I glance at my watch, but it is difficult to see the hands with my tear-filled eyes. 'She gets home just after 5 p.m. Oh God, I can't tell her!'

'I'll stay. I will tell her.' Bob squeezes my hand. He turns to the policeman and woman, who have resumed their places on the sofa. 'What happened?'

'I'm sorry, Mr Woods, but your daughter was stabbed. Abi died at the scene on a beach in Cape Town. It would have been quick.'

But they don't know that, do they? How long was my baby fighting for her life? Why wasn't anyone there to help her? Where were Becky and Ethan?

'Becky?' I ask.

'Who is Becky?'

'Abi's best friend,' I say. 'She was meeting Becky and Ethan in Cape Town. That's why she went. They've been travelling on their gap year, and Abi went for three weeks to spend some time with them.'

The detectives glance at each other. 'We are not aware of any other victims. It seems that Abi was alone when she was attacked. We will, of course, liaise closely with the team in Cape Town. Can you give us contact details for Becky and Ethan?'

Bob takes over then, because I can't. My mouth opens and closes again. The tears rip through my chest. Why? Why did it happen to Abi?

I THINK BACK to just three days ago. Abi was so excited to go to Cape Town. Unlike many of her friends, she decided not to take a gap year and accepted her place at Durham University to read history. We were so proud of her. No one in either of our families had been to university. Bob studied electrical engineering at a college in Crawley; I got some basic hairdressing qualifications, but mainly learned on the job. Although Abi said she just wanted to get on with her degree and not waste a year travelling, we all knew the real reason was she couldn't afford to lounge around for a year. Or more to the point, we couldn't afford to support her. Bob is a good man, and whilst our divorce was acrimonious at the time, he has never failed to pay child support and is as generous as he can be towards our girls. But he has a new wife now and a five-year-old son. Abi and Ella are no longer his first priority.

It had crossed my mind that Abi might be jealous of Becky and Ethan as they went off on their six-month grand tour of Africa, but Abi assured me that she was fine about it. Although there is only four months difference in age, Abi was born in July and Becky in October, so Abi ended up the year ahead of Becky at school, not that it stopped them from being the best of friends. Of course, things changed with Abi at university and Becky still at school.

Abi loved university; she made plenty of new friends and told me she enjoyed her course. Apparently, her second-year exams went well, and she reckoned she might even get a first if she worked really hard next year. For the entire two years at uni, she had a part-time job as a barista at Café Blanco, and this past year she saved up so she could pay for her flight to Cape Town, excited about meeting up with Becky and Ethan. I was disappointed that she didn't come home straight after her second-year exams, but she explained she needed to work more shifts to pay for the holiday. I understood.

It was the middle of June when Abi eventually returned to Horsham, just five days before she was due to fly. I asked her where she was staying in Cape Town.

'I'll see when I get there.' She shrugged in that infuriating manner young people have of assuming that everything will just pan out.

'Cape Town isn't like Durham or even Newcastle!' I exclaimed. 'You need to pre-book accommodation. Have Becky and Ethan booked anywhere?'

She shrugged and rolled her eyes.

'Do you know that Cape Town is one of the murder capitals of the world?' I asked. How prophetic that was.

'Chill, Mum!' She groaned. 'I'll message Becky.'

I watched as her fingers raced across the screen of her phone, not for the first time marveling how quickly she typed. The phone pinged several times.

'They haven't booked anywhere yet,' Abi said. 'It's no big deal!'

I disagreed, so I sent an email to Ruth, Ethan's mother, and Natasha, Becky's mother, both lifelong friends, and asked if they knew where the kids were planning on staying in Cape Town. Natasha came back to me first.

Becky said Abi is sorting accommodation.

I ground my teeth. Typical Abi.

'Abi, you're meant to be sorting out somewhere to stay,' I shouted upstairs.

'Whatever,' she replied.

Abi, Becky and Ethan might have considered it no big deal, but I disagreed. I spent the next two hours researching places to stay in the vicinity of Cape Town, cross-checking between Trip-Advisor and various accommodation booking sites. Eventually, I settled on a small town half an hour south of Cape Town called Kalk Bay. It looked delightful with a harbour, quirky shops and beautiful beaches. And so, I booked two rooms in a charming bed and breakfast in Kalk Bay, a couple of streets up from the beach. The photograph of the landlady showed a white woman in her fifties, with a wide, open smile and a mane of brown hair piled on top of her head. The house looked stunning – all white walls, teak floors and brightly coloured paintings.

June was not the best time of year to visit Cape Town, but that didn't seem to dampen Abi's excitement. The furthest she had travelled was Turkey, so this was an experience of a lifetime. I insisted on driving her to Gatwick Airport and waving her off. She strode through the airport several steps ahead of me with a large rucksack on her back, and it struck me that she walked with a new confidence, as if during the past year she had found herself. Her hair was streaked with highlights, done well and not by me. My little girl had morphed into a beautiful young woman after two years away at university.

After she checked in, I accompanied her to the gates at passport control.

'Bye, Mum,' she said nonchalantly.

But I had a feeling then. *Don't let her go. It's not safe.* Or is it only with the benefit of hindsight that I thought I may never see her again?

I grabbed her and pulled her into an awkward hug. I buried my face in her hair, breathing in the cherry blossom scent of her shampoo, along with a new expensive-smelling perfume. I put my hands on her cheeks and tugged her face towards me, placing a lingering kiss on her soft, peach-like forehead.

'Euch, you're embarrassing me, Mum!' she said, laughing as she pulled away. 'I'm only going for three weeks.'

'I know.' But that sense of unease niggled in my abdomen. 'You will take care, you promise me?'

'Yeah. Stop worrying!'

'It's just that Cape Town–'

'I know. You've told me a thousand times. It's not safe. I'm a big girl now, Mum. Chill!'

'Text me as soon as you arrive.'

'Will do!' she said. And then she blew me a kiss and turned away, striding through the gates. I watched as she grabbed a little transparent plastic bag, and then she gave me one last wave before disappearing out of view.

I never saw my daughter again.

2

The next couple of days pass in a blur. The doctor prescribes me something to help me sleep and to dull the pain during the days. Although I know I shouldn't, I take double the recommended dose. It numbs my brain and dampens my feelings.

Bob told Ella. Ella is the quieter, gentler, less confident of my two daughters. I have always worried about her more. She clung onto her father as if she were a toddler, begging him not to go, as if she knew that I wasn't strong enough to provide her with the emotional support she needed. But Bob did leave. This is not his home.

'We will get through this,' I said, wiping away her tears. But I knew that was a lie. No parent can ever get over the death of their child. Not really.

It is Ruth and Natasha who rally around. We were at school together and have been best friends for thirty years, supporting each other through the highs and lows of our lives. As each of us married and had children, our friendship ebbed and flowed, but at its core, it has been consistent. Ruth and Alan moved away to Cambridge for five years, but when they returned to Horsham, it was as if they had never gone. For a while, about a decade ago, when Justin, Natasha's husband, was doing incredibly well, I felt as if Natasha thought she was above us, but that period didn't last long. Our families are bound together like ivy climbing up an old tree. We are each other's keyholders, godparents – more like relatives than friends. But perhaps what has made our friendship incontrovertible is that our children get along so well. Becky, Natasha and Justin's daughter, is like a sister to Abi, and it's only been these past couple of years that they have drifted apart a bit, simply because Abi left school a year before Becky.

Ruth knocks on my door and pokes her head around. I force myself to sit up in bed. I have no idea what day of the week it is. I glance at the clock. It's gone 10 a.m. I never sleep that long. And then I remember. Abi is dead. My beautiful daughter is never coming home. I can't stop the grief that grips my body in convulsive waves.

'Hey,' Ruth says. She sits on the side of my bed and rubs my back as I hug my arms around my knees.

'Where's Ella?' I sniff.

'She's downstairs eating breakfast. She's talking about going back to college.'

That sets me off again. I can't bear the thought of not having her within my sight. When I get the sobs under control, Ruth takes my hand.

'Becky and Ethan are back in England. They flew home yesterday.'

'Okay,' I say. My voice is small. Does Ruth know how lucky she is having Ethan safe? Does Natasha realise how grateful she should be that Becky is back at home?

'Why weren't they with Abi? Why did they leave her all alone on that beach?'

She squeezes my hand. Her palm feels hot and slightly sticky.

'The thing is, Becky and Ethan weren't even in Cape Town.'

'What?' I pull away from her and tug the duvet up to my neck. 'Were they delayed? I don't understand.'

Ruth shakes her head. She keeps her black afro hair very short, almost boy-like. It suits her because she has a small round face, with high cheekbones. 'Ethan and Becky were in Durban. They weren't due to arrive in Cape Town for another four days. They flew home directly from Durban.'

'No, that's not right. Abi was meeting them in Cape Town. That's the whole reason she went there.'

'Perhaps, but she wasn't due to meet them for another few days. It seems that Abi was out there by herself.'

This doesn't make sense. I try to force my memory to recall the exact words Abi used, how she told me that she was spending three weeks with her oldest friends. I booked two rooms at the Airbnb in Kalk Bay. Did I commit her to spending money unnecessarily? It doesn't compute, and I wonder if my drug-addled brain is failing me.

'I want a drink,' I murmur.

'It's ten o'clock in the morning,' Ruth says. She stands up and pats down her black jeans. 'And you don't drink.'

'Can I talk to them?'

'Becky and Ethan? I'm sure you can. The police lady is here. She wants to talk to you.'

I frown; then I swing my legs out of bed. 'Do they have any news? Do they know what happened?'

Ruth shakes her head sadly.

I grab an oversized sweatshirt and a pair of joggers and pull them over my nightdress. I walk into the bathroom and stare at myself in the mirror. My face has got lines and blotches that weren't there a week ago. I wonder if I've turned white overnight underneath the chestnut brown hair dye. It happened to one of my customers a few years back. I splash my face with cold water, but it doesn't calm my bloodshot green eyes. I can't be bothered to put on any makeup or get properly dressed, so I pad downstairs barefooted.

Linda Hornby, Ruth and Ella are seated around the kitchen table.

'Good morning, Grace. How are you feeling?' Linda asks. She is a pale woman: light flaxen hair, skin almost translucent and stenciled eyebrows over those light blue eyes.

'I'm feeling crap, as you might if your daughter had been brutally murdered!' I don't know why I'm being rude to her. It isn't my normal style.

'Mum!' Ella says, pushing her chair back so it screeches along the kitchen floor. She flees the room.

I hurry after her and shout up the stairs, 'Sorry, darling.'

Ella glances over her shoulder at me, but her lips are tight and tears are welling in her eyes. I consider going up after her, but Ella strides into the bathroom, and I can hear her locking the door. I shuffle back into the kitchen and sink down onto Ella's vacated chair.

'Mr Woods has flown out to Cape Town in order to make an official identification of Abigail,' Linda says.

'What? Why? But I wanted to go!'

'He thought it was best if you stayed here, to look after Ella. It will be a very distressing experience for Mr Woods.'

'But she's my daughter too.'

Ruth whispers into my ear as she squeezes my hand, 'And you have another daughter, who needs you. Grace, you must stay here and be strong for her.'

SOME HOURS later Ruth has to go to work. She is an air hostess and travels every few days. I am glad she has been here for me because she is super calm in the direst of circumstances. But now I need to let her go back to her normal life, to be with her husband, Alan, and son, Ethan, and to return to her job. Tonight she is flying from London Heathrow to Boston Logan and back again, one of her shorter international journeys.

And when Ruth leaves, in comes glamorous Natasha. Of the three of us, Natasha is the most outgoing, the one who has been the most upwardly mobile, the brightly coloured butterfly. When she turned forty, she decided to ditch her life as a housewife and train as a life coach. She did a few courses, some that necessitated her staying in London for several days at a time, others online. A year later, newly qualified, she added a few letters after her name and opened her own practice. She has a small room at the side of the house with a private entrance where she consults two days a week. A few of her clients visit in person; the rest are helped via Skype. I've never really understood what it is she does, but it seems to give her satisfaction that she's helping people. It's hard not to admire Natasha.

After discarding her Burberry macintosh, she sweeps me up into an embrace, muttering, 'I'm so sorry, darling,' again and again. 'I've found someone to keep an eye on Mum in Paris, so I can be here to look after you.'

'Thank you,' I say as I inhale her floral perfume. I know it's been tough for Natasha too, having her elderly, arthritis-riddled mother in France and having to jet backwards and forwards to keep an eye on her. Her mother's second husband was a Frenchman, and it was a shock to everyone when they emigrated to just outside Paris over a decade ago. Natasha had hoped that in their later years, her mother would choose to return to Sussex, but that hasn't happened.

The telephone rings.

'Do you want me to answer it?' Natasha asks.

I shake my head and reach over for the phone. It's Linda Hornby.

'Have you got any news?' I ask, my voice eager.

'Just that Mr Woods has identified Abi's body. I'm sorry, Grace, but it's definitely her.'

I don't wail or cry any more, even though I wonder if Bob might have made a mistake. It is possible, especially if in death, Abi doesn't look like Abi anymore. There have been mistaken identities, I've read about them in the tabloids. I suppose my face displays my dismay, because Natasha grabs my hand and squeezes it tightly.

I sink down into my favourite armchair. It's soft and just the right shape to support me.

'Tell me everything,' Natasha says as she sits on the sofa opposite. But there is nothing to tell her other than I have a gaping wound in my heart.

THE NEXT MORNING, Bob comes straight over to my house after getting off the night flight. He looks terrible: sunken eyes with dark purple rings and three days of stubble. His breath smells sour. I have brushed my teeth extra well this morning because last night I did what I promised myself I would never do again. I drank. We only had half a bottle of brandy in the house, but that was enough. It took the edge off the pain.

Ella went to college this morning. I made her promise to text me during every break. For the first time, she didn't roll her eyes. She just threw me a sad look.

'Did you bring her home?' I ask Bob as he puts down a small suitcase in my hallway.

He shakes his head.

'But why not?' I ask, my voice quivering.

'Let's sit down,' he says wearily.

Bob follows me into the living room. He walks with a stoop as if he's aged at least a decade during the past week. 'I couldn't bring her home. They're carrying out an autopsy in Cape Town.

I met the investigating officer, and he promised me he will find out who did this, who killed our girl.'

'But Abi shouldn't be all alone in South Africa! It's not right.' My hand rushes to my face, and I bite the inside of my mouth until I can taste blood. 'How long will the autopsy take?'

He sighs. 'I don't know. They didn't give a timescale.'

'And you didn't ask?' I stand up and pace the small living room. This is typical Bob. Laid-back, not asking the right questions.

'We have to run with the process.'

'But I want to have a funeral and celebrate her life.'

'I know, Grace. And we will. But it takes time.'

He leaves then. We don't touch each other, even though I know that he is as broken as I am, that he is the only other person in the world who can truly share my grief. I wish he would reach out to me, but he doesn't. He has Sue, his new wife. I know I need to stop calling her his new wife. They've been married for six years, but to me, she'll always be the impostor.

Mid-morning, Natasha returns. I haven't cleared up from breakfast; in fact I haven't cleared up from last night's supper either, but Natasha doesn't seem fazed. She picks up the dishes and puts everything in the dishwasher, rummaging under the sink to find a dishwasher tablet, and then switches the machine on. She takes a kitchen wipe and spray detergent and cleans down the countertops and the mucky table. I think how the Natasha of old might have made a snide comment about my filthy kitchen, but today she just throws me worried glances. When the kitchen is sparkling clean, she makes us both a cup of tea and sits down at the kitchen table.

'I'd like to help you, Grace. Use a few of the skills I've gained as a life coach. How would you like to feel once we've finished talking?'

'What?' I can't help scowling at her.

'If we could change just one thing to make you feel better, what would that be?'

'Take away the pain. It's like it's the end of the world. As if I'm living in a nightmare. As if someone has made a terrible mistake, and Abi will walk in through that door and everything will be alright.'

'What are *you* doing to take away the pain?'

'Sleeping pills. Tranquilisers. I'm not sure what the doctor has given me.'

'Oh, Grace, try to avoid them. I'll get you some homeopathic remedies.'

'Look, I know you mean well, Natasha, but I don't want a life coach, I want a friend.'

Natasha leans her head to one side, and her burnished gold hair cascades over her shoulder as she nods. There is a flash of disappointment, but then she picks herself up.

'Justin is organising a special school assembly next week to help everyone deal with their grief. It's hit the teachers and the pupils really hard.'

I nod. Abi, Becky and Ethan went to the same school, the one where Natasha's husband, Justin, is the headmaster. For a while, I wondered if it would be healthier for Abi and Ella to go to another school, where they didn't know any of the teachers, but it soon became apparent that Justin wasn't going to give the children he knew well any special treatment. If anything, he was particularly tough on all of our kids.

'He's asked for a photograph of Abi that they can blow up and have at the front of the assembly hall. Can you give me one?'

I burst into uncontrollable sobs.

3

It's the first time I have been out since it happened, the first time I have got into my little red Kia. Everything mundane is once again a first. With Abi. Without Abi. It doesn't seem right that the sun is shining and that people are carrying on seemingly without a care in the world.

I drive across town to the new, fancy estate where the Bellovers live. Natasha did well marrying Justin. In fact, Ruth did well marrying Alan. It's only my life that hasn't followed the upwards trajectory. Divorce meant downsizing for both Bob and me, although since he's remarried, he is on the up again. I have no idea how much Natasha and Justin's house must be worth, but certainly upwards of a million. Don't get me wrong. I'm not jealous. Far from it. I have a liberty that Natasha and Ruth will never have, living my life as I choose, only having to think about my girls. As a hairdresser, my work is flexible and I am self-employed. I have a small manageable house and enough cash to comfortably cover the mortgage, although it did mean that my daughters didn't get the it-toys or designer clothes for Christmas and birthdays. Before my life was devastated, I was even mooting the idea of dipping my toe into dating. That won't be happening now.

I pull up in front of the Bellovers' wide red-brick house. They have a crunchy gravel drive and manicured flower beds either side of the shiny black front door. Natasha was so pleased with the house. They bought it off plan and she worked with an interior decorator, who upgraded what would have been a standard five-bedroom modern house on a new estate into something she called 'elevated'. It may not be to my taste, but I do recognise it's very lovely.

I use the large gold hare doorknob to announce my arrival. Natasha swings open the door and throws her arms around me.

'How are you doing, lovely?' she asks.

'Okay,' I say feebly. 'It's just so weird that life can carry on without her.'

She nods sympathetically as she leads the way through the oversized square hallway, which is about the size of my living room, down a corridor into the open-plan kitchen, her kitten heels clip-clopping on the pale, marble tiled floor.

'Hello,' I say, surprised to see Justin at home. And then I remember. It's a Saturday.

'Hello, Grace. I am so sorry.' Justin stands there awkwardly. I suppose it isn't appropriate for him to give me a hug. 'I am utterly devastated, as we all are.' He is wearing chinos and a white polo shirt that almost shimmers with brightness against his closely cropped ebony hair. Justin has confounded every stereotype, morphing from the poor mixed-race boy, the son of a single mother, into a much-loved and highly respected pillar of society.

I nod. 'Thanks. And thank you for organising the special school assembly.'

'Everyone is distraught. Teachers and pupils alike.' He bites his lip and looks away, as so many people seem to do at the moment. 'If you'll excuse me, I need to get going,' he says, holding up his golfing gloves. 'Take care, Grace.'

He throws Natasha a cursory kiss and strides out of the room. I hear the door close behind him and his car start up.

'He's off for his regular Saturday game of golf. I suppose I shouldn't begrudge him, he works so hard, and it's always particularly stressful at the end of the school year. But it's tournament after tournament at the club, and it would be nice for him to be at home occasionally at the weekend, especially now that Becky has returned.'

I throw her a half smile. I'm just relieved I'm not shackled to a man who prefers golf to me.

The kitchen is all sparkling white. White kitchen units, white marble countertops, a giant fridge hidden behind wide white doors contrasting to the black ovens and black sink. Initially, I'd thought the black sink was a good idea, as it wouldn't show up the dirt so much, but then I changed my mind and reckoned I would prefer to know where the dirt is lurking.

Natasha holds a mug under her boiling hot water tap and hands me a cup of builders' tea. She doesn't need to ask how I like it. Natasha, Ruth and I must have drunk gallons of tea together over the years, and gallons of wine, for that matter.

'Can I speak to Becky?' I ask.

'Yes, of course, but Becky is really fragile, Grace. I can't begin to imagine how horrific this is for you, but please go gently with her. I don't want a repeat... you know.' Natasha may be the one to bring levity to our friendship group, but when it comes to her daughter, she is earnest. It's not surprising. It's easy to forget how hard it was for Natasha to fall pregnant, how she endured round after round of IVF, and when Becky was born, it was a miracle. But then Natasha went through a bout of postnatal depression, and it wasn't until Becky was five or six that their family life was back on an even keel. You would have thought that Natasha would have spotted it in her own daughter, but when we see someone every day, we often miss the things that are obvious to those on the outside.

Becky has had mental health issues since she was fourteen. It was Abi who first noticed it, telling me how Becky was throwing away her packed lunches, at most eating an apple or a celery stick. It's easy to miss all the signs: how her clothes began to get too big; her periods stopped; her passion for sport increased. I don't blame Natasha for not seeing it. Sometimes it's easier to hope these difficulties will pass without intervention or blame them on adolescence. We rallied around for Becky and Natasha, and with a lot of counselling and support from the school, Becky got through it. The bulimia seemed to be under control, and the panic attacks became more infrequent. Natasha was beside herself with worry as to how A Levels and university applications might stress Becky further. We had countless conversations when Natasha shared her fears that Becky might have a relapse and how she blamed herself for being a bad mother and not adequately helping her daughter.

As it turned out, none of us needed to worry, because Becky got a boyfriend. Becky and Ethan tried to keep things under wraps for a while. As families, we have always been so close that they worried it would be a bit like dating a sibling. But it was the best thing for Becky. With Ethan there to support her in person and Abi at the end of the phone, she sailed through exams. Once I asked Abi whether she was envious of her best friends being in a relationship. She laughed at me. 'Ethan's lovely, but he is absolutely not my type, and he's a year younger than me!' I never found out what was Abi's type.

Natasha clip-clops to the bottom of the stairs and shouts, 'Grace is here, darling. Can you come down?'

She returns and places a hand over mine. Her nails are always perfectly manicured with a French polish. I'm usually attentive to mine, too, as no one wants their hair done by someone with bitten nails, but today they are raw and red from where I have bitten the skin at the sides.

'I'm worried about Becky,' Natasha says in a low whisper. 'That she might be on the verge of a breakdown. She is totally riddled with guilt for not being there to save Abi. She hasn't stopped crying for the past three days.'

She's not the only one.

We both look up as Becky shuffles into the kitchen wearing Ugg slippers, skinny jeans and an oversized T-shirt with the name of an African elephant sanctuary emblazoned across the front. Even the way she walks looks fragile. Her dark, frizzy hair appears greasy, held back from her head in a rubber band, and there are rings under her eyes. She clutches her arms around her torso, ribs showing through her thin T-shirt. 'I'm so sorry.' She turns away from me as she sobs.

'Hey, come here,' I say, holding my arms out towards her. I have known Becky since she was born; she is as close to being my third daughter as anyone could be. I hug her tightly. She is taller than me, taller than Natasha, and for a moment, I wonder who is comforting who.

'Would you like a juice, darling?' Natasha asks when Becky peels away from me.

She shakes her head and grabs a bar stool from under the edge of the island unit.

'I don't know why Abi was there,' Becky says, sniffing.

'She told me she was flying out to meet you,' I say.

'Yeah. But we weren't meeting for another few days. I've got the texts.' She takes her iPhone from the rear pocket of her skinny jeans. After scrolling for a while, she finds the messages she's looking for, then slides the phone along the white marble work surface.

I read through the texts. Becky is right. Her messages clearly state that she and Ethan can't wait to meet up with Abi on 3 July, yet Abi's flight arrived into Cape Town on 28 June. Why did Abi lie to me? Why did she go to Cape Town five days before she was due to meet up with her friends?

Tears fall down Becky's cheeks, and sobs rack her slender frame. 'I'd have been there for her. I love Abi. She's the sister I never had.' Becky slides off her stool. Natasha leaps over to her daughter and wraps her in a bear hug. I can't look. It makes me miss Abi even more.

When Becky has calmed down, Natasha steps away and reaches up to take a little bottle from the shelf.

'Five drops of this under your tongue.' She holds a pipette up above Becky's mouth. 'Go and listen to some nice music, or switch on Netflix and watch a movie.'

Becky sniffs and trudges out of the room.

I want to ask Becky more: how did Abi seem to her when they last spoke? Did she have a boyfriend I didn't know about? Did she give any hint as to why she might have gone to Cape Town early, or was it a genuine mistake? But if the latter, why hadn't Abi been in contact with Becky when she discovered her friends weren't there?

But I can't push it. Not now. Becky is a wreck and suffering just like I am.

'I'm going to make an appointment for her to see the counsellor again,' Natasha says, walking towards her giant larder cupboard and opening the door. 'She's taken this really hard.' I have never seen anything quite so well stocked outside a shop. She removes a box.

'Good idea.' How I wish I could do the same for my daughter.

'Have you heard any more from the police?' Natasha undoes the cellophane packaging on the box of finest mixed biscuits and tips them onto a white-and-blue porcelain plate. 'Here.' She shoves them towards me, but I'm not hungry.

'No and...' My words get choked up. That's what happens. I

am absolutely fine for a few minutes, and then grief hits me like a hammer on my head.

'Hey. Have a few drops of this.' Natasha passes me a little vial of Rescue Remedy. When I can control myself sufficiently, I put several drops under my tongue. I doubt it'll work, but I'm prepared to give it a try. I'll take anything at this point to dull the pain.

And then there is a loud rap on the door.

'It's probably Ethan,' Natasha says.

'Good. I want to talk to him.'

I follow Natasha to the front door, and it is indeed Ethan. He throws Natasha a quick smile. He is wearing loose-fitting jogging bottoms and a grey T-shirt. With his jet-black buzz cut and a pair of Ray-Ban sunglasses on his head, he looks considerably taller and broader than the last time I saw him.

'Ethan!'

He seems shocked to see me and fumbles with his words.

'Sorry. Not very good at this,' he says, his eyes downcast. 'I'm really sorry. I can't believe what happened. I'm going to miss Abi so much. We all are.'

'I know,' I say softly. 'Did she mention that she intended to arrive in Cape Town a few days before you and Becky?'

He frowns. 'No. But to be honest, I haven't spoken directly to Abi since before we left for our travels six months ago. All the arrangements were done between Becky and Abi.'

'Did Abi have a boyfriend?'

He shifts from one foot to another and glances away.

'Um, I don't think so. I really don't know. You're best talking to Becky about stuff like that.'

Ethan slinks past me and I listen as he takes the stairs two at a time. For a new house, the floors are very creaky. I hear his footsteps overhead and then the closing of a door.

As I follow Natasha back into the kitchen, I try to work out what it was that didn't sit comfortably during that conversation.

And then I realise. Ethan has exceptionally beautiful green eyes outlined with dark lashes. Even when he was a little boy, he used to hold other people's gazes, as if he had some secret ability to know what was going on inside their heads. That gaze stayed with him, even through the awkwardness of puberty and adolescence. Yet now, it is gone.

He didn't once meet my eyes.

4

The hours merge into days, and then it's a week since Abi died. I am trying so hard to keep things together for Ella. Although she went back to six-form college for the last few days of the academic year, now she's lounging around at home, listening to music at high volume and slapping black and grey paint on canvases in her bedroom. I thought about returning to work too, but there is no way that I could keep my composure in the salon. It's that pitying look in people's eyes that catapults me into grief.

Bob is being surprisingly kind. He pops by after work most evenings, just for half an hour or so. I think he's worried I'm going to slip back into my old ways, and he wants to check that Ella isn't living with an alcoholic. I can't believe how strong I've been. After finishing off the brandy, I haven't touched any alcohol. We haven't got any in the house.

But I can't sleep. I doze off for an hour or so and then wake with a start. Every night, I've been tiptoeing across the hallway and curling up in Abi's bed, quietly sobbing myself to sleep. I'm awake early, so I return to my room and Ella isn't any the wiser.

One night, when I couldn't sleep, I went into Abi's room and switched on her laptop. It was just lying there on her desk, closed, stickers plastered all over its case. I would never have dreamed of looking at it if she were still alive, just as I never looked through my girls' diaries when they were younger. I didn't understand mothers who felt they had the right to sneak-read their children's private thoughts. Anyway, the last thing I wanted to see was hateful words about me. But this is different. My Abi is dead, and I need to connect to her.

My hands were shaking as I lifted the lid and pressed the start button. It asked me for a password. I know it's bad practice, but the three of us always used the same passwords. Either 100AcreWoods or W!nn!ethePooh. I held my breath. I tried both; I tried variations, but nothing worked. I switched off the machine, closed its lid and shed tears into Abi's pillow.

AND STILL I don't know anything about how Abi died. I've never been very good at sitting on my hands, waiting for information to come my way, and I have never felt such an overwhelming need for the facts. Someone must know what happened to Abi, and I am determined to find out.

On day nine, I call Detective Inspector Pete Fairisle.

'You must know something,' I insist.

'It's very tricky dealing with foreign police forces.'

'But haven't you sent someone out there to help with the investigation?' My voice sounds a little too high pitched and hysterical.

'We just don't have the resources, Mrs Woods. But the police in Cape Town are very capable, and the autopsy will be completed soon.'

'When will they give us the results?'

He is silent for a while, and I wonder if the line has been cut. Eventually he says, 'I'm afraid that you won't get the results of the autopsy.'

'What do you mean?'

'In South Africa, the results are only shared with the investigating officer and not with the family. It's quite different to here in the UK.'

'But they'll tell you, won't they?'

'I'm not sure. But rest assured, as soon as I know anything, I will be in touch.'

'But I need to know! Was Abi murdered knowingly, or was it a random stabbing?'

'Grace, if I may call you that.'

I don't respond.

'It is always so much harder when someone is killed abroad. I'm afraid that we don't have any control over the investigation. When the autopsy has been completed, we can arrange for Abi's body to be repatriated, and then we can carry out another autopsy here in Sussex. I don't know when that will be.'

'But I want a funeral. We need to lay Abi to rest. And we need answers.'

'Of course you do. May I suggest that you go ahead and organise a memorial service. Perhaps you could have a private funeral in a few weeks, when the UK autopsy has been completed.'

'And what about her phone records? She was getting a local SIM card for her phone so she didn't have to pay international rates. Can't you track that?'

'Our South African colleagues are looking into phone records.'

'You *are* chasing the team in Cape Town for answers, aren't you?'

'Rest assured, we are doing everything that we can.'

But I don't believe him. I just don't. I am sure if it were his daughter, he would be over there now, chasing up all loose ends, finding out exactly what happened. But it's not his daughter. She was mine. And now she's gone.

. . .

'I WANT to go to Cape Town,' I say to Bob on the phone. 'I want to see where Abi died. I want answers.'

'We all want answers,' he says dejectedly.

'Can you lend me the money to go?'

He splutters. 'I had to borrow for my own flight, so there's not a hope in hell I can afford to buy another one for you. Any spare cash is going to have to be spent on Abi's funeral. Let it go, Grace.'

We are both silent. Eventually, he says, 'I was going to call you anyway. I was wondering if Ella would like to spend the weekend with Sue, me and Tommy?'

'No, she wouldn't.' I cross my hands in front of my chest. I cannot bear the thought of letting Ella out of my sight.

'Grace,' he says, sighing. 'Alright. I won't say anything for now, but don't be unreasonable.'

I change the subject. 'We need to organise Abi's memorial service. The policeman said it'll be ages before we can have a funeral. A proper funeral with her body.' My attempt at stifling my sobs is futile. I hear Bob sniff.

'Right. Let me know what you want me to do.'

IN THE END, it's Ruth and Natasha who take control of organising Abi's memorial service. I contribute very little. My ability to think and to process seems to be diminishing by the day. Ella gets involved too, putting out messages on Facebook so that all of Abi's university friends are told the time and the place. I wonder how many will attend, now it's the summer holidays. Ella tells me that Abi's Facebook and Instagram pages have been inundated with messages of condolence. I will look someday, but I can't yet. It's too soon.

'Grace, are you ready?' Ruth opens my bedroom door and

finds me seated on the edge of my unmade bed. I am wearing a black sleeveless dress, but I haven't been able to force myself to get up to put on any makeup. It is just too overwhelming. She bustles in and kneels down on the floor in front of me. 'Hey, sweetie, you need to get ready. The car will be here in fifteen minutes.'

'I want a drink.' My voice is deadpan.

'I know you do. And I do too, but you've been so brave and so strong. Don't give in today. You need to be there for Ella.'

I look at her now. My lovely friend. She looks tired too. I wonder what all of her strange working hours as an air hostess have done to her body clock. Ruth never complains though, and I suppose if she didn't want to carry on with her job, she wouldn't have to. Alan is the European sales manager for a Dutch greenhouse manufacturer, and he must be on a decent wage.

I stand up and walk into the bathroom. It's a tip. Ella has used some of my make-up, but I don't have the energy to chastise her. I swipe some blusher over my cheeks, put some concealer under my eyes and a pale apricot lipstick on my lips. There's no point in using eyeliner or mascara; it'll run down my cheeks.

'Have you got any dark glasses?' Ruth asks as I emerge from the bathroom.

I nod and fetch them from my chest of drawers.

I hear Ruth out in the hallway. 'Ella, are you ready?'

Ella responds immediately to Ruth's question. I gulp when I see her. With a touch of makeup and wearing one of Abi's old dresses, she looks so like her sister.

'I've never been to a funeral,' Ella says. I squeeze her hand.

RUTH HAS ORGANISED for the service to be held in the local humanist church. Neither Bob nor I are into religion. We got married in a registry office and didn't bother to get either of our girls christened. Does that make us bad people? I hope not. Besides, how can you have a proper funeral without a body? Ruth suggested we invite everyone who knew and loved Abi and have a celebration of her life, a true remembrance.

'Is Alan coming with Ethan?' I ask as Ruth, Ella and I slide into the black Mercedes she has organised to transport us to the service.

'I'm afraid Alan can't come today.' Ruth gazes out of the car window. 'He's in Nairobi looking at some greenhouses, and he couldn't get out of the trip. He sends his apologies. Ethan is coming with Becky and Natasha.' I sense tension in her voice.

According to Ruth, the church seats one hundred people, but by the time we arrive, the place is packed; young people are standing at the back of the room. I am heartened that my daughter was so popular. I walk self-consciously to the front row, where Bob is already seated. Ella climbs in first and sits between Bob and myself.

I don't know how we get through it. I think I shut down. Behind my dark glasses, I can close my eyes and pretend that I'm floating on a cloud, with Abi on my left and Ella on my right. We are looking down at the earth, the beautiful azure sea and astonishing jagged mountains with snow-capped peaks. From time to time, the words of the celebrant – Ruth told me he's not a vicar – pierce through and drag me back to reality. And then there are the songs, chosen by Ella and not in the slightest bit reverent. But when some of Abi's friends from school walk up to the front and sing 'Angels' by Robbie Williams, every person in the room cries. Bob squeezes Ella so tightly, it must hurt her. Is there a God? If so, how could he be so cruel to take my girl rather than taking me?

Somehow Ruth and Natasha get me out of the church and into the car.

'Where's Ella? I need Ella.'

'She's fine. She's with Bob and Sue. They're right behind us.'

And so I sit on the back seat with Ruth holding my left hand and Natasha holding my right hand as we are driven for ten minutes to a hotel for the reception, somewhere I have never been before.

'Do you want to freshen up before we go in?' Ruth asks, holding out a little compact mirror. I nod. I look a wreck.

The hotel is a typical country house hotel with chintz furnishings and a lovely natural garden. The weather is warm, and as I look through the large lounge area, I see people are congregating outside on a wide terrace. This should be a wedding, not a funeral. There are plenty of familiar faces as well as many young people whom I don't recognise. Who are they all? Did they love Abi when she was alive? Were they kind to her?

'You go and be with Justin,' I say to Natasha as I spot a sign for the ladies' toilets.

Her eyes flutter to the left. 'I'm sorry, but Justin couldn't make it today. He had a governor's meeting, and you know what they're like. He always gets so stressed about them, and he couldn't change it, not when they're organised that far in advance. He sends his apologies and condolences, of course.'

I am disappointed. Justin should have been here. He was Abi's headmaster during her high school years, and he should be representing the school.

'I'll go and freshen up,' I say.

'I'll come with you,' Ruth insists.

'It's fine. I'm fine, Ruth. I'll join you in a moment.' She lets me go.

I walk down a narrow corridor lined with botanical prints. To my relief, there is no one in the toilets, so I lean over the marble sink and splash water on my face, patting it down with a white flannel cloth. My eyes are raw and red and the concealer has wiped away. I touch up my face and slip the sunglasses back on, and once I've adjusted to the darkness, I leave again. A waitress carrying a tray of filled glasses of wine passes me in the corridor.

'May I?' I say, swiping a glass before she can respond. I know I shouldn't. Of course I know I shouldn't, but today it is my daughter's funeral and I am allowed one glass. Surely I am?

The problem with not drinking for several years and then drinking again is that the effects are immediate. My body craves this, and the relief that courses through my veins is indescribable. Yes, I know I shouldn't and I won't again, but today…

I walk outside to where most people are congregating and spot Natasha standing next to a rose bush, talking to Ethan, Becky and a young woman I don't recognise. Before anyone sees me, I quickly tip back the contents of my glass, place it on a table and walk towards them.

'Mrs Woods.' A girl of Abi's age steps into my path. Her hair is in dreadlocks and she has a tattoo on her right forearm, a contrast to her demure short-sleeved black dress. I can't read what the tattoo says. 'My name is Katy, and Abi and me share a house. I'm going to miss her so much. We're all gutted.'

I nod. I'm unsure what to say.

'And Alex and Dom over there, plus Nia and Jadyn, we are all Abi's housemates.'

She grabs hold of a boy's arm. He is mixed-race and beautiful with large almond eyes and flawless coffee-coloured skin. 'This is Jadyn.'

He nods at me and lowers his eyes. Did Abi mention the names of any of her housemates? They don't sound familiar, but then it's as if my memory has been lobotomized. All I can recall is Abi saying she was sharing a house with a great bunch of kids.

'We can't believe it,' he says.

'Yeah. She was so looking forward to going to South Africa.' Katy takes a sip from a glass of Coca-Cola.

'Did Abi have a boyfriend?' I ask.

They both look up, a little startled.

'No, not that I'm aware of,' Katy says.

'Do you know who she was planning on meeting in Cape Town?' I ask.

'Her old friends from home. I can't remember their names.'

'Becky and Ethan,' I prompt.

'Yeah, that sounds right.'

'And no one else?'

Katy frowns. 'Not that I know of. She was well excited about going.'

'I know.' I shake my head. 'She saved up for months. She told me that she took every shift she could as a barista.'

Katy and Jadyn frown at each other.

'What is it?' I ask.

'Did you say "barista"?' Katy asks.

'Yes. She worked at Cafe Blanco.'

'No, she didn't! It's me who works at Cafe Blanco. Abi didn't have a job. She said her dad was wealthy and she didn't have to worry about stuff like that.'

My mouth falls open. I stare at the young woman. I take my sunglasses off and peer at her again.

'Once again, I'm so sorry, Mrs Woods,' Katy says, shifting uncomfortably from foot to foot. 'If I can do anything.' And then she slips away, following Jadyn as they weave between all these people who have come to mourn my daughter.

My twenty-one-year-old Abi, who fed me a string of lies.

5

In the days after Abi's memorial service, I don't say anything to my friends about the revelation that Abi didn't work as a barista. I can't bear the thought of them looking at me with their pitying expressions, all the while thinking what a terrible mother I am for not knowing what was really going on in my daughter's life. I don't even tell Bob. He blames me for our divorce, even though he is the one who moved on quickly, finding a new lover and then a wife within a year of our separation. I don't want to give him further reasons for criticising me, and I certainly can't face the risk of him insisting Ella go to live with him. So when I offer to drive up to Durham to collect Abi's belongings, I do so with bated breath. Bob sounds relieved.

Through social media, Ella contacts Abi's housemate Katy, who says she'll let me in. Even though it's the summer holidays, she is still living there. Perhaps she hasn't got a home to go to.

It's a long way. Bob drove Abi last September, at the beginning of her second year, with a car loaded full of cast-off cushions, rugs, lamps, pots and pans. I have only been to Durham once, at the beginning of Abi's first year. She was so excited, and of course we were too, proud of her and buzzing about the new, limitless future that was hers for the taking.

But as I drive up the A1, I try very hard not to think about that first journey. I do whatever I can to distract myself from thinking about Abi. It's not easy. I put on the radio at high volume, listening to music, but switching stations every time a sad song is played. After five exhausting hours, interspersed by a couple of lousy coffees at motorway service stations, I arrive in the beautiful, ancient city of Durham, with its imposing cathedral and Norman castle, and follow my satnav to where Abi lived.

It is a small red-brick terraced house with white window frames and a red front door on a cul-de-sac, in an area that must have once housed miners and their families. All the streets in this part of town are dominated by a vast railway viaduct that connects London to the north-east of England. There is little suggestion that this part of town belongs to such a picturesque city. I park on the opposite side of the road, get out of the car and stretch, and then I am startled when a train thunders overhead. It feels as if the earth is moving. My heart is thumping as I cross the road and rap on the front door.

'Hello,' Katy greets me as she opens the front door. Despite it being early afternoon, she looks as if she has just got straight out of bed, wearing a crumpled T-shirt and cotton shorts. Her dreadlocks are coiled on top of her head.

'Come in.' She stands to one side and I walk down the narrow corridor that smells of burned food laced with a hint of marijuana. 'Abi's room is upstairs, first on the left. Do you need any help?'

'I'm not sure. I might need a hand putting everything into the car. I've brought some empty bags.' I hold up a couple of holdalls and a roll of bin liners.

'I miss her so much,' Katy says, biting her lip.

I nod. Katy edges past and walks up the narrow stairs covered in blue fraying carpet. I follow.

'In here.' She opens the door. 'My room is next door, so give me a shout if I can do anything.'

I swallow hard before thanking her.

THE ROOM IS COMPACT. Just big enough for a single bed and a surprisingly large pine wardrobe that dominates the space. There is a narrow built-in desk that looks as if it was made from a scaffolding plank and a chair with scuffed wooden legs. Abi has done as much as she can to make the space her own. There are posters on the walls, some familiar old ones that she had at home, such as the seascape with a sole yacht beneath a sunset. But there are other pictures that I haven't seen before, including one of a baby with its tongue stuck out, holding its fingers in a V shape. Candles line every surface, and the scent of incense hangs in the air.

I can't halt the tears as I sink onto her bed. I finger the duvet cover, which we bought together two years ago. It feels worn and bobbly now from over-washing. I remember how she couldn't decide between the blue floral pattern or the red tartan. She chose the red tartan in the end. It takes me a few minutes until I feel strong enough to stand up. Wiping my tears away, I walk to the wardrobe. I swing the wooden doors open and stare at the rail of clothes. Trailing my fingers along them, I pull one dress after another off the rack.

These are not Abi's clothes.

These are expensive designer dresses.

Abi wears clothes bought from H&M and Topshop. I gasp. The dresses are both short and long, mainly black, low cut, figure hugging, and most definitely not student-wear. And then I see the row of high heels. Gingerly, I pick one pair up. They are gold and strappy. What the hell? Abi hated these sorts of clothes. She used to joke that she would never be able to walk in high heels. I remember the end-of-year prom at school, how she wanted to wear her Doc Martens with an evening gown, and it was Becky who persuaded her that she looked ridiculous. At the end of the rail are a few of Abi's clothes, the things I recognise: a pair of scruffy jeans, some dungarees, leggings with holes in. There are some open shelves above the rail, and I see a couple of familiar sweatshirts and a jumper I knitted her last year.

And then I think. Perhaps one of the other girls has put her belongings in Abi's wardrobe now she's no longer here? I walk into the corridor and knock on Katy's door. Music plays quietly.

'Hey,' she says as she opens the door.

'Um, all of those smart clothes hanging in Abi's wardrobe, I was wondering who they belonged to?'

Katy pulls her head back in surprise. 'They're Abi's. None of us have even been into her room, I promise!'

'I'm not accusing you of anything. It's just I don't recognise those clothes.'

She shrugs, but I notice a slight colour tinge her pale cheeks.

'They're Abi's, I promise.'

'But where did she get the money to pay for them? Or was she given them? And why did she need to wear fancy dresses like that? She's a student!'

'I'm sorry, but I don't know. She used to go out from time to time and she always looked smart.' But Katy's face reddens even more and her eyes dart around. She's lying.

'Did Abi have a boyfriend?'

'No.' She shakes her head vigorously.

'Are you sure?'

'Of course I'm sure. She wasn't even that into boys. She and I–' Katy hangs her head low and a solitary tear drips onto her bare foot.

'She and you, what?' I prompt.

'We had a bit of a thing a few months ago. I thought she might have said something.'

'A thing?'

'I really cared for her, more than she did for me.'

'You mean you had a relationship with Abi?' I exclaim, my jaw falling open.

'She swings both ways. Most of us do. It's the person we're attracted to. It's normal.' She shrugs.

It may be normal for Katy, but I'm still taken aback.

'So you really have no idea how she got all of those clothes or when she wore them?'

'Sorry.' She tugs at the dreadlocks on top of her head. 'Abi and me weren't doing the same course or anything.'

'Is anyone else living here at the moment who might know?'

'Nope, it's only me. The others have all gone home or are working or travelling. I can give you the names of some of Abi's friends if you like, or just look on Facebook. We've all left messages.'

I nod and return to Abi's room. Did I know my daughter at all? Was she gay? And does it even matter? I suppose not. I have always told my girls that so long as they are happy, I don't mind who their partners are.

I start packing Abi's belongings into the two large suitcases she has stored under her bed, but my hands shake as I fold the dresses. What was my daughter up to? My packing becomes hasty and careless, shoving her belongings into bags, into bin liners. I can't look through her things; it feels too invasive and too overwhelming. I will sort through them when I'm home. I pick up the lamp off her desk and a little mug full of pens and pencils. At the base of the mug she has sellotaped a small piece of paper with what looks like a password. GH254k!zz29] Carefully, I remove the piece of paper and place it into my wallet.

I leave all the books related to her course piled on her desk, but everything else is now stuffed in bags. The walls are bare, the bed stripped, and I just need to get out of here as quickly as possible. After dragging everything down the steep stairs, I shout goodbye to Katy. She pops her head out of the door and waves at me.

I KNOW I shouldn't be driving all the way home; it's irresponsible when I'm so tired and emotional, but I am desperate for my bed and to be able to hug Ella. I stop regularly, drink copious coffees and tins of Red Bull. Whenever possible, I stay in the slow lane. Fifteen hours after I left home, I am back. Exhausted, emotionally devastated, but in one piece. I lock the car up and drag my weary self into the house.

The lights are off in Ella's bedroom, so I don't wake her. I make myself a couple of pieces of toast with butter and marmalade and take the plate upstairs and into Abi's bedroom.

'What were you doing, my darling?' I whisper as I sit down at her desk. I open the lid of her laptop and start it up. Very slowly, I type in the digits from the password I found under her mug. I hold my breath as I hit return. It works. I'm in.

I wait until everything is loaded and then click on her emails. Unlike me, Abi was organised. She has four folders: home, uni, sweet and other. What is sweet? Do I want to know? I hesitate before clicking on the folder, and see strings of emails from people with strange names, mainly consisting of numbers and letters. And then I see an email from an organisation. Sweetner.net. I click on the link, and when the page loads, I let out a wail.

It's a sugar-daddy website. My beautiful girl was prostituting herself.

I work backwards through the emails. She started this nearly eighteen months ago, using a fake email address and a fake name. She calls herself Anya. And then I find the photos.

Her face is heavily made up, with huge eyelashes and pink shining pouty lips. In some she is barely dressed, in provocative poses, wearing lacy underwear; in others she is wearing beautiful dresses and she looks like a film star. But why? Why did she feel she had to do this? I know she didn't have much money, that we couldn't support her in the way that Natasha supports Becky, but Abi was always brought up knowing right from wrong. She knew my feelings about sex, and we openly discussed everything. This must be my fault; my fault for choosing to divorce Bob when I felt that all the love had dissipated from our marriage, when I felt so worn down by the bickering and the snide comments and the perpetual put-me-downs. If I hadn't forced our divorce, would our girls have had a more stable, secure upbringing? Should I have sacrificed my happiness for theirs?

I slam the lid down on the laptop.

Who knew about this? Did Abi's friends know what she got up to in her spare time? Was Katy lying to me? Or was Abi selling herself because she felt that was the only way she could support herself as she incurred all of that student debt?

It makes me feel nauseous and deeply ashamed. How could Abi do something like this?

This is too much for my frazzled brain to compute. I drag myself to my bedroom, pull off my clothes and collapse into bed. But just as I am drifting off to sleep, my body jerks awake.

Did Abi's death have something to do with one of those sugar daddies?

6

The next morning, I am awoken by the phone. I fumble for it and press answer.

'Grace, it's Bob. I've just heard from the police. The South Africans have released Abi's body, so we can bring her home.'

'That's great.'

'Yes and no. It's going to cost fifteen grand.'

'What!' I drop the phone. I can hear Bob's disembodied voice. I clamber out of bed and pick up the phone. 'Did I hear you correctly?' I ask. My voice sounds breathless.

'Yes. We can choose to have her cremated in Cape Town, but then there will be no further forensic investigation or input from the British police, or else we repatriate her and a full post-mortem inquest can take place in England.'

'Oh God,' I murmur. This is all too horrific. Where are we going to get that sort of money from? I can't ask Bob to remortgage his house with his new young family. It will have to be me, and I'm not even sure if I'll be allowed to do that. 'What are we going to do?'

'I don't know. Let's talk again this evening. I've got to go to work now.'

Bob hangs up.

I collapse back into bed. We can't get our daughter cremated in Cape Town. I need to know what has happened to her. She needs to be back here in England with us, where she belongs. It feels as if I have flu, the way my bones ache and my head pounds, but mostly my heart feels as if it has been shattered into a thousand tiny pieces. Fifteen thousand pounds. What the hell are we going to do? And then I remember. I told Abi to take out travel insurance for her holiday. I nagged and nagged her, and she promised me she did, but now I just need to find the details. I shrug on a large jumper and go into her room. Ella's door is still firmly closed, and I am careful not to wake her.

I open Abi's laptop again and log in. I go through all of her personal emails from the last month, but there is absolutely nothing about travel insurance. I have no way of knowing if she actually did take it out. I can't even access her online banking because I don't have her bank card or her PIN numbers. In fact, my own daughter has become an enigma, and I simply don't know what to do.

An email pings in and goes straight into the Sweetner folder. It sickens me, so I slam down the lid and walk into the bathroom and take a long, hot shower. I can sob in the shower, where Ella won't hear me.

I am getting dressed when the phone rings again. I am tempted not to answer it, but eventually I do.

'How are you?' Ruth asks.

'Been better. We've just discovered that it will cost fifteen thousand pounds to repatriate Abi's body. We can't afford to do it.'

There is a long silence and eventually Ruth says, 'That's terrible. What are you going to do?'

'I don't know.'

'I can see if I can pull any strings by talking to the airline. Or how about crowd funding?'

'But then the whole world will know about us and Abi.' I let my voice trail away. I suppose they will soon enough anyway. There have already been some short reports on her death in the newspapers.

'Leave it with me. On another note, I'm going to do a shop. Do you need anything?'

I haven't got the energy to go downstairs and check the fridge, so I thank her for the offer and decline.

A COUPLE OF HOURS LATER, Natasha sends me a text message.

'Justin and I will pay for the repatriation. Abi was my goddaughter and it's the least we can do. Justin will talk to Bob. Love Nx'

I am bowled over. I knew they had plenty of money, but to spend that much for a friend is extraordinary. As it sinks in, I let the tears flow again.

And that is how Ella finds me when she eventually surfaces, sitting at our kitchen table, a total mess.

She clutters in the cupboards to find a bowl and a box of muesli, but it isn't until she's sitting down that she looks at me, her hair piled up on top of her head with a purple scrunchie.

'What's happened?'

I tell her about the repatriation in the broadest of terms, missing out the bit about the postmortem, and then I ask, 'Do you know of something called Sweetner?'

'Isn't that a sugar-daddy website or something?' She speaks with her mouth full.

I nod. 'Did you know that Abi was on it?'

'What!' Ella lets her spoon clatter to the table. 'That's gross. Did she have to do you-know-what?'

'I don't know, Ella. It's all a shock. I don't want you to tell anyone, alright? And certainly not your father. He would go ballistic.'

'I can't believe that Abi would do that.'

'I can't believe it either. Perhaps there was some mistake.' I wish I really believed that. 'Please don't tell Dad, Ella,' I repeat.

She nods. I hope she won't let me down.

IN THE MIDDLE of the afternoon, Sergeant Linda Hornby calls me.

'What's happened?'

'We have received some news from our South African colleagues. They have discovered CCTV footage from outside a bar in Cape Town, and they believe that it is Abi talking to someone. Unfortunately, the person she is talking to is standing in the shadows, and they can't see any specific features. The police think it was most likely that Abi was just in the wrong place at the wrong time.'

'Why do they say that?'

'We will know more soon, I am sure. I just wanted to bring you up to date and find out how you are.'

I swallow. I wonder if I should tell her about Abi being on Sweetner.net? Is it relevant, or am I just airing my daughter's dirty laundry in public? I can't bear the thought of it getting out into the media, the shame of us all being judged. How likely is it that someone she met on Sweetner followed her to South Africa, or did she hook up with someone she met online? Would she really have been that stupid?

'I understand that Abi's body is being repatriated imminently,' Linda says. 'Hopefully, we will know more when the postmortem has been carried out here. But at least some progress is being made.'

Then I hear another phone ringing in the background and Linda says, 'Do you mind if I take that? Call me any time.'

So I don't tell her. I will tell her, but not quite yet.

I certainly don't expect the doorbell to ring a couple of hours later, and I am shocked to see Linda Hornby and Detective Inspector Pete Fairisle standing on the doorstep. I don't recall him wearing black rectangular glasses on the day he told me about Abi's death, but perhaps my memory has expunged the detail.

'Can we come in?'

I nod. What has happened now? Why are they here?

I lead them into the living room and they sit down.

'Grace, I'm going to get straight to the point. We have received the autopsy report from Cape Town. Did you know that your daughter was pregnant?'

I think I'm going to faint. The room starts spinning and I see bright flashes in front of my eyes, and then as I'm about to sink into blackness, Linda Hornby pushes my head between my knees.

'Breathe,' she says. 'In and out, slowly in and out.'

A few moments later, Ella is standing in the doorway. 'What's happened?'

'Can you make your mum a cup of tea, love?' Linda asks. 'Put a couple of teaspoons of sugar in it.'

'This is evidently a shock to you,' DI Fairisle says as I sit back up in the chair.

I nod.

'We assumed that might be the case. Did Abi have a boyfriend?'

'Not that I'm aware of. In fact, I've only just found out that she had a relationship with a girl.'

'It's not very likely that her pregnancy had anything to do with her murder, but obviously we have to take that into account,' Linda Hornby says softly.

'I can't believe she would have been that stupid. We talked about things like that. How many weeks was she?'

'We think fourteen. Enough for her to be aware that she was pregnant.'

I gulp. Why didn't she tell me? I would have helped her. Or had she decided to keep the baby? Surely not. Abi was ambitious. She wanted to be a lawyer, to seek out justice, to make the world a better place. She would never have made it to law school with a baby in tow. I think back to how she was the few days before she went to Cape Town. She'd seemed happy, excited, young and carefree. I certainly don't recall being worried about her, or feeling that she was carrying a heavy secret she couldn't share with anyone.

DI Fairisle runs his fingers through his greying hair and stands up. 'We will stay in close contact with the police in Cape Town, and as soon as her body is returned, we will liaise with the coroner.'

'Take care,' Linda says.

I nod and try to smile, but I suspect it comes out as a grimace.

7

ANYA'S BLOG FROM THE SUGAR BOWL

JANUARY 28TH

A bit about me:

I'm twenty-one years old and reading history at one of the Russell group universities in England. And I'm about to become a sugar baby. I'm writing this blog because I want to chart my journey from a poor student saddled with massive loans to, hopefully, a solicitor working in one of London's leading firms. That's my ambition, anyway.

Tonight I'm putting up my profile on one of the leading sugar-baby websites, sweetner.net. I'll let you know how it goes!

JANUARY 29TH

Why I'm becoming a sugar baby:

Well, it's the money obviously, but also the connections. I come from a poor family. Mum and Dad don't earn much, and I'm the first person in our family to go to uni. They can't pull any strings for me, open any doors or other such clichés. I met a girl in the year above me here at uni. It seemed like she was loaded; she wears all this fancy gear, designer clothes and is happy to flash the cash in the college bar. Anyway, she told me about being a sugar baby and kind of took me under her wing. I'll call her Angel, because she's become my guardian angel. My first reaction was, shit, you're a prostitute. I guess she realised I was thinking that because she quickly told me that she's got a boyfriend and that she doesn't have sex with any of her sugar daddies. I think I believe her.

JANUARY 30TH

I thought about putting a copy of my profile up here, but in case any SDs (sugar daddy) search for me online, I reckon it's best if I don't. But thanks to Angel and the tweaks she made to my profile, OMG – I've had a stack load of interest. Within the first twenty-four hours I had thirty-three profile views, eleven "favourites" and seven messages. I've been emailing and texting my first POT (potential, for you newbies out there).

D lives and works in a city just half an hour away from uni; he's a lawyer (yippee!) and his profile pic suggests he's one of those salt-'n-pepper silver-fox types. I hope this doesn't sound boastful, but I look pretty sexy in my profile pics. Amazing what some lacey underwear, false eyelashes and a swipe of red lippie can do! (Thanks to Angel, again. She took my photos and tweaked them on a photo app.)

So I'll give you guys a quick precis on some of the messages I've had. "I'm looking for a willing baby to give £££s to every week. You up for that?" Didn't you read my profile? No sex... So no, you idiot, of course I'm bloody not! I blocked him. Another was, "Message me if you'd like to see you-know-what..." Ergh, yuck. I most definitely don't! Anyway, D's message was sensible, almost a bit boring, but better that than sleazy.

----

*Loads has happened – some good, some bad. I had my first M&G (meet and greet) with D. I did what Angel suggested, and we met at Costa Coffee at 5 p.m. on a weekday. Hardly the most romantic place, but then I had to remind myself that this is an ARRANGEMENT, not a date! He texted me an hour beforehand to double-check we were still on, and I had such high hopes. Before I go into the details, here are the things I did first. And you **must, must** do these too because your safety is the number one most important thing.*

Set up a separate email just for your SRs (sugar relationships). Get yourself another phone and phone number before you message your SDs. Once you've exchanged a few messages with your POT, take all your conversations off the website (Sweetner.net in my case). Text him, and if you think there's a rapport, discuss the allowance amount or PPM (pay per meet). This is the best, best advice that Angel gave me. I made it clear to D (my first POT SD) that I was new to the bowl (the sugar dating lifestyle), so we messaged each other (emails actually) about the arrangement. I told him I wanted a monthly allowance and would be free to meet up once a week. D said he was fine with that but wanted to do a PPM (pay per meet) for the first three times we meet up, just so we can be sure the chemistry is there and that we both agree we want to pursue a relationship. That freaked me out a bit, because I normally associate chemistry with sexual chemistry (you can tell I'm a humanities major and not a scientist, can't you?!), so I reiterated that I am only interested in platonic relationships. He said he was too. Relief! Anyway, he said that if it works out, he's going to pay me a monthly allowance of £900, and he'll pay £200 for those initial PPMs plus travel expenses, food and drink etc. I was frickin' over the moon about this, but Angel told me I'd sold myself short. Anyways... back to that first meeting.

Tell a friend where you're going, and/or ideally have a tracker on your phone, get dressed up, and you're set to go.

So... back to D. He was sitting at a table near the back of Costa Coffee. The good news is, he does look a bit like his photo, but he's at least five stone heavier than when his profile pic was taken. But hey, it doesn't matter what he looks like, does it? I tried so hard to come up with conversation topics, asking him about his work, what he likes to do in his spare time, where he last went on holiday. But it was like pulling teeth. Either he was shy, or he didn't like me or shit knows, because in the end the conversation stopped altogether, and then he leaned across the mucky table, placed a sweaty hand over mine and said, "You're so beautiful, I don't think I could spend an evening with you without wanting to make love to you." Holy shit! I left my half-drunk Caramelatte and got the hell out of there! I may well meet an SD that I want to have sex with, but there is no way in hell that I'll be doing that with D.

I was really disappointed, but Angel told me that it's par for the course. Apparently I've got to meet up with loads of guys before finding some genuine ones. No different to the vanilla world (normal dating without strings attached).

So the next POT I texted, it was obvious really early on that he wanted to be an FWB/FB ('scuse the lingo here, folks, it means "friend with benefits"/"fuck buddy"). I blocked his number, like I'd blocked D's. In fact, right now I'm thinking this is a waste of my bloody time. I've got two big essays I need to hand in next week, and this SB stuff is distracting me too much. Might be the last post on this blog...

8

It isn't until I hear their car doors slam and the engine start up that I realise once again that I didn't tell the police about Abi being on Sweetner. Is it relevant? Should they know? They're going to think my girl was such a tart, and I shudder at the shame and humiliation. I don't want them to know. I don't want anyone to know. It's impossible to grasp the fact that she was pregnant, that I could have been a grandmother at forty-six, that Abi seemed perfectly happy about being pregnant. Or did she not realise? None of this makes any sense.

It's time to read through all of Abi's emails. I start with her folder titled home.

There is nothing about her trip to South Africa; she hasn't mentioned it to anyone in her messages, and all I find is the booking for the return flights on British Airways. I wish I had her mobile phone, but according to the police, it is missing and they haven't been able to track down the mobile number for the pay-as-you-go SIM Abi bought in Cape Town. The phone wasn't in her crossbody bag, or in her Airbnb room, or anywhere on the beach where she was found. That's why the police think that it was a random killing. Perhaps she was stabbed for her phone and for cash. I used to chastise the girls for talking on their phones when they were out and about. It's asking for trouble, isn't it? But Abi used to laugh, saying her old phone wasn't worth anything, and if someone stole it, they were welcome to it. She'd be able to claim on her insurance for a new upgraded phone. But it's one thing walking around comfortable safe Horsham or strolling along the cobbled streets of Durham; pacing the gritty streets of Cape Town with a mobile phone in hand is quite another story.

I KNOW that I am going to have to read through all of her emails on Sweetner.net, but it sickens me. How I wish I could have a drink. My body craves numbness; perhaps not even numbness, just a little relief from the pain and horrid maelstrom of emotions that cramp my sternum and swirl around my head. It's been nearly ten years since I drank any alcohol, with the exception of the brandy and that single glass of wine at Abi's memorial. I'm sure that I can control it. Just one glass of wine. Surely I deserve one glass of wine. But it means going out to the off-licence, and I am so tired. Besides, what will I tell Ella?

I used to have a problem with alcohol. My friends called me an alcoholic, and once, Ruth tried to get me to attend an Alcoholics Anonymous meeting. She tricked me by saying she wanted me to try out a new restaurant. We met outside a nondescript building. 'Are you sure you've got the right place?' I asked, frowning. Ruth nodded and led me inside. When she opened the door to a room off the hallway and I saw all of those people sitting in a circle, I stormed straight back out again. I was livid with her. Absolutely livid. I didn't talk to her for nearly a month.

I was not an alcoholic. I am not an alcoholic. I was a heavy drinker, and there is a huge difference between the two. Alcoholism is a medical condition. Alcoholics simply can't control their drinking; once they start, they can't stop. It's a physical craving and a mental obsession. Nothing matters to them except drink. Years ago, I had a friend whose mother was an alcoholic. 'My mum would walk over babies to get a drink,' she said. I wasn't like that. I used to drink to obliterate my feelings. I used it as a crutch, but I still had control. I would never drink and drive. I could stop drinking; I simply chose not to.

Alcohol became my companion because it helped me block out the memories of the worst year of my life, the year I turned twenty-one. How very ironic that Abi's twenty-first year was also the worst of her life. And her last.

Mum died of cancer in the February of that year. It wasn't unexpected, but for me, it was; at that age, I never actually thought it would happen. Five months later, Dad died. The police said that it was an accident, that his car spun on a slick of oil on the road, but I think he wanted to die, that he couldn't cope with life without Mum. So it was just Will, my younger brother, and me. I survived, at least I thought I did. When I received my parents' modest inheritance, I decided to set up my own hair salon. Natasha, who back then was working in a bank, helped me write a business plan. I listed everything I needed to set up the new business and reckoned I had plenty of money to get me going. My next step was to find a premises.

The estate agent was a man called Liam. A few years older than me, he was a cocky know-it-all with trousers that were too tight, black hair and piercing blue eyes, pretending to be suave and sophisticated. Young, naive and hurting, I fell for his charms as he showed me various properties, each more unsuitable than the next. He kissed me on a second viewing of an old shop near the station. But the kiss turned into something more, and then he forced himself on me, and well, I didn't cope. It was one trauma too many.

I should have gone to the police. I should have told someone. I should have accepted that I had been raped, but I didn't. I hid it from Natasha and Ruth, and I hid it from myself. *It must have been my fault; I must have led him on.* It's only the wisdom of age that lets me look back and realise that I never stood a chance. Even Bob doesn't know. Instead, I told my friends that I had a change of heart about the business, that it was too risky to open up my own salon at such a young age. Do I regret it? Of course I do. For a while, drink became my companion and my saviour.

And then I turned to alcohol all over again, in a less dramatic way, when my marriage broke down. I let my girls down then and swore I would never do that again.

But these days I can just about control that longing for alcohol, so I click on the folder Abi named Sweet and scroll through the emails. Over the past few months, she conversed with three people on a regular basis. Loaded-Len, PapaWilliam and Jared B. These men sicken me. How dare they exploit young girls.

I read through the messages. They don't say much, just confirm the times and places they are going to meet or when they are going to video chat. I gasp as I realise how often Abi went to London. At least once a week, and I knew nothing about it. The train journey is expensive, and it takes at least three hours from Durham one way. And then it dawns on me. She didn't have to pay; they covered her travel expenses and no doubt bought her all those fancy clothes. Did she have sex with these men? Did she stay overnight in luxury hotels? Suddenly, it makes me so angry. If Ella weren't in the house, I would scream and hurl plates at the wall, but I can't. I have to keep control for my youngest daughter.

I take a piece of paper from the printing tray of Abi's printer and tear it into smaller and smaller pieces, and as I do so, there is the ping of an incoming email. It's from Jared B. I click on it.

'Anya, sweetie, I haven't heard back from you. I know you

said you were going on holiday, but I thought you would be home by now. I need you. Normal time, normal place tomorrow? Double sugar ps Bae, let's go freelance x'

The sleazy bastard. What the hell does all of that mean? I go onto Google and do a search for the words I don't understand. *Bae* is a term of endearment, and *freelance* means he wants to take everything offline. From the message, I would assume their relationship has been 'offline' for a long time. I am flabbergasted to discover there is a whole lexicon of terminology used in the sugar-baby world; there are even websites offering advice to babies and daddies alike. I shiver with repulsion. If I had known this, could I have done more to protect Abi? Has the suppression of my past affected my daughter's relationship with men?

As I scroll down, I see another message that arrived two days ago from PapaWilliam. It simply says, 'I'm missing you'. I try to imagine the sort of men who send messages like this. Are they selfish creeps, like the man who raped me, or are they troubled or lonely? What is it in them that makes them seek out young girls?

I need to get access to Abi's bank details to see how much money she's been earning through these arrangements, but for sure it was enough to buy the clothes and to travel to Cape Town.

This is all so seedy and wrong. Although I don't want the police to know about Abi's involvement with Sweetner, I reckon I have no choice but to tell them; after all, it may impact the investigation. If these men have done anything illegal, I want to know, and I want them to suffer like I'm suffering right now. I find Linda Hornby's business card, the most empathetic of my police contacts, and call her direct line.

She answers immediately.

'There's something I need to tell you about Abi, but I don't want anyone to know. It's highly confidential.'

'Everything you tell us is in confidence and only disseminated on a need-to-know basis,' she promises.

'It may not be relevant, but I discovered Abi was a sugar baby and using a website called Sweetner.net. Do you know it?'

'No, but I am aware that a lot of young people are turning to what they call "arrangements" to manage their student debts. I'm afraid that if it is a consensual arrangement, there is nothing illegal about it.'

'But it's amoral!' I exclaim, realising that I sound like a middle-aged prude. Perhaps I am.

'Is there any evidence that the relationships Abi had were threatening or difficult?'

'Not that I'm aware of. But as she was pregnant and didn't have a boyfriend, well, it just stands to reason that one of these men might have been the father.'

'Possibly, but without further evidence it will be difficult to prove anything. I had a message from our police colleagues in Cape Town, and we are having a conference call with them first thing tomorrow morning. They want to update us with their progress.'

'That's good.' I wonder if the person seen on CCTV was one of the Sweetner men.

'I'll keep you posted, Grace,' Linda says before saying goodbye.

Perhaps Linda would be more outraged if she were my age with a young daughter, but she doesn't look a day over thirty, and I doubt she has kids. Even though the police say they are working on the case, I can see that it's going to be up to me.

As I put the phone down, my initial reaction is anger, but then I have a moment of inspiration.

The sleazy sugar daddies all think Abi is still alive.

I'm going to lure them somewhere and meet them. Look them in the eye and tell them how disgusted I am with their behaviour. And perhaps I'll be able to find out if one of these men impregnated my daughter or even had anything to do with her death.

I draft a message to send to all three men, apologising for being out of touch and explaining it's a bit difficult to get to London at the moment. I suggest that we meet at the Hilton Hotel at Gatwick Airport. And then I realise I will have no idea who these men are. If it were really Abi writing these emails, they would recognise each other. I need to come up with a way to spot them. I add another sentence. *I loved South Africa. Can you bring me a protea flower? If it's real, you'll be in for extra special treats, but dried or fake will do too. I expect to see it in your lapel! Love, Abi*

Just before I hit send, I remember that she's not Abi to them – she's Anya. I change the name and let out a sigh of relief that I didn't screw it up before I have even begun. And then I hit send. Yes, I feel disgusted, but I want to snare these bastards. I will make them pay for what they've done to my beautiful daughter, for exploiting her.

DAMN, I so need a drink.

'Mum, we're out of milk!' Ella shouts upstairs.

Normally, I would tell her to go to the corner shop and buy some, but now, as the light is fading, I'm nervous of her going out alone. Besides, it gives me the opportunity to buy other things.

'I'll go,' I say.

I shove my wallet, phone and keys in my pockets and stride down the road to our little convenience store. As I open the door, Mrs Patel looks up and sees me. Her face creases.

'I'm so sorry, love,' she says.

I nod. I'm not sure I can speak. Last week, Abi's tragic death featured on page three of the local newspaper. I hurry to get a pint of milk and select a mid-range bottle of wine, which I can't really afford.

'I'll buy a bag, too,' I say as I hand over the change.

She smiles at me. 'You take care.'

I stride up the road, holding the bag slightly behind me. I know it's ridiculous, but I don't want to be seen carrying a bottle of alcohol. I'm aware that only my closest friends know the truth about my relationship with alcohol, and it's unlikely that either Ruth or Natasha will be passing. I suppose it's the guilt. I reassure myself that that's why I'm not an alcoholic. I still care.

I stand at the bottom of the stairs to make sure that Ella is up in her room; then I pop the milk in the fridge, grab a glass and climb up the stairs to my bedroom. I hide the bottle and the glass in the wardrobe before going to Ella's room to tell her I'm having an early night. Yes, I feel disgusted at myself. Yes, I know it's wrong and verging on pathetic. But how would you feel if you had just been told your twenty-one-year-old daughter had been murdered, that she was pregnant, that she was unsure about her sexuality, and that she was a sugar baby pleasuring sleazy old men? I think I can forgive myself a glass or two of wine.

After saying goodnight to Ella, I go into Abi's room. This is the home of the Abi I knew and loved. The little girl who had a penchant for all things pink; the fluffy white cushion on her chair; her childhood teddy bears lined up on the windowsill. The teenager who morphed from pinks to grunge, who never failed to tell me that she loved me. I will never change this room. I want it to remain exactly as it was the last time Abi slept here. I sit on the bed and bury my face in her pillow, as I have done every night since she died. But it no longer smells of Abi, and how will I ever recapture her scent, that uniqueness that was my daughter?

9

My mobile phone wakes me. My heart is hammering as I fumble for it. Is it the police? I groan. Last night was a mistake. I have a pounding headache and a revulsion so profound, I wonder if I will ever be able to shake it. I finished the bottle. A decade of strong willpower destroyed in one swoop.

'Hello,' I answer without checking the screen.

'Hi, Grace. How are you doing this morning?' It's Ruth.

'Okay,' I say, but I can tell from her voice that I'm not kidding her.

'Natasha and I were wondering if you'd like to go out for a light supper tonight. Just something quiet and only the three of us.'

'It's kind of you, but I'm not sure–'

'Natasha is paying.'

'I think Natasha and Justin have done enough for me.'

'Hey, I know you don't want to go out, but it might do you good. We're not going to give up on you that easily. How about the Hornby Arms at 7.30 p.m.?'

I sigh and I agree simply because I need to get Ruth off the phone. My stomach, so unused to alcohol, is clenching and I really don't want to throw up.

After staggering to the bathroom and drinking two glasses of cold water, I stare at myself in the mirror. My hair has lost its lustre, and dark red wine stains my front teeth. My skin looks sallow, and I'm sure I have wrinkles around my eyes that weren't there a couple of weeks ago. They'll be crying lines. After swallowing a couple of paracetamol, I force myself to stand under a freezing cold shower for three minutes. It's penance. I emerge feeling marginally better.

I make myself a strong coffee and then fire up Abi's laptop. Two of the three men I emailed on Sweetner.net have replied. PapaWilliam has suggested meeting for lunch. That surprises me. I assumed Abi would only meet men in the evening. Jared B says he can meet me at 6 p.m. after work. Still pretending to be Abi, or rather Anya, I agree to both, reminding them they need to bring me a protea flower. Only Loaded-Len hasn't replied.

Being a hairdresser, I don't have many smart clothes, but I feel that today I need to look as official as possible. I wear a black blazer and match it with some black trousers and a cream scoop-neck top. I start to put on makeup and then decide what the hell. Let them see the pain all over my face.

Ella shouts up the stairs, 'I'm spending the day with Rachel. See you later, Mum!' Rachel is her best friend and, conveniently, lives two streets away.

'Have you got Find Friends on your phone?'

'Yes. I'll text you when I'm there.'

How everything has changed. Just a few weeks ago, Ella would have rolled her eyes at me and bitten my head off for me wanting to keep an eye on her. Now she is volunteering the information.

'Have fun, love,' I say.

. . .

I AM EARLY, but even so, my heart is hammering as I walk through the doors of the hotel into the massive open-plan reception and lounge area. It is a vast enclosed courtyard with three storeys of corridors and bedroom doors discernible on three sides. I try to remember that I am invisible, that no one knows why I'm here or what I am doing. It is easy to be anonymous, just another businesswoman waiting for a colleague. Keeping my eyes on my mobile phone, I skirt away from any hotel staff and find a seat with a good view of the entrance. I place *The Times* newspaper on the table in front of me and pretend to read the pages.

'Hello, Madam. Can I get you anything to drink?'

I jump.

'Just a black coffee, please,' I say, and then regret it. There is no way I will be able to navigate a cup of coffee to my lips without trembling and spilling it.

And then, on the dot of 12.30, I see him. A middle-aged man wearing navy corduroy trousers and a tweed jacket, carrying a protea flower in one hand and a small bag from Space NK in the other hand. He has a full head of hair, greying at the temples, horn-rimmed spectacles and a chin that merges into his neck. I jump up, and as I try to avoid a waiter carrying a platter of food, I almost barge into him.

'Excuse me,' he says as he attempts to skirt around me.

I put my hand out. 'PapaWilliam?'

He stops dead. He pales and his grey eyes dance from side to side behind those glasses.

'Who are you?'

He speaks with a deep voice and a cut-glass accent.

'My name is Grace Woods. I'm the mother of Abi, but you know her as Anya.'

He sways. For a moment, I wonder if he's going to faint, or even worse have a heart attack, his face goes so pale.

'We need to talk,' I say, pointing to the table for two to our left.

'Why isn't Anya here? Has something happened to her?'

'Please, let's talk sitting down,' I say.

I wonder if he's going to turn and march straight out. There's nothing I can do to stop him if that's what he chooses. Perhaps I haven't played this cleverly.

But then he nods imperceptibly and follows me to the table.

As soon as we sit down, the waiter arrives with my coffee. 'Would you like a drink?' I ask. He declines.

He lets out an audible sigh. 'I suppose you're here to tell me I'm a dirty old man and to stay away from your charming daughter.'

'Yes and no,' I say. I am taken aback that he hasn't put up a fight, and I'm somewhat thrown.

'How is she? Did she enjoy her trip to Cape Town?'

I stare at this man who is acting like an avuncular uncle as opposed to a desperate, sex-starved middle-aged loser. I mustn't be swayed by this act. 'She's dead.'

His jaw drops open and he grips the edge of the table. 'No!' he whispers. 'No.'

'It's true. She was murdered in Cape Town. Were you there?'

'What? No. Of course I wasn't there. What are you talking about?'

'Abi died from stab wounds on a beach in Cape Town. I collected her belongings from the house she was living in at university, and I discovered that she is what you call a sugar baby on a website called Sweetner.net. I read your messages and I wanted to meet you.'

His face crumples and for a brief moment I feel sorry for this man. But only for a brief moment. He is an exploitative, filthy piece of...

'I am so sorry. So desperately sorry.' His voice cracks and he puts his hands over his eyes. His fingernails are clean and neatly cut, and I note he doesn't wear a wedding ring. When he removes his hands, there are tears on his cheeks, and his lower lip is quivering. *Did he actually care for Abi?*

'Did you have sex with my daughter?'

He shakes his head vigorously. 'No. I loved Anya – sorry, Abi – like a niece or a godchild.'

'I don't believe you.' I narrow my eyes at him.

He shakes his head and takes a white cotton handkerchief out of his pocket, blowing his nose noisily. When he has stuffed it back into his jacket pocket, he places his hands on the table and leans forwards. His eyes are downcast.

'I admit when I first joined the website, I was looking for sex. I am a fifty-five-year-old widower. My wife died five years ago and we didn't have any children. The first time I met your daughter, she looked so young–'

I interrupt him. 'Because she was.'

'Yes, I know. And I knew straight away that my intentions were wrong. I have never slept with a prostitute, and I knew I could not bed a young, articulate, intelligent and beautiful girl like Anya.'

I don't correct him.

'But I found her charming. During that first meeting, she shared all of her dreams with me, how she wanted to become a barrister, but her divorced parents were poor and were unable to support her. She explained that she was doing this work because she didn't want to leave university with enormous debts. And I realised that she could have been my daughter, the one my wife and I could never have. So yes, I did give her money and I bought her presents: dresses, jewelry, perfume.' His eyes dart to the Space NK bag on the table. 'And I don't regret it. I cannot believe such a wonderful young woman is dead.' He shakes his head, lifts his glasses up and dabs his eyes again. 'What happened?'

And so I tell him the little that we know. I recall how Linda said the team were having a briefing call with the South African police, and I wonder if there is any news. I pick up my phone from the table, but I have no missed calls or messages.

'I am so sorry, Mrs Woods. Life can be desperately cruel. I am not sorry for having gotten to know your daughter, but I am deeply ashamed as to how we became acquainted and what my initial intentions were.'

This conversation has not gone the way I expected. I thought he would be defensive and leave as quickly as possible, but this man seems utterly thrown by Abi's death. Should I believe what he's saying? Is he spinning me a web of lies to expunge his guilt? And could he be the father of Abi's unborn child, regardless of what he is telling me?

'She was pregnant,' I say, my eyes firmly on his.

'Oh dear God!' He shakes his head repeatedly. 'She didn't tell me.'

'Were you the father?'

He leans right forwards across the table and looks me straight in the eye. 'I never laid a finger on your daughter. The only physical contact we had was when I kissed her on the cheek when I met her, and again when we parted ways. I treated her like a daughter and I cared for her like a daughter.'

I notice that he defined his relationship with Abi as like a niece a few moments ago, and now he's saying she was like a daughter to him, but am I splitting hairs? I don't want to believe this man, but I do.

He leans back in his chair and sighs. 'If I may, I would like to tell you a little about myself. I am a psychiatrist with a thriving private practice in central London that I have run for twenty-five years. I was a long-time carer to my wife, who died of multiple sclerosis five years ago. I am a middle-aged man with more money than I know what to do with, thanks to inherited wealth, and I earn well enough from my practice. I was lonely. When I dipped my toe into the murky waters of sweetner.net, I knew it was wrong, but sometimes people with the very best of intentions do bad things. Your daughter was the only friend I made on that website, and she brought a smile to my face. Yes, I have had many women chase me, but they always want something. Money, normally. At least on Sweetner, the transactional side of the arrangement is transparent. I met Anya once a fortnight. I paid for her travel and took her out for dinner or lunch. Sometimes we went to a concert or the theatre, but she enjoyed the ballet the most. I then paid for her to spend the night in a hotel room in central London and I went home. We spoke on the phone once or twice a week, depending upon her schedule.'

'No sex?' I ask him dubiously.

'I promise, Mrs Woods, that I never had sex with your daughter.'

I lean back in my chair and let out a groan. I really don't want to like this man or to believe him, but I do. In many ways he is like me. Middle-aged and alone. At least I have my girls. No, my girl.

'What are the police doing to try to find the murderer?' he asks.

'So far they haven't come up with much. I'm expecting to hear more today.'

'I really can't express my condolences sufficiently. What a tragedy! What a terrible loss. If I am feeling this level of desolation and pain, I cannot imagine how badly you are affected.' He takes his glasses off again and blinks rapidly before placing them back on his nose. 'If there is anything that I can do, anything at all, please reach out to me.'

To my surprise, he fumbles in his wallet and hands me a business card.

Dr William Jennings, FRCPsych. Harley Street, London.

'The epitome of respectability,' I say sarcastically as I read it. He shifts uneasily.

'I am truly sorry. If there is anything I can do to help you and your family, please call me.'

'You can find Loaded-Len. He's the sugar daddy who hasn't got back to me.'

William's face darkens for a moment. I wonder if each of the men thought they had an exclusive arrangement with Abi.

'Never mind,' I say quickly.

He stands up and extends his hand. 'I wish we hadn't met in these circumstances, Mrs Woods. Please accept my sincerest apologies.'

I find myself accepting his handshake. He then glances at the protea flower and the small bag, obviously meant to be a gift for Abi.

'Please take them away,' I say.

He nods, picks them up and walks briskly towards the hotel exit.

I HAVE a lot of time to kill before meeting the next man from Sweetner, almost enough time to go home and come back again, but instead I decide to wander around Crawley. I grab a sandwich for a late lunch and aimlessly walk the streets. Eventually, I find a coffee shop and read the newspaper that I have been carrying around all day. I try calling Linda, but get her voicemail twice. Ella has sent me a couple of text messages saying she intends to stay at her friend Rachel's house for supper, too. It suits me. I think about William and I have to assume he was genuine. Why would he have given me his business card if he wasn't? I regret not taking a photograph of him, but hopefully there will be some online.

And then I am back in the hotel. It's busier now and I struggle to find somewhere to sit near the door, so instead I have to stand.

He is five minutes late and holding the stem of an artificial protea flower in the same hand as his briefcase. He strides straight past me and then stands in the reception area, obviously looking for Abi. Jared B is younger, perhaps early forties. He is wearing a dark navy suit with slimline suit trousers. His inky eyes are deep set and his hair jet black. There is something about him that scares me, and for a moment, I wonder if I should just disappear. But then I remember. I am doing this for Abi. I need to know about these men. I need to know who was the father of her baby, and whether any of these men followed her to South Africa. I take a quick, discreet photo of him with my phone; then I put it in my bag and walk towards him.

My stomach clenches as I tap him on the shoulder. He swivels around to face me.

'Yes?'

'Are you waiting for Anya?'

He takes a step backwards, narrows his eyes at me, and then he walks as quickly as he can towards the exit. I have to run to keep up with him, and only reach him when he is outside on the pavement, dodging travelers pushing trolleys laden with suitcases.

'Wait! Please wait!' I shout. 'I'm not the police. I'm Anya's mother and I just need to talk to you.'

He stops then and swivels around to face me, his eyes narrowed.

'What do you want?'

'Abi, or Anya as you knew her, is dead. And she was pregnant.'

He pauses for a long moment, and I can tell that he isn't sure whether or not to believe my words. 'Look, Mrs, I am sorry for you and for your daughter. It's a great shock, but it really has nothing to do with me.' He tries to walk away again, but I grab his arm.

'You were sleeping with her, Mr Jared, or whatever you're

called. I am aware of Sweetner. At the very least, you owe me the truth. When did you last see her?'

'I don't owe you anything,' he hisses. I recoil slightly from his stale coffee breath. 'I had an arrangement with Anya, and if you are implying that I might have got her pregnant, I most certainly did not. If it's money you want, I will go to the police to report you.'

'I don't want money, you bastard. I want...' And then I wonder, what *do* I want? 'Did you go to Cape Town?'

'What? I have never been to Cape Town. Look, I'm sorry for your loss, but would you please let me go.'

'I've got a photograph of you, and I can find out your real identity through Sweetner,' I bluff.

He glances around as if to check whether anyone knows him, and then he takes a step closer to me. He speaks in a low, threatening voice. 'I have a wife. I have three children. Never, ever approach me again. Do you understand?' He then turns and strides away.

'You bastard!' I yell at his retreating back.

10

I am still shaking when I get on the train to Horsham. I got a really bad feeling about Jared or whatever his real name is. I hope he treated Abi well. I pray he did. It was obvious he was scared that I am going to expose his sordid behaviour to his wife, but he is wrong about that. William gave the impression of genuinely caring about Abi, whereas Jared was only interested in himself. The bastard.

Just as I'm leaving Horsham station, ready to walk home, I get a phone call from Linda.

'Sorry to be ringing you so late, and apologies for not returning your call earlier. We have some news from Cape Town. The police have arrested a man called Kungawo Nkosi. He is a local man, living in a township in Cape Town called Nyanga. He's illiterate and a drug addict, and the police believe he killed Abi for drug money. I'm so sorry, Grace.'

I sit down on a low brick wall and my shoulders slump.

'So it was a random killing?'

'Yes. I'm afraid Abi was just in the wrong place at the wrong time. They tell me there were 298 murders in the Nyanga precinct last year.'

'But Abi wasn't in a township, was she? She was found on the beach near Kalk Bay.'

'That's correct. But it's believed this man made his way to Kalk Bay and attacked Abi for money. It explains why her cash and phone were missing. If you recall, the police found her passport and preloaded bank card in her money belt, which was strapped around her waist, but a wallet with money or debit cards was never found.'

'It doesn't make sense. Abi knew that if someone threatened her, she should hand over her wallet and phone. She was streetwise. We talked about it.'

'I'm sorry, Grace, but the Cape Town police are charging this man. They say they have conclusive evidence that he killed her for drug money.'

'But only two days ago they had a sighting of Abi with a man outside a bar.'

'That could have been anyone. It was a red herring.'

'So it's all over?' I ask, blinking away the tears from my eyes.

'Yes. They've found the killer. He is already in custody. His trial will be heard by a judge and two qualified assessors. Similar to in the UK, the court will only convict if it is convinced he is guilty beyond all reasonable doubt. But he has form; he's served several prison sentences to date, including for dealing drugs and grievous bodily harm. It's expected that the trial will be a mere formality, and it's likely he will get life imprisonment.'

'Does that mean you won't be investigating any further?'

'There is no reason to believe that Abi's death was anything other than an opportunistic killing by a local man. We will, of course, continue to offer you all the support you need, but there is nothing further for us to investigate. I will call Mr Woods to notify him straight away.'

I can't trust myself to speak anymore. A life, taken so brutally, so unnecessarily, and what for? Money for drugs.

'Is there someone who can be with you, Grace?' Linda asks.

'I'm fine,' I whisper, but my voice is a quiver.

'Are you sure?'

'Yes. Goodbye.'

And then I burst into tears.

I don't know how long I sit on that low wall, my head in my hands. The phone rings twice, and then I panic it might be Ella. I wipe my eyes with the back of my hand and peer at the phone. Damn. I had totally forgotten I was meant to be seeing Ruth and Natasha this evening. It's the last thing I feel like doing. I'm midway through composing a text bailing out when the phone rings again.

'Where are you?' Ruth asks.

'Outside the railway station,' I say, trying to keep my voice even. But Ruth is an old friend and she knows.

'I'll be with you in three minutes.'

RUTH PULLS UP in her silver Volkswagen Tiguan. Natasha is in the front passenger seat, and she jumps out of the car before Ruth has put on the handbrake. She leaps towards me and, in her typically exuberant manner, throws her arms around me.

'What's happened, love?' She stands back to peer at me. She's wearing high gold wedges and a pink floral maxi dress.

'They've charged someone with Abi's murder. She was murdered for money by a drug addict.'

She hesitates and then says, 'But that's a good thing, isn't it, now you know what happened and that someone is in custody?'

'Yes. Maybe. It's all so confusing.'

'Come on, let's get you in the car. We'll cancel the table at the pub. Ruth has said she'll rustle us up some pasta.'

'Thanks, Ruth,' I say as I climb into the back seat. 'I'm not very hungry, though.'

Ruth throws me a look of concern. 'Where have you been? You're looking very smart.' She peers at me in the mirror.

'I've met up with some...' I then change my mind. Do I really want my friends to know about Abi being on Sweetner? Do I want them to know that she was pregnant? Will they care? Will they judge me and her? I shut my eyes and try to think.

'They've charged someone with Abi's murder,' Natasha tells Ruth.

TEN MINUTES LATER, we're in Ruth's kitchen. Ruth and Alan's house couldn't be more different to Natasha's. For starters, it's old. I think Ruth told me the history of the cottage years ago, but I can't remember now. It's just outside Horsham and backs onto fields. Inside, the ceilings are low and criss-crossed with beams. There is a small green Aga in the kitchen, and a butcher's block is a makeshift island unit, although how Ruth does anything on it besides chopping, I've no idea. The fabulous chunk of wood dips dramatically into a crater in the middle. The windows are small, and the house is always dark. Bob never liked their house; I think it's cosy, and I can fully understand why Ruth loves it. Typically olde English, it must be a tonic and a refuge for her when she returns from all of her travels as an air hostess.

Alan saunters into the kitchen, a half-drunk glass of beer in his hand. A few years older than us, he has a receding hairline that he tries to hide with a comb-over. It does him no favours. With a rotund stomach and eyes that bulge slightly, Alan has always reminded me of a child's drawing made from a series of circles. A round face on top of a round body with egg-shaped limbs.

'You're back early,' he says, giving Natasha and me a quick peck each on the cheek. With the four of us in the small space, it feels cramped.

'We've decided not to go out after all,' Natasha says. 'Ruth is going to rustle up some pasta for us.'

Alan opens his mouth as if to say something, but then clearly thinks better of it. I notice that Ruth has her back to her husband and remains silent. He takes another beer out of the fridge.

'I'll keep out of your hair, then,' he says. 'Behave yourselves.'

'Is Ethan here?' I ask.

'No. He's at our house with Becky this evening,' Natasha replies, with an almost apologetic tone to her voice.

Ruth pours herself and Natasha a glass of white wine and gives me a glass of sparkling water. I never used to mind them drinking in front of me, but now I want some wine, too. I almost say something, but instead, I blurt out one of my other secrets.

'Abi was on a sugar-baby website.'

'What?' Natasha's eyes are round and wide.

Ruth lets a spoon clatter into the sink. She turns around to stare at me, but then, noticing the tears swelling up in my eyes, she speaks. 'Oh, Grace, I'm sorry. That must have been such a shock for you.'

'Yes.'

Neither of my friends look at me, but their expressions betray the melee of emotions that pass through their heads. No doubt Natasha is wondering whether Becky was on the website, and then thinking that no, her daughter is a good girl, not like my Abi. And in that moment I decide to share the double shock; I have nothing left to lose.

'Abi was pregnant.'

Natasha is the first to react. 'Oh my God, Grace. Pregnant! That's so sad. Do you know who the father was?'

'No, but I intend to find out. I know the South African police think that the druggy killed Abi, but I still wonder if it was someone off Sweetner.'

'But she wasn't a prostitute!' Ruth exclaims. 'Girls on sugar-baby websites are like companions for older men, and in return, they are given gifts or their student loans are paid off.'

'Come on, Ruth. Don't be naive. Of course sugar babies sleep with their clients. Are you saying their relationships are only platonic?' Natasha scoffs.

'It's not exploitative in the way that brothels are.' Ruth runs her fingers through her short hair. 'The girls have a much greater degree of control. I have a work colleague whose daughter is on one of those sites, and thanks to being a sugar baby, she has finished university debt-free.'

'So you're saying it's acceptable? It's easy for you to say, you've only got a son. Sorry, but I think it's sordid.' Natasha takes a large glug of wine.

'Shut up, both of you,' I say. 'We're talking about my dead daughter here.' I stifle a sob.

Natasha does her usual and embraces me, muttering that she didn't mean to upset me. But I'm not in the mood for niceties, so I push her away.

'I'm a bloody awful mother. I had no idea what Abi was up to, and the last bloke I met, he was creepy as hell.'

'What do you mean, you met?' Ruth turns away from the stove to face me, her wooden spoon dripping sauce onto the floor.

'That's what I was doing at a hotel in Gatwick, why I'm dressed up like this. I pretended to be Abi and I met two of Abi's sugar daddies. That was before the police rang me. As her friends say Abi didn't have a boyfriend, it stands to reason that one of those sugar daddies must have got her pregnant. I want to know which one.'

'Did she seem stressed before she left for Cape Town?' Ruth asks, returning to the stove and vigorously stirring the saucepan with the wooden spoon.

'No. She was happy and excited.'

'Perhaps she was happy about the pregnancy,' Ruth suggests. 'Perhaps she wanted to keep the baby.'

Natasha and I catch each other's eyes and frown. Abi was focused on her degree; she wanted to be a barrister, and she knew exactly what Bob and I would have thought about her having a baby aged twenty-one.

'Do you remember that case about a newly married woman being killed in Cape Town, and everyone thought her husband had paid a hit man?' I ask. 'Well, after that it came to light that the police are under strict instructions to solve any murders of tourists as quickly as possible. They don't want long trials or investigations that are likely to be covered by the international media. The country simply can't afford to scare off foreign tourists who might think the place is too dangerous to visit. Well, I think that's what's happened here. They've laid the blame on an easy target. It's general knowledge that the police are corrupt. I've just got a really bad feeling about it.'

'Oh, Grace,' Natasha purrs. 'I can't begin to imagine how difficult this is for you, but surely you have to trust the police? You can't condemn a whole police force as corrupt – that's ridiculous. Besides, the police in the UK would carry on investigating if they thought it was suspicious.'

'I agree,' Ruth says as she reaches up into a high cupboard for some plates.

I feel a surge of anger towards my two best friends. They don't understand, and they're not making any efforts to do so.

'Either pour me a glass of wine or change the bloody subject,' I say.

They change the subject.

11

I really wasn't in the mood to gossip with my friends, and shortly after 9 p.m. I asked Natasha to drop me off back at home. Besides, I needed a drink. I've asked myself many times over the years why I never told Ruth and Natasha about being raped. In the early days, it was shame that sealed my lips, and now decades after the event, what happened to me aged twenty-one seems irrelevant. They thought my descent into recklessness was the result of losing both my parents in the same year. For sure, I was shoulder-deep in grief, but being raped added that element of self-destruction. I loathed myself. I hated my body, I hated my weakness, and I lost the self-confidence of youth. I never opened my own salon and instead got a part-time job as a hairdresser and frittered my inheritance on alcohol and partying. That was until I met Bob. Yet, although in many ways Bob saved me, I never even told him the truth.

And now, here I am. Back in that black fog, grief edged with self-loathing both rearing their ugly heads once again. What a useless mother I must be for knowing so little about her daughter. The more I think about Abi being stabbed to death by some stranger requesting money for drugs, the less likely it seems.

Yes, I know it's possible. A stranger being stabbed happens everywhere in the world. You can be in the wrong place at the wrong time and have your life snuffed out in an instant. But Abi was hiding things. She was hiding a pregnancy, being a sugar baby and going to South Africa early to meet an unknown boyfriend. Call it a mother's intuition, but I think she died because of her life, not due to a stranger's depravity. Of course, my friends are right. Who am I to question the police? What do I know about justice on the other side of the world?

I hop into the car and drive to an off-licence on the other side of town. I buy a case of white wine, two bottles of vodka and a bottle of brandy. Of course I shouldn't. It's stupid, but I think I deserve it. I stopped drinking overnight twice before, so I am confident I can do it again. I just need the edge to be taken off my feelings for the next couple of weeks.

ELLA IS BACK HOME, but she is upstairs in her room, so I bring the case and the vodka inside and carry them straight up to my bedroom. I shove them inside my wardrobe, crushing clothes in the process. I open a bottle of wine and pour myself a glass. I then run a hot bath and soak in the tub, drinking my wine. It seems oh-so-very civilised.

By the time I've got out of the bath and am climbing into bed, I'm totally exhausted and don't feel like any more wine. I am so proud of myself for drinking just two glasses.

But I can't sleep. Perhaps Abi didn't know she was pregnant, but at fourteen weeks, that seems quite unlikely. It can happen, though. And I still haven't heard from the third Sweetner sugar daddy, Loaded-Len. I wonder whether he went to Cape Town with Abi and killed her. It would make sense that he wouldn't reply to her messages, because he would know that she was dead. The more I mull over that theory, the more probable it seems.

. . .

I HATE first thing in the mornings. In the instant that I wake up, I am calm and normal, but then I remember. Abi is dead. My life will never be the same. My baby is gone. But at least this morning I feel a sense of purpose.

I call Sergeant Linda Hornby.

'Good morning Linda,' I say, relieved she answers my call. 'I've managed to track down two of the men Abi was spending time with via Sweetner.net. One of them seemed really dodgy, but there is a third man who hasn't responded to any messages. I think he could be a suspect. Can you force the website to release the identity of the man who hasn't responded? His pseudonym is Loaded-Len.'

She is silent for a long time. 'Are you still there?' I ask.

'Yes. The thing is, Grace, Abi's murderer has been found and charged. None of the people using Sweetner have done anything wrong. It's not a police matter. I understand that you find it distasteful and immoral, but it isn't illegal. I also understand that you want to find out the identity of Abi's boyfriend, or whoever got her pregnant, but I strongly advise that you don't pursue this. It would be much better if you could talk to a counsellor. Why don't you have a chat with your doctor?'

'I don't need any support,' I say curtly and end the call.

I HAVE BEEN a hairdresser all of my adult life. For the past ten years I have worked full time, mostly in a salon that we abbreviate to HHH. Helena's Hairdressers Horsham was set up by Helena over a decade ago, and it has a good reputation in West Sussex, especially as we prefer to use dyes with as few chemicals as possible. I have rented a chair from Helena for the past three years, which means I am listed as one of HHH's hairdressers, but I am self-employed. I also have a few private customers whom I visit in their homes. It's a precarious business being a hairdresser. I don't get sick pay or time off for holidays, and although the last thing I feel like doing is returning full time to the salon, I know that I have to continue with some of my clients; I simply can't afford to pay my bills without it.

I have two appointments with regulars this morning, and I'm already running late. I leave a note for Ella that I'll be home for lunch, and hurry out.

The salon is bright and airy with full-height mirrors in front of each black leather chair, plenty of green plants and aromatherapy diffusers pumping out essential oils. The sink section has a row of massage chairs and soothing low lights. The other stylists are all lovely towards me, but Helena must have briefed them to refrain from asking me any questions, so I just get lots of offers for coffee and kind smiles. In between my customers, I have a few minutes to spare, so I nip into the staffroom at the back of the salon and go onto my phone to search for Sweetner's contact details. All I can find is an online form and their office addresses. Their head office is in California, and they have offshoots in London, Paris and Madrid. Telephone numbers are not listed anywhere. I'm stumped.

'Grace, your client is here.' Amy, the new trainee, is a waif of a girl, and she speaks so quietly she's almost inaudible. My telephone pings, but I haven't got time to look at it, so I shove it back in my bag and return to the salon. Mrs Dawson is one of my regulars, and fortunately for me, she doesn't indulge in chatter, instead making the most of the bountiful supply of women's magazines that Helena keeps in the salon.

Once Mrs Dawson has left, I collect my belongings, wave a hasty goodbye to everyone, and walk downstairs and onto the street. As I'm striding along the main shopping street, I remember the ping on my phone. I stop and take my phone out of my brown leather bag. To my surprise, it's an alert on Snapchat. I open it and, to my horror, see that someone who calls themselves Abi's Ghost has added me as a friend. I remember Abi installing the app on my phone about three years ago, laughing at me that I was such a luddite. The girls sent me messages on it occasionally, but more latterly we moved to WhatsApp. My hand is shaking as I click to accept the friend request, and then just a couple of seconds later a message comes through.

Dear Mum,

Abi here – or rather my ghost. You need to step back and stop probing. I'm dead and there's nothing you can do to bring me back. You won't be able to find out where this message came from, so don't try. I don't want the world to know that I was on Sweetner, and there are some raunchy videos out there that you would hate, so stop prying. My life is over and you need to let me rest in peace.

Love,

Abi x

I THINK I'm going to throw up. I lean against the brick wall between two shops and bend over, gulping big breaths of fresh air to try to halt the sensation of heaving. Who the hell would send me a message like that? Could there be anything crueler than to send a message pretending to be their deceased child to a mother?

'Are you alright, love?' A woman, about my age, is peering at me.

'Yes, fine. Thank you.' I stand up straight and smile at her. It takes several long minutes for me to stop shaking, and when my stomach feels vaguely stable, I try calling Linda, but all I get is her voicemail. I don't leave a message. Instead I call Detective Inspector Pete Fairisle.

He picks up on the first ring.

'It's Grace Woods. You're investigating the murder of my daughter Abi.'

'Yes, Mrs Woods. How are you doing? How can I help you?'

'I've had a Snapchat message from someone pretending to be Abi's ghost, and it's horrible.'

'I'm sorry to hear that. It does sound very cruel. Did you screenshot it?'

'What?'

'Snapchat deletes the message as soon as you come off the chat. Is it still there?'

I ask him to hold on whilst I look at the app again. To my dismay, the message has gone. Not only that, my only two friends on Snapchat are Abi and Ella. Abi's ghost has disappeared.

'It's gone and the sender has vanished too. I can't believe it!'

'Mmm,' DI Fairisle says. 'Unfortunately, there's not much we can do at this stage. If it happens again, screenshot the message and we can look into it. Was the sender threatening you with anything?'

'No, not really. I'm not sure.' And now I just feel confused. I read the message and it upset me, but I can't even remember exactly what it said.

'If you receive anything else or are worried, don't hesitate to get back in touch with Linda or myself.'

After we finish the call, I stare at my phone as if it is the offending item. I can't believe anyone would be so cruel – and who sent it? Was it one of the sugar daddies? When I walk past the local co-op, I go inside and stride straight to the till. Behind the cashier is a screen hiding shelves of cigarettes from view.

'I'll have twenty Benson & Hedges, please. No, make that forty.'

. . .

BACK AT HOME, Ella has left me a note to say she's spending the afternoon with Rachel again. I go upstairs and grab one of the bottles of vodka. I take it, a glass, the cigarettes and a lighter to our small back garden, which is my pride and joy. During the years I have been living alone, I have found solace in my little garden, watching it change during the seasons, nurturing the plants and making it as beautiful as I can. Although it's postage stamp sized, I have a small bed set aside for my cutting garden, depending upon the season, filled with sweet peas, delphinium, dahlias and tulips. I have an old crockery jug that I picked up at a car boot sale some years ago, which I like to keep filled up with flowers cut from my garden. But today, even my beloved plants can't dispel the misery. I take one of the wrought-iron chairs and place it on the lawn, and then I pour myself a large measure of vodka and light a cigarette. I don't know how long I sit there, stewing in my own misery, but eventually I need to go to the toilet. When I stand up, the garden spins. It's hard to put one foot in front of the other, and I'm proud of myself that I make it up the stairs without having an accident. But then I think about Abi again, and I tumble into her room, collapsing onto her bed in a fit of sobs.

I assume I pass out because by the time I awake, the light outside is fading. I can hear the clatter of someone in the kitchen. Ella, I hope. I sit up and rub my eyes. The room isn't spinning anymore, and all I have is a thudding headache. I stagger to the bathroom, throw cold water on my face and drink straight from the tap.

'Hi, darling,' I shout from the top of the stairs, but my voice sounds weak.

'Hello, Mum. Just making myself an omelette. Do you want anything?'

'Could you put a piece of bread in the toaster for me?'

'Sure.'

When I come downstairs, Ella throws me a really strange, quizzical look. 'Are you okay?'

'As okay as is possible under the circumstances.'

'Was it you who left an empty bottle of booze and a pile of cigarette stubs in the garden?'

'Shit,' I mutter under my breath. I decide that honesty is the best policy in the circumstances. Ella stares at me, her eyes wide, her hands on her hips.

'No, Mum, not again! You promised. And what about all those lectures you gave Abi and me about not smoking? It's so hypocritical.'

'I admit it, Ella. But with everything that's happened, I just wanted to... Look, there's no excuse. It was a bloody awful idea, and I'll be suffering for days as a result. I'm sorry. I've got to pop out to Ruth's house now, but we can talk when I'm back in an hour.'

I give her a quick kiss, which she shrugs off.

MY PLAN IS to talk to Ethan, hopefully alone. I recall Ruth saying she was flying today and Alan was also away. Ethan has always been into programming, and he has a place at university to read computer sciences. I am sure he'll know about apps and whether it's possible to recover a deleted message. Besides, I haven't had the chance to have a one-to-one with Ethan, to find out if what he said originally was true, that he has barely had any contact with Abi over the past year.

As I open my car door, it strikes me that I probably shouldn't be driving. Although I don't feel drunk anymore, the alcohol will still be in my system. I curse. I can't take the risk, so I call a taxi. Whilst I'm waiting, I stand a few doors down and smoke a cigarette. After a few puffs, I stub it out in disgust at myself.

Fifteen minutes later, I am at Ruth's house. I ring the door-bell, but to my dismay, Ruth herself answers.

'Hello. This is a surprise.'

'Actually, I was here to have a word with Ethan. Is he home?'

'No. He's staying the night with a friend. But come in.' Ruth stands back to let me pass.

'Was your trip cancelled?' I ask.

'Trip?'

'I thought you were flying today.'

'No.' She looks at me quizzically. I must have been mistaken. 'Anyway, what did you want to talk to Ethan about?'

'I need some help with my phone, and as he's the wizard at all things technical, I was hoping he might be able to help me.' I follow her through the corridor and down a step into their living room. She sits on an armchair and I sit opposite Ruth on the sofa. And then I decide to tell her.

'I got a Snapchat message from someone pretending to be Abi's ghost. But because it came in on Snapchat, it's gone now.'

Ruth lets out a whistle. 'Bloody hell, Grace. That's really mean. Who would send a message like that?'

'I'm assuming it's one of the men on Sweetner.' I wipe away a tear. Ruth comes over to give me a hug.

'Grace?' She recoils slightly. 'Have you been drinking and smoking?'

'Yes, and it's hardly surprising, is it?' I retort. 'You'd want a few drinks too if you were in my position, desperate to find out what happened to your daughter and who the father of your dead grandchild was.' I run my fingers through my hair and tug a section so tightly, a bunch of hairs come loose in my fingers. 'I need to talk to Ethan and Becky again.'

She stands up. 'I know you are going through hell, Grace. But you've just fallen off the bloody wagon! Don't you think it's more important to start putting your life back together again so that you're there to support Ella?'

'Oh, please don't judge me.'

'I'm not judging you. I'm trying to help you.' She glowers at me.

I stand up. 'All I want to do is talk to Ethan and get his help with Snapchat.'

'I think it would be better for everyone if you left Ethan alone.'

'Why?'

'He's suffering too, Grace. We all are. I'm trying really hard to support you, but...' She waves her hands around in the air as if she's exasperated.

'Forget it,' I say as I leave the room.

12

I wish Abi's phone had been found. It would have answered so many questions, and now I have to chase for answers myself. I can't stop thinking about the Snapchat message. Would a grown man use such an app for communicating? Isn't it more likely that it was sent by one of Abi's contemporaries? Ethan or Becky perhaps. Maybe that's why Ruth didn't want me to talk to Ethan. Or Katy? If she was in a relationship with Abi, perhaps she has something to do with all of this, but quite how, I can't work out.

I am aware that Ethan and Becky spend most of their time hanging out at Natasha's house, no doubt because Becky has a spacious bedroom with an en-suite bathroom tucked away on the third floor. The next day, after work, I drive straight to the Bellovers'.

Becky answers the door.

'Hello, love. Is your mum home?'

'No, she'll be back soon though.'

'Actually, it's you I'd like to have a quick word with. Is Ethan here?'

'No,' she whispers. She bites her lip and scratches her wrist.

It's obvious she doesn't want to talk to me, but she's well brought up and polite, so she stands back to let me pass.

'Do you use Snapchat?' I ask, noting the huge bouquet of lilies in the hallway.

'Not often.'

'I had an unpleasant message about Abi,' I say, peering at her to see if I get any reaction. She reddens.

'It wasn't me!'

'Sorry, Becky. I wasn't implying it was. Look, I know it's really difficult for everyone. You've lost your best friend. I've lost my daughter. But surely you knew what Abi was up to? Who her boyfriend was?'

Becky bursts into tears, her bony shoulders shaking, her thin arms clasped around her narrow torso. 'I miss her so much,' she says through her sobs.

'I know you do, love. We all do. And that's why I need to know what you know.'

But her sobbing becomes more violent, hiccups, breathless, and I wonder if she is going to choke.

I stroke her arm. Surely this is an overreaction, unless she's hiding something that is eating her up? Or is this just the way Becky is? Emotional, overwrought, anxious, troubled? That's why I had wanted to talk to Ethan rather than Becky.

When I hear the crunch of tyres on the gravel outside and the slamming of car doors, I am mighty relieved.

'Helloo!' Natasha shouts as she slams the front door behind her. I hurry into the hallway.

'Lovely surprise,' she says, placing her shopping bags on the floor and giving me an air kiss.

'I'm afraid I've upset Becky,' I say quietly. 'I asked her some questions and she's sobbing now.'

I expect Natasha to be annoyed, but she seems unsurprised, resigned even. 'An overreaction, undoubtedly. We have an appointment with the counsellor next week.'

I follow her into the kitchen, but Becky has disappeared.

'Help yourself to a cup of tea whilst I go and have a word with her,' Natasha says.

A few seconds later, I hear raised voices and the slamming of a door. Natasha reappears. I raise an eyebrow.

'Don't ask,' she says, shaking her head.

I feel like a glass of wine, not a cup of tea, but decide not to say anything. It seems, however, that Ruth has been talking.

'Gather you're drinking and smoking again,' Natasha says. She's never shy of pulling punches.

'Hardly surprising under the circumstances. If you're offering, I'll accept.'

'I'm not.' Her face is deadpan.

'Ruth wasn't very keen on me talking to Ethan. She had a real go at me, actually.'

'You need to be kind to her.'

'What?' I scowl, insulted that Natasha might be implying I've behaved in any untoward manner to Ruth.

'What I mean is that Ruth is having a tough time. Not like you, obviously, but things aren't great at home.'

'What do you mean?'

'You promise you'll keep this to yourself?'

'Yes, of course.'

'Ruth thinks Alan has been having an affair.'

'An affair!' I splutter. The thought of boring, unattractive Alan having an affair seems very unlikely.

'Ruth is convinced about it, but she didn't want to tell you when you've got so much on your own plate.' Natasha twirls her golden hair between her fingers. 'It's not surprising if you think about it. They're both away so much. Ruth is off flying at least half of every month, and Alan is in Kenya more than he's at home. And now Ethan is back living at home, they've been trying to ensure one of them is around for him. As a result, they barely ever see each other.'

'Poor Ruth. What's she going to do about it?'

And then the front door slams and Justin walks in. Natasha has her back to him, and she puts her finger over her mouth, indicating I need to change the subject. I nod.

'Hello, Justin,' I say more brightly than I feel. I owe this man, considering he spent so much money on repatriating Abi to England.

'Hi both.'

'Good day?' Natasha asks.

'Just another stressful day in paradise,' he says sarcastically. 'I'll leave you two to it. I've got a load of paperwork to get through.'

'Justin looks exhausted,' I say, noting the rings under his eyes and the grey pallor to his face.

'He's under a lot of pressure at the moment. His deputy head has just given notice, and it's often the way at the end of the school year. Reports, sorting out capital projects to be completed over the summer, reviews. In fact, it's so bad he's even pulled out of the golf tournament he was meant to be playing in.'

I raise my eyebrows. Justin used to take everything in his stride. I think back to when we were teenagers. All three of us fancied Justin, who was in the year above us, captain of the rugby team and on track to go to Oxford. I'm sure there wasn't a girl in the school who didn't have a secret crush on him. His toffee-coloured skin and black, almond-shaped eyes, matched to his muscular frame and intellect, were a heady mix, along with that unspoken thought of how impressive it was that a boy from such an underprivileged background could crash through all the ugly social and racist barriers to achieve so much. No one was more surprised than I was when he grabbed me as I walked past him in a darkened corridor at a school disco during my lower sixth year.

'Oi!' I said, ready to kick whoever had the audacity to grab me, until I realised who it was: Justin Bellover.

'I've been watching you. You're a good dancer.'

'Thanks,' I said, blushing deeply.

And then he kissed me. Justin and I were an item for three weeks, which in the heady days of sixth-form life, was a long time. He broke my heart by dumping me to, as he explained, 'concentrate on his exams'. In fact, he started dating another girl. When Natasha got together with Justin after he graduated from Oxford, I was in part a little bit envious. Justin adored her, and they were the first of my friends to walk down the aisle.

In the early days of their marriage, Justin would still flirt with me, throwing me a wink or acknowledging in some little way that we had history. But these days he barely looks at me. Of course, I haven't got the funds to keep myself as trim and beautified as Natasha does, but even so.

'Are you back at work full time?' Natasha asks, bringing me back to the present.

'No,' I say. 'Part time. Oh, Natasha, I wish I had enough money to go to Cape Town myself. I might be able to find out what really happened.'

She shakes her head at me. 'That's a really bad idea. You have to leave these things to the police. What would going there actually achieve?'

I don't know. All I do know is that there I must find out more about my beautiful daughter's death.

IT'S on my drive home that I get the idea. I need to contact the landlady where Abi stayed. I trawl through my emails to find her address, and I send her a message.

Dear Karolyn,

*I am the mother of Abi, who was murdered on the beach whilst she
was staying at your Airbnb. I would dearly love to talk to you to find
out how she was during the days before she died. I know this is a
huge imposition, but if you're up for this, please let me know.
Kind regards,
Grace Woods*

THE NEXT MORNING, I wake to a reply from her.

*Dear Grace,
My heart bleeds for you and your family. The police declined to give
me your contact details and said I shouldn't make contact. I am glad
you have reached out to me and would be happy to speak to you.
Shall we connect on Skype? My skype name is Karolyn-Kalk-Bay.
We are just one hour ahead of you. I'll leave Skype on today.
My thoughts are continually with you,
Karolyn*

As soon as I see Karolyn's face, I know that I like her. She has a
mop of brown curly hair pinned on top of her head, a wide
mouth, sparkling eyes and large dimples in both her cheeks.
Her face is tanned and lined and I can't see a scrap of makeup.
It's hard to discern her age.

'Grace, if I may call you that. I am so sorry. Abi was such a
delight.' Karolyn's South African accent is strong, and her
words, I am so sorry, sound more like *I ehm so sorry*.

'I was just wondering how Abi seemed to you the day she
died?'

'Happy, excited, full of the confidence of youth. She played
with my dog and then said she was going out for the day.'

'To do what?'

'I can't remember if she said, but she was very excited about meeting up with her boyfriend.'

'Boyfriend?' My heart skips a beat.

'I told the police this. She said her family and friends didn't approve of her boyfriend. I didn't like to pry.'

'But as far as we knew, she didn't have a boyfriend.'

Karolyn's face falls. 'I wish I'd asked her more, but you know, I try not to ask my guests too many questions.'

'Of course.'

'Did you see her with a man?'

Karolyn shakes her head and we're both silent for a moment.

'Would you like to see around my house? I can show you where Abi slept?'

'Yes, that would be lovely.'

Karolyn flips the camera on her iPad and shows me her bright and airy living room, with a dark wood floor and rattan sofas and chairs piled high with cushions in bright colours: tangerine, neon green, raspberry. There is a wide glass coffee table under which a Staffordshire bull terrier lies, one eye open as he watches Karolyn. She walks through some patio doors into a courtyard garden filled with brightly coloured blooms, some in pots, others planted underneath tall foliage, blowing gently in the wind. There is a small pond in the centre of the garden with a little water feature in the centre.

'We can see the sea from here,' she says, pointing the iPad in another direction. And there is the azure ocean sparkling in the distance. It is beautiful and I am glad that Abi enjoyed such a stunning location during her last days.

'I'll take you back inside now and show you where Abi stayed.' She walks me through the living room and into a light-filled open-plan kitchen that has shelving units stacked with brightly painted crockery. And then we go through a small corridor, and she turns right into a large bedroom with white muslin curtains that are blowing in the wind, a large mahogany-framed bed topped with a white duvet cover and bright orange cushions. Through the window there is another glimpse of the sea.

'It's beautiful,' I whisper.

'You know Kalk Bay is not a dangerous place, Grace. There are many places on the Cape that are dangerous for tourists to visit, but here, I think we have had one killing in the past decade. It is a small town with galleries and cafes, and we have a working harbour, where fishermen go out daily and return to sell their fresh catch. We even have a couple of resident seals in the harbour. I hope one day you will visit.'

I absorb what Karolyn is saying, and for a moment all I hear is the faint crackle that transmits between Cape Town and Sussex.

'Do you think it was a random killing?' I ask Karolyn.

She turns the iPad around so I can see her face. 'I find it strange. You know the police sometimes like to solve crimes quickly here. We cannot afford for tourists to stay away. Yes, it may be a random killing, and there is a terrible drugs problem in many of the townships and elsewhere, but this murder was solved very quickly.'

'They say that he admitted guilt.'

Karolyn shrugs her shoulders. We smile at each other. I know for sure that if we lived in the same place, she and I would be firm friends.

'Do you have any children?' I ask.

'A son who lives in Australia and a daughter who lives here in Cape Town. I can't begin to imagine what you are going through. If you ever want to come to South Africa, my home is yours. It would be a pleasure.'

'Thank you, you are so kind.' My eyes well up with affection for this stranger and desolation for my daughter.

· · ·

I PUT the phone down and make myself a cup of coffee. I consider putting a glug of brandy into it, but as I glance at the clock on the kitchen wall, I see it's not even 9 a.m. The more I think about it, the more I am convinced that Abi was killed by a sugar daddy. Perhaps she was meeting a new man, someone based in South Africa? But it seems more likely that it is one of the three she already knew; after all, why would I receive a message pretending to be Abi's ghost from someone who didn't even know I was suspicious about who killed her?

13

The letterbox rattles and the post plops to the floor. I hear Ella stomp to the front door. She talks to me as she walks back into the kitchen.

'Mum, is it ok if Rachel and I go shopping in Crawley today?'

'Have you got any money?'

She passes the post to me. 'Dad gave me some. I want to buy some new jeggings.'

'Alright. Message me during the day, please.'

Ella has changed. Two months ago she would have rolled her eyes at me if I'd asked her to stay in contact, but now our need to stay close is mutual. I flip through my post. It's mainly bills. My fingers hover over my mobile phone bill. I know I should have gone digital for my bills, but I still have the need for that bit of paper; otherwise I fear I'll forget to pay them.

Abi's phone bill. Just because we don't have her phone doesn't mean that we can't check what numbers she dialed. I call Bob.

'When you were sorting out Abi's stuff, did you cancel her phone bill?'

'Damn. No, I forgot that one.'

'Don't worry. I'll do it.'

WE HAVE all used the same network provider, to ensure that we get specials on family deals. With a copy of Abi's death certificate in my bag, I walk to the centre of town and into the mobile phone shop. The place is deserted; the only sales assistant is a young man with a face full of acne, who looks younger than Abi was.

'My daughter died, and I would like to settle her bill and transfer the phone number to my account. Can you do that for me?'

His eyes dart around the shop before eventually resting on my chin. 'Yes, that's awful. Sorry.'

I hand over the death certificate. From the look on his face, I doubt he has ever seen one before.

'Her phone number?'

I say it out loud. After confirming Abi's details, he asks for my own. His fingers dance across the keyboard, and in no time he smiles briefly and announces it's all done.

'Please can I have a copy of Abi's last bill,' I ask.

'Um, I'm not sure if I can give you that. It's data protection.' His voice fades away.

'I know you must have your rules and regulations, but I have just lost my daughter.'

'Yeah, sorry. I don't think I'm allowed to.'

I lower my voice and lean forwards. 'Just think how your mother would feel if you were killed.'

His mouth drops open and he takes a step backwards. I realise then how threatening my words sounded.

'Sorry,' I say, shaking my head. 'I didn't mean to–'

'No. It's ok. I'll do it for you.' He presses a few keys, and then a printer, hidden under the desk, starts whirring. A few awkward moments later, he hands me several sheets of paper.

'Thank you,' I say.

'Sorry for your loss,' he mumbles.

I HAVE an hour before my first client in the salon, so I walk to Costa Coffee, order myself a latté and take a table near the back of the coffee house. Carefully, I look through all of the numbers that Abi used to call. Mine and Bob's pop up the most. In fact, I am surprised that there are so few numbers, and then realise that she would have contacted her friends via apps or social media. The young don't seem to talk so much on the telephone anymore. But there is another number that she called regularly, sometimes daily, or at least three times a week. And the calls lasted anywhere up to an hour. Nervously, I dial the number from my telephone.

'Sorry, the number you are trying to reach has been disconnected.'

I dial it again, just to be sure. I get the same message.

That is bizarre. Did this person throw away their phone and delete their account after Abi died?

I call Linda and explain about the phone number.

'Yes, it does seem strange,' she admits. 'It's a tricky situation, Grace, because Abi's murder has been solved. Look, leave it with me and I'll discuss it with the DI. I'll get back to you.'

'Thanks,' I say, but I have my doubts that the police will do anything further.

DURING MY BREAK, I check my mobile phone to make sure that Ella has arrived safely in Crawley. I have two messages from her, including one where she has photographed herself in the mirror of a changing room, having tried on a spaghetti-strap dress she has bought.

'Grace, there's a call for you,' Amy, the new trainee, says.

I frown. Normally, the girls book my appointments for me and I don't talk to my clients on the phone.

'It's a man.'

'I don't do men's hair.'

'He doesn't want a haircut. He's says it's personal.'

I don't understand why anyone would call me on the salon's number, so I hurry after Amy. Fortunately, Helena is drying a client's hair, so is unaware of the call.

'Hello?'

'Mrs Woods, this is William Jennings; we met at Gatwick.'

'Yes, Dr Jennings,' I say, my heart quickening. Why is he calling me? I never told him where I worked – or perhaps Abi did?

'My apologies for calling you at work, but I have no other means of contacting you. I have taken the liberty of employing a private detective.'

'What! Why?' I am astounded.

'I want to help you, Mrs Woods. When we met, you mentioned someone called Loaded-Len.'

Goodness. I said his name as a throwaway remark. I am flabbergasted that Dr Jennings remembered.

'Yes.'

'My private investigator has identified him.'

'How?'

He laughs. 'I'm not sure that I want to ask how he acquires his information. But nevertheless, he assures me that Len is a seventy-four-year-old retired judge who lives in York. He has a penchant for young girls, but he had a vasectomy twenty years ago and consequently cannot be the father of your daughter's unborn child. Furthermore, he was unfortunate enough to have suffered a stroke just three months ago and apparently is now wheelchair bound. I assume that is the reason he has not replied to you.'

'Wow,' I say, sitting down on the stool behind the reception desk. As I look up, I see Helena glaring at me.

'Dr Jennings, I can't talk here at work, but just before I go, Abi used to call a particular phone number on a regular basis, but now the number is out of service. Do you think your private detective might be able to help us with that?'

'I don't know, but I can certainly ask.'

'Thank you,' I say. 'I'll call you later with the number.'

Later on, when I'm back home, I send him a message with the telephone number that was listed repeatedly on Abi's phone bill. I wonder what William's private investigator will discover. I hope that it will lead to whoever is trying to scare me.

14

M y face is wet with tears when I awake, a heaviness in my chest. There is a knock on the door and it opens. Ella walks in holding a tray.

'Happy birthday, Mum,' she says as she places the tray on the end of my bed and opens the curtains. I have totally forgotten that today is my birthday.

'What's up?' she says as she turns and sees me wiping my face dry with the edge of the duvet cover. She sits down on the bed and puts her arms around me.

'It's not fair, is it?' she murmurs into my hair.

'No. We will miss Abi every day, but never more so than on special days like birthdays and Christmas.'

'I'm no good at baking cakes, like she was,' Ella says.

'Don't worry, darling. Just having you here is enough.'

She nods, but I know this isn't the upbeat birthday atmosphere she was hoping for. I glance at the tray. She has made me toast, a cup of coffee, a bowl of cereal, and there is a little vase with a single sprig of delphinium, my favourite flower. She hands me an envelope. Ella has painted me a beautiful card depicting a Cornish cove and seascape. It was the last holiday the three of us spent together.

After eating my breakfast, watched by Ella, I stretch. 'I'd better get going. I've got to get to the salon.'

'Um, I don't think so,' she says, blushing slightly.

I look at her askance.

'You're not going to work today.'

I frown.

'You need to call Natasha. She didn't want to ring too early, in case she woke you.'

I do as Ella instructs.

'Happy birthday to you!' Natasha sings down the phone line, unashamedly out of tune. 'How are you?'

'Mmm, ok. It's hard without Abi.'

'Of course it is, love. That's why Ruth and I are taking you out for the day. It's all been approved by Helena. Don't worry about your clients; they've been postponed until next week. Casual clothes. Be ready in an hour.' She puts the phone down.

'Have you all been in on this?' I ask Ella, who is grinning at me now.

'Yup.'

AN HOUR LATER, I am sitting on the back seat of Natasha's car.

'We're having a day out at the new spa at the Elder Crown Hotel. It's our birthday present to you.'

'Wow!' I exclaim. 'That is so kind.' The owners of the super-luxurious country house hotel have spent millions on upgrading its spa, and it was reviewed in the local papers just last month.

Half an hour later, we pull up in front of the turreted hotel. The spa has been constructed on the side of the historic house and is all glass and straight lines.

After a herbal tea, we are shown into sumptuous changing

rooms, with marble sinks, rain showers, heated floors and plump leather sofas. The assistant hands us each fluffy white dressing gowns and soft slippers.

'What treatments have you booked?' I ask.

'You're having a full-body scrub followed by an aromatherapy massage. After lunch you're having reflexology, a head massage, and then you're getting a manicure and a pedicure,' Natasha says.

'Thank you so much,' I murmur, although I do wish I'd had notice. I would have shaved my legs and made sure I was suitably prepped for such an occasion.

My masseuse is a beautiful Indian girl with a lilting accent and a firm touch. I think it's the first time I have truly relaxed since Abi was taken from us. I find myself floating off into a dream state, my body heavy, my mind stilled as I inhale the aromatic scents and sink into the warm bed.

When she wakes me, I struggle to come to.

'When you're ready, please take a seat at reception. You can keep your dressing gown on for lunch. One of my colleagues will take you and your friends through to the dining room.'

When I meander through to the reception area, which is shrouded with palm trees and is furnished with chairs and tables more suited to the Orient than West Sussex, I am the only guest there.

'Hello, Madam. Would you like a glass of champagne while you wait?' The waitress is holding a bottle of champagne and an empty glass.

'Thank you,' I say, wondering if I can drink it quickly before the others arrive. I am out of luck. Ruth pads in, her hair damp and sticking up, framing her small head like a hedgehog. She furrows her brow as she looks at my glass, but she doesn't say anything. I wonder how she's holding up in light of her marriage difficulties. I recall how both Ruth and Natasha were my stalwarts during my marriage breakdown, and I feel sad that she thinks she can't confide in me now. I could do with thinking about someone else's problems rather than being so focused on my own. But I'm not going to betray Natasha's confidence, so I just smile at her. And then Natasha arrives, with a shiny bright face.

'How were your treatments?'

'Divine,' I say.

'Mine too,' Ruth says.

'Ladies, are you ready for lunch?' the waitress asks.

I quickly finish my champagne, and we follow her into a small dining room and then outside onto a patio that sits above lawns that fall away to fields and woodland in the distance. The air is warm and scented with lavender from the bushes that are growing around the edge of the patio. We are handed menus featuring largely vegetarian dishes with fancy-sounding names.

'I'll have the avocado and smoked salmon ballotine with the jeweled salad and brittle, please.' It is one of the few dishes that makes sense to me.

'Would you ladies care for a bottle of sparkling wine with your lunch?'

'Thank you,' Natasha says. I catch Ruth frowning at her.

'I can manage to drink just one glass, you know. I don't need to drink myself into a stupor every time.'

'Sorry,' Ruth mutters.

'So, how have you been?' Natasha asks, breaking the atmosphere.

'I think I might be making some progress,' I say as I lean my head back to feel the sun on my face. 'Dr Jennings, who is one of the sugar daddies, has employed a private detective to help us track down the other sugar daddies.'

'Shit,' Natasha says. 'That's awful.'

'This Dr Jennings, do you trust him?' Ruth asks.

'Actually, I do.'

'Mmm.' Natasha plays with a whole-meal bread roll. 'Don't

you think he's being a bit too helpful? Perhaps he's deflecting from himself to throw you off the scent, or maybe he's doing this out of guilt.'

'No,' I say firmly, taking too large a gulp from my sparkling wine. 'I'm sure he's genuine, well, as sure as anyone can be. I really don't think he's guilty.'

'Are you sure you're not being naive, Grace? You can't forget that he's a sleazy geezer. He's a sugar daddy, after all. Not exactly blame-free.'

'You've got it wrong!' I cry.

I look at my two lovely friends and see the disdain on their faces, and although they're doing so much for me and treating me to a glorious day out, I can't stop myself from crying. I push my chair back and hurry down the steps of the patio onto the lawns. Even so I can feel the eyes of the other diners on my back.

I find a larger rhododendron bush and stand behind it so I'm shielded from view. Throwing my head backwards, I stare at the bright blue sky and then take a series of deep breaths. When I feel as if I have my emotions under control, I hurry back towards the terrace. Natasha is walking towards me.

'Hey.' She puts a hand out towards me.

'Sorry. An overreaction there.'

'It's fine,' she says, linking her arm in mine as we walk back up the lawn. 'Neither Ruth nor I can begin to imagine what you're going through.'

'I know, but even so. All you're both doing is being lovely towards me.'

Ignoring the other diners' stares, I dart Ruth a watery smile and murmur, 'I'm sorry.'

'Nothing to be sorry for.' She raises her glass. 'Happy birthday.'

'Thanks,' I say. 'And thank you for this and for being such wonderful friends. I don't deserve either of you.'

I finish my glass of sparkling wine, but when the waitress comes over to refill all of our glasses, I put my hand over the top of mine. I'm trying. I'm really trying.

AFTER LUNCH, we're led back to the spa reception.

'Did you enjoy your lunch, ladies?'

'Thank you, we did,' I say.

'Once your afternoon treatments are finished, we have an afternoon tea for you along with some Free From cakes, prior to your departure.'

I'm surprised how full I feel from my relatively modest but very delicious lunch. Ruth and Natasha are led away by their therapists, and then another girl arrives for me.

After rinsing and scrubbing my feet, my therapist starts massaging the soles of my feet. My session of reflexology is painful in parts, but also deeply relaxing. And then she gives me a pedicure, and once again, I feel totally chilled out.

'We normally suggest you get dressed before we do your manicure, so you don't mess up your nails.'

'Sure, that's fine. I'll get dressed.'

I am the only guest in the changing rooms, so I quickly put on my jeans and blouse, slip my feet into my sandals and admire my newly painted toenails. Then I grab my bag. As I'm walking back to the treatment room, I do a quick check of my phone. Although Ella knows where I am today, I still want to double-check in case I have any messages from her. I don't. But then my phone rings. It's a withheld number, and immediately I think of the police, terrified that something might have happened to Ella. I have to remind myself that she's with Rachel, that Rachel's mum is sensible and she would call me if there were any problems.

I press accept to the call.

'Grace Woods?'

The voice is weird and sounds like a robot. It's indistinguishable as male or female.

'Who is this?' I ask.

'You need to let Abi rest in peace. Do you understand?'

'No. Who are you?'

'If you continue your futile digging, then you'll lose Ella, too. And if you go to the police or tell anyone about this, including your friends and ex-husband, Ella will die a slow and tortuous death.'

'Who is this?' My hand is shaking as I hold the phone up to my ear. 'Who is this?'

'Remember what I've said.'

And then the line cuts off.

What the hell? My breath is coming out as short pants, and any good from the day's relaxing therapies has evaporated from my body. I stare at my phone, and then I look at the last call received, but it says number withheld. Of course it does. Whichever bastard is trying to scare me is too clever to leave obvious trails.

'Is everything alright, madam?' My therapist is standing in front of me. I can see from the look on her face that she disapproves of my use of my mobile phone.

'No. I need a drink.'

'I will sort that out for you,' she says and scurries away.

I meant it metaphorically not literally, but if they want to furnish me with a drink, I'll happily accept. I collapse into one of the leather armchairs, but it's as if my brain is unable to process anything. Ella. I need to call Ella, to make sure she's ok. She is at Bob's house today, spending time with the new Mrs Woods and their toddler.

'Ella, are you alright?'

'Yes. Why shouldn't I be?'

'Nothing. Nothing. I just wanted to check.'

'You're sounding strange, Mum. Aren't you having a nice time at the spa?'

'Yes, lovely. Just missing you, that's all.'

'Okay.' She drawls the word as if she doesn't believe me.

'I'll see you later, love.'

'Dad says he'll drop me back home this evening.'

THE THERAPIST IS BACK with yet another glass of sparkling wine. I accept it eagerly and drink it in a couple of glugs. She looks on disapprovingly. If she knew what was going on in my life, she might not be quite so sanctimonious.

'Are you ready to have your nails painted?'

It's the last bloody thing I feel like doing. I'm skittish now and want to go home, but I know that Natasha and Ruth have gone to such an effort to make this into a lovely day for me, I mustn't disappoint them. I follow the therapist back to the treatment room, where she has laid out a vast array of varnishes in different colours.

'Which colour would you like?'

It seems so trivial to be selecting colours when a stranger has just threatened me and my daughter. I shrug.

'Sorry, I've got a bit of a headache. Why don't you choose a colour that you think will suit my skin tone?'

'Goodness.' She looks horrified. 'I hope the treatments haven't brought that on. Let me get you another glass of water.' She stands up and walks to the other side of the room, where she pours a pitcher of water infused with cucumber and orange slices into a tumbler. I would prefer another glass of sparkling wine, but I don't say anything.

She selects an apricot colour that I would never normally choose and don't really like, but it seems churlish to say anything. Instead, I muse over what the caller said. Someone is very unhappy that I'm probing into Abigail's life. Either this person murdered her, or they are worried that I'm going to find out something that they want hidden. Can I risk going to the police? I'm sure I should, but if they really do hurt Ella? I shut my eyes. I can't think about it.

It seems to me that my therapist wants to get rid of me quite quickly, and I don't blame her. She does my nails in record time, and before long, I'm seated back in reception and offered another glass of sparkling wine. This time I accept it. I try so hard to ignore the urge to drink more, but it's overwhelming. I am scared; I am in pain; I need something to diffuse the agony.

By the time Natasha and Ruth emerge, all fresh faced and beautified, I am more than tipsy.

'What a glorious day,' Natasha effuses as we sit down for our afternoon tea. They bring us another bottle, but Natasha abstains, as she's driving, and despite Ruth's worried glances, I polish off most of it.

'Sorry I'm drunk,' I slur, as I eat a slice of the chocolate birthday cake (probably made with courgettes and sweet potato) the hotel made especially for me. 'But it's my birthday and my heart is broken.'

Natasha places her hand over mine. 'We know, honey.'

'Thank you for being such amazing friends, and for today and everything.' I wipe away the tears.

'We're just sorry you're having to go through such hell,' Ruth says.

I want to tell them. I so want to tell them, but I'm scared. And in the car on the way home, I pretend to sleep, or perhaps I do, because then we're at my house and I'm tumbling out of the car, and when Ruth offers to see me inside, I shrug her off and thank them for the lovely day and hurry away so I can grieve alone.

'BLOODY HELL, Grace, are you drinking again?'

Bob's voice wrenches me from a dream where Abi, Ella and I are prancing along a Cornish hilltop. I pull myself up from my reclining position on the sofa. There is a half-drunk bottle of red wine on the coffee table, and my glass is empty.

'Yes,' I say. 'It's my birthday.'

'Shit, Grace. You haven't drunk in nearly a decade.'

'Things are different now.'

'I know, but it's not good for you.'

'Where's Ella?'

'She went upstairs to her room.' He stands in front of me, his arms crossed over his chest.

'I had a phone call. Someone threatened to hurt Ella unless I stop looking into Abi's death.'

'What!' Bob exclaims, letting his arms drop by his sides. He starts pacing around the small room.

'I got a phone call from someone with a Dalek-sounding voice. It was horrible.'

He stands still and frowns at me. 'Are you sure you're not imagining it? Don't you remember when you used to drink too much, you told the most implausible stories. Your imagination literally controlled your brain. It's probably happening again.'

'No, Bob, it's not. This is real and is nothing to do with alcohol. I wasn't even drunk when I got the call.'

'Have you told the police?'

I shake my head. 'The person told me they would kill Ella if I told anyone: you, my friends, the police.'

Bob bites his lower lip. I used to find that habit charming. I don't anymore. 'Can I see your phone?' he asks.

My head pounds as I haul myself up and walk to the kitchen, where I always dump my handbag. I rifle inside it, but I can't find my phone.

'Shit,' I murmur under my breath. I tip the bag upside down, and all the detritus comes out: my wallet, chewing gum, tissues, a lipstick, a half-used packet of cigarettes, a cheap plastic neon green lighter, house keys and car key and my sunglasses. But no phone. I hear Bob walking into the kitchen behind me.

'My phone's not here. I must have left it at the spa.'

He rolls his eyes at me. 'Losing Abi has been unbelievably tough on you. On all of us. But you've got to stop the drinking now. You know how out of control it got before, and it's obviously happening again.'

'No, Bob, it isn't!' I can't help but raise my voice at him.

'Don't do it, Grace.'

'You're not my bloody husband anymore! You don't get to tell me what to do!'

He turns on his heel and strides out of the kitchen. I hear him shout goodbye to Ella, and then he is gone.

15

Wednesdays are my late nights in the salon. I start work at 2 p.m. and accept clients right through until 9 p.m., although it's normally only in the run-up to Christmas that I'm in the salon that late. Today I have a full afternoon, but then there is a last-minute booking at 8.30 p.m. for a woman who has an unexpected event to attend. She begged the salon for an appointment, and kindly, Helena gave it to me. Although I desperately need the clients and the money, I am finding it difficult to muster my normal enthusiasm for beautifying people. The woman, who must be my age, has grey roots showing through her black hair and a tired face with a square jawline. When she announces that she wants a full head of colour with highlights and a cut, I can't stop myself from glancing at my watch. She catches me looking, and her dark eyes plead with me as she stares at me in the mirror.

'It's a funeral, not a party,' she says, in a low voice.

I nod and go to collect the colour chart. I promised myself that I would not let alcohol dictate my life, but I can feel that resolve slipping. I have started filling my water bottle with vodka. I don't drink it all in one go, but just take the occasional sip to dull my pain. But it's been a long day today, and there is just one sip left in my water bottle, one last covert gulp of vodka to get me through the next couple of hours.

The last few days have not been good. Mondays are my days off, so after ringing the spa and receiving confirmation that my phone had been handed in at reception, I asked Ella if she would like to come with me and I would pay for her to have a manicure. She threw me a look of disdain and turned away from me. I suppose her rejection isn't surprising. This morning, she found me passed out on the sofa, empty bottles and cigarette ends on the coffee table.

I cleared up. I made some futile apologies about having had a terrible birthday, and although there was no excuse, well... that was my excuse.

'You chose to be like that,' she spat at me. 'I wanted to cook you supper, to give you a proper birthday.'

I hung my head and apologised. Ella was scornful, and she's been monosyllabic to me since. I suppose I deserve her disdain, and the last two nights I've tried to keep off the alcohol, limiting myself to regular, little sips during the day, just to keep the edge off my fear and grief, without tipping me into drunken oblivion. And I've been extra vigilant about not driving. I will never drink and drive.

The other thing I didn't do was ring the police. My phone log shows that I received a call from a withheld number, but that is the only evidence I have. I cannot take the risk of putting Ella in harm's way, so all I've done the past two days is work and watch television. I haven't been on the internet; I haven't done any more probing.

By the time I have finished my new client's hair, which is now a shiny mahogany and falls in soft curls to her shoulders, I am the last hairdresser in the salon. After paying, she hands me a ten-pound note.

'Thank you for staying late. You've done a great job.'

'Sorry about the funeral,' I say.

Tears well up in her eyes. 'My sister.'

I bite my lip. It's sad, but at least she had half a life, I want to say. Not like my Abi, who never made it to proper adulthood.

After sweeping the floor around my station, I double-check that everything is switched off and then collect my bag, turn off the lights and set the alarm.

I am bone weary as I trudge through the deserted streets of Horsham, and when a taxi cruises past, I am tempted to hail it for the short distance home. But I don't. It would defeat the object of working late and having bonus cash in my wallet. My legs ache from standing for so many hours, my feet are swollen and sore, and my neck feels knotted and uncomfortable. On top of all of that, I have a pounding headache, probably because I haven't eaten properly all day and have been sipping at my vodka-filled water bottle.

AFTER A FEW YEARS of hedonistic partying, I met Bob. He came to fix the fuse board in my rented flat, and somehow or another, he never left. My love for him became stronger than my love for alcohol, and when I said 'I do' on our wedding day, I knew that I was also saying 'I do' to another promise. No excessive alcohol ever again. And I kept that promise for ten years, but when our marriage disintegrated, I started drinking again. One glass of wine after work became two or three, and by the time our decree nisi came through, I was consuming a couple of bottles a night all by myself.

And then Bob found out. He came to collect the remainder of his belongings a day before I thought he would. He discovered an empty bottle under my bed and a full bottle at the back of the wardrobe. Bob threatened me. He said he would fight for full custody of the girls unless I stopped drinking immediately. I knew he meant it. Not to be cruel, because Bob is not a cruel man, but because drinking would not only ruin me, it would also ruin my girls' childhoods. Occasionally I wonder if I should have stayed married to Bob; I doubt I will find anyone else, but Bob and I didn't love each other anymore. We tolerated each other; we didn't talk; we had morphed into housemates who just happened to share custody and love of our children. We bickered. We became resentful of each other. It wasn't enough, and I don't begrudge him for finding a new woman who could give him so much more.

I'M NOT FAR from home now. The roads have got darker, street lights more scarce, and this is the section I like the least at night. A small park runs down one side of the road, and a church and a large car park are on the other side. I find it creepy at night. I pick up my pace and then feel relief as headlights from a car coming from behind me light up the road and pavements ahead. The street is deserted. The car is driving slowly. Very slowly. It is just behind me. I turn to look, but the lights blind me, so I step closer to the far side of the pavement, away from the road, alongside the hedge. I walk faster, almost trotting. The car keeps pace, just a metre or so behind me. This isn't right. There are no houses here. I look again, trying to make out who is driving. But I can't see. When I try to look at the driver, the headlights burn my eyes, so that when I glance away, I see darting pricks of light.

And then I run. But even so, the car is just behind me, driving a little faster now to keep up. I look again. It's a small car, dark-coloured, I think. A Ford Fiesta, perhaps. I don't know anyone who drives a compact car like that. But then, as I turn to look, my shoe catches on an uneven section of pavement and I stumble, my heart in my mouth. I let out a scream as the car swerves towards me. A tyre mounts the low pavement. It's going to hit me.

On purpose.

I scramble into the bushes just in time, letting out a scream as I wait for the pain, the thud of being hit by a car. How can one brief moment extend like this?

But then the car pulls away and, with a squeal of the brakes, accelerates down the road until its rear lights disappear into the horizon. I try to catch the number plate, but I'm not fast enough. The car is gone. My whole body is shaking, my breath irregular pants. And a screaming, screeching sound is in my ear, or perhaps that's the sound I was anticipating, but it never came.

Someone wanted to scare me.

Someone purposefully drove their car towards me.

Someone just tried to kill me.

My eyes dance around. Is there anyone here? Will the car come back for me? I stand up and wipe my hands on my trousers. They feel gritty and sore. I fumble in my bag for my phone and jab 999.

'Which service do you require?'

'Police.'

'How can I help you?'

'I need to speak to Detective Inspector Pete Fairisle.' My voice is trembling.

'Which police station is he with?'

'I don't know!' I exclaim. 'Horsham?'

I can hear the man clicking on a keyboard.

'Sussex police. What is it regarding?'

'Someone just tried to kill me!'

'What is your name, and where are you?'

'Grace Woods. I'm in Horsham, the road by the church just before Begonia Avenue.'

'And what happened, Grace?'

'A car tried to drive into me. On purpose.' I am running now, homewards, and my breath sounds ragged.

'Is the car there now?'

'No, it drove off.'

'Are you somewhere safe?'

'I'm running home. I'm nearly there.' I sprint up the small path to our semi-detached house and drop the phone as I try to juggle the phone and my keys. I can hear the policeman's tinny voice coming from the ground. I open the door and grab my phone. 'I'm home now.' I slam the front door behind me, pull the safety catch across and lean against it, panting loudly.

'I will organise for a patrol car to come and visit you. What is your address?'

'I want Detective Inspector Pete Fairisle, or Linda Hornby, who works with him.'

'Why do you want to talk to them in particular?'

'Because my daughter was murdered and they were investigating!'

'I will try to get hold of DI Fairisle. Please stay on the line.' I marvel at how the man's voice stays the same even after I have told him my daughter was murdered. I suppose it's testament to the daily horrors the police have to face.

'Mum, what's going on?' Ella stands at the top of the stairs, wearing skinny jeans and an old grey hoodie, her brow furrowed, her eyes narrowed.

'Someone tried to... Never mind. Can you get me a drink? There's wine in the fridge.'

She scowls at me and mutters, 'Get your own bloody drink,' before turning on her heels. Her bedroom door slams.

The police operator comes back onto the phone line. 'I'm afraid that DI Fairisle isn't working tonight, and there is no one available on his team. I will dispatch officers to your address, and my colleagues can take your statement.'

'Forget it.' I don't want to have to explain everything to yet more strangers.

'If your life was endangered, we need to–'

'Look, I don't mean to be rude, but I just want to speak to Fairisle. Please can you ask him to call me?'

'Yes.'

'Thank you.' I hang up and slide my back down the front door, to the ground. Am I really in danger? Is Ella in danger? After a few long moments when I examine the scratches on the palms of my hands, I haul myself up and stagger to the kitchen. I know I'm weak. I hate myself for it, I really do, but I need to dull all of this pain. I pour myself a large glass of wine and then another one, drinking both in quick succession. I make myself a piece of toast and flop in front of the television. I drink some more wine, quickly losing count of the number of glasses.

Sometime later, the front doorbell tugs me awake. I must have dozed off because my neck is cricked, and as I sit up, the room swirls. I've drunk too much again. I wonder how quickly my body will adjust to alcohol. Twenty years ago, I rarely got hangovers. I suppose my body became tolerant to all the booze.

The doorbell rings again. I'd better hurry. I don't want to disturb Ella. As I move across the room, I knock over a side table.

'Coming!' I say. At least I think I say that. I struggle with the security lock on the door and eventually get it open. A police-woman and a policeman both in uniform stand on the doorstep.

'Grace Woods?'

'Yes.'

'We understand that you were attacked earlier this evening. May we come in?'

'Um, do you have to?' I mumble. I grab the doorframe to keep myself from slipping to the ground.

'Are you alright?' the policewoman asks.

'I wanna talk to Linda. She knows what's been going on.'

'Who's Linda?'

'She works for you. Dunno what her last name is.'

'Why don't we come inside, have a sit-down, and you can give us a statement as to what happened.'

I shake my head. That is a bad idea, because now I can feel the alcohol sloshing in my stomach and I think I'm going to throw up.

'It's ok. Sorry.' I shut the door in their faces. I just make it to the downstairs loo in time and vomit violently.

I DON'T REMEMBER GOING to bed, or finishing another bottle of wine or setting my alarm clock, but clearly I did all three, because it's 7 a.m. and the alarm is going. It feels like it's hammering the inside of my head. I slam my hand on the button to shut it up, and turn over in bed, dropping back to sleep.

I am awakened by a door slamming. I groan as I turn to look at my alarm clock. It's 8.15 a.m. and I've got a 9 a.m. client: a regular. I wonder if I can cancel, but then recall that I've already cancelled on her twice. Perhaps Helena can take her on. But if that happens, then I'm losing money, and there's only so long Helena will be sympathetic towards me. And then I remember Ella's look of disgust yesterday evening, and that was before the police came and I drank even more and... I want to cry I feel so ashamed of myself. Drinking is one thing, but being so careless as to let people know you're doing it is quite another. I have to pull myself together.

I swing my legs out of bed and realise I'm still wearing yesterday's underwear. I wait for a moment to steady my head and then walk to the bathroom. I drink from the cold tap before washing. I feel terrible. I take paracetamol and ibuprofen and hope they'll do the trick. If I don't hurry, I'm going to be late.

I cake the makeup on and tie my hair back. Hopefully, I look respectable. After a quick bowl of cereal and a black coffee that burns my tongue, I realise I don't have enough time to walk to work. I will have to drive. Besides, I don't want to walk. What happens if the bastard who scared me last night returns to complete the task today?

I hurry out to the car and stuff some chewing gum into my mouth in the hope that it will remove any hangover breath. As I'm pulling out onto the main road, I realise I probably shouldn't be driving. I feel compos mentis, able to be in control of the car, but I'm under no illusion that I'd be over the limit if I got stopped. I drive carefully, slower than usual, abiding by all the speed limits. And then I'm pulling into the small car park behind the salon with just two minutes to spare. I reverse into a space and then, crunch.

Shit. I've hit another car.

I jump out and to my dismay realise I've reversed into Helena's convertible pale blue mini, her pride and joy. The bumper is bent and I've smashed my rear brake light.

I let out a yell. I can't afford to get all of this fixed, and what will it do to my insurance premium? It's all my bloody fault. If I hadn't drunk so much last night... But I can't go there. What is done is done. I get back into the car and manoeuvre it into the tight parking spot. Not only am I late, but I've just bashed my boss's car.

Helena is drying the hair of a client. She must have started early this morning. And I can see my lady sitting on the banquette waiting for me. She's flicking through a magazine.

'Can I have a quick word?' I ask Helena.

'Can't it wait?'

I shake my head. She apologises to her client and follows me to the back of the salon.

'I've just reversed into your car and bashed your bumper,' I admit.

She looks at me but doesn't speak.

'Obviously I'll pay for the damages, or at least my insurance company will. I'm so sorry.'

She then places a hand on my arm. 'It's alright, Grace. It's only a car. I'm worried about you. Do you think you should be working?'

I nod. Not only do I need the money, but I need to be out of the house. If I was stuck at home all day, I would drink myself into oblivion, desperate not to have to confront my grief and fear. And Ella and I would get on each other's nerves.

'In which case, your client is waiting.' She nods her head towards the waiting area. 'And don't worry, Grace. It's not the end of the world.'

I have to control myself from not bursting into tears. Sometimes kindness can be as blindsiding as grief.

16

During my mid-morning break, I check my phone and find a message from Linda. I call her back.

'Hi, Grace. What happened? I had a message that someone tried to hurt you last night.'

'A car drove at me whilst I was walking along the pavement.'

'What time was that?'

'I'm not sure exactly but probably between 9.30 and 10 p.m.'

'Did you get the number plate?'

'No. It was dark and the headlights blinded me.'

'The make and model of the car?'

'No. I think it was dark coloured and quite small. A Ford Fiesta perhaps.'

'Mmm. And my colleagues say you were a bit worse for wear and didn't allow them into the house to take a statement.'

'Yes.' I hang my head. If only I hadn't been bloody drunk. I can tell from Linda's voice that she's not taking my claims seriously, or at least not seriously enough. Should I tell her about the threatening phone call? But then I think of Ella, and I simply can't take any risks.

'If anything else happens, call 999 immediately and give a full statement.'

'I will do.'

Bloody useless, that was.

I spend the morning thinking about the sugar daddies. I wonder if I should contact William and ask his private investigator to do some more digging, but then I recall what Ruth and Natasha said. Is William really genuine? Could he be behind all of this? It seems more likely that it's Jared B. He was an angry, threatening man. I pull up his photograph on my phone and stare at it. Yes, he looks like a thoroughly unpleasant individual, and it breaks my heart that Abi had to spend time with him. I load the picture into Google's reverse image search, but the supposed matches look nothing like the man I met. Jared isn't a common name, but even so, I get millions of results. I scroll through the numerous photos of men called Jared, and none of them are Jared B. I suppose it's quite probable that Jared isn't even his real name. I give up. It's futile.

I AM RESOLVED to keep Ella safe and decide I need to tell her what's been happening; otherwise she's likely to take my words of warning with a pinch of salt, thinking I'm just being unnecessarily overprotective. That evening I cook roast chicken, Ella's favourite. As we're sitting down to eat, Ella puts her mobile phone on the table next to her.

'We need to talk,' I say as I cut up my first bite of chicken.

'Mmm.' Ella has put her fork down and is scrolling through her phone.

'Please put your phone away.'

She ignores me.

'Ella, I have some important things to discuss with you.' I try to keep my voice level, but it's hard.

She rolls her eyes and looks at me.

'I'm about to tell you something that you must never, ever tell anyone else. Do you promise?'

'Shit, Mum, you sound like a kid.'

'This is serious, Ella. Your dad knows, but no one else, and it has to stay that way, for your safety.'

'What?'

Someone is threatening me. Threatening us. Whoever it is doesn't want me to dig into Abi's life or death, and they're threatening to hurt us.'

'What, me?'

'Yes, you too.'

'But I'm nothing to do with this!'

I reach for my phone and show her the photograph I took of Jared B. 'Have you ever seen this man before?'

'No. Who is he?'

'He's dangerous. If you ever do see him, you need to call the police immediately.'

'Who is he?'

'A sugar daddy. He might have had something to do with Abi's death.'

'Why aren't the police protecting us? Why haven't they arrested him?'

'Because I can't tell them everything. The person has threatened to hurt us if I go to the police.'

'This is all your bloody fault!' Ella shouts at me. 'Don't you realise? If you can just accept that Abi is gone and there is nothing you or anyone can do to bring her back, then we could all get on with our lives in peace. But no. You're a drunken obsessive, and all it's doing is making us miserable. Do you really think Abi would want this? You're pissed off your head every night. It's disgusting! It's not surprising Dad left you.'

Ella chucks her cutlery onto her plate, pushes her chair back and storms out of the kitchen.

'Ella!' I shout after her futilely.

Maybe Ella is right. Perhaps I should accept that the man behind bars in a Cape Town prison is the murderer of Abi, that the life she lived beforehand was one of her choosing, and that it's irrelevant now who fathered her child. They're both dead. I can't do anything to bring her back. I stifle a sob. I think about all the things that will never happen. Abi's excitement and pride on graduating. Getting her first job. Introducing us to her fiancé, and me helping her choose a wedding dress and being the proud mother of the bride. Worrying as she goes through her first pregnancy, and then the joy of being a grandmother. All of those things that are a rite of passage, just the simple everyday norms that we all expect to experience on our journey through life. I get up and walk to the fridge. The bottle of wine that I thought was there has gone. I look through the cupboards and none of my bottles are there. The vodka, the wine. All gone. What the hell? Did I hide them upstairs in my bedroom and have I forgotten? I run upstairs and turn my bedroom upside down. Nothing.

I knock on Ella's door. She doesn't answer.

'Ella, did you do something with my bottle of wine?'

'I chucked it out. I chucked out all your bloody booze.'

'You what!' I exclaim, clenching my fingers. 'How dare you!'

'Fuck off!'

'Never, ever talk to me like that!'

I need a drink now, and in future, I'm going to have to be more careful. In a fury, I grab my purse and walk out of the house towards the off-licence two streets away. It's still light outside, but even so my heart is racing through a mixture of fear and outrage towards Ella. Just as I'm about to walk into the shop, an old woman hobbles out. She's muttering to herself, her sallow cheeks sunken from rotten teeth, a plastic bag in her wizened hand, bottles clinking.

That could be me in a few years. Ella is right. How could I not see that my daughter is trying to protect me? I gulp, and before I can change my mind, I turn and stride as quickly as I can back home.

I open the front door.

'What are you doing?' I ask Ella.

I stare at the suitcase at the bottom of the stairs and Ella, who is sitting on the second to bottom step, her jacket over her knees and phone in hand.

'I'm leaving.'

'What do you mean, you're leaving?'

'I'm going to Dad's. I don't want to be here anymore, with you drunk every night and on some crazy mission that's not going to make any difference.'

'No,' I say. 'I'm not going to be like that anymore. I promise.'

She shrugs and looks away.

'Please stay, Ella.' I wring my hands hopelessly, but she won't meet my eyes.

TEN MINUTES LATER, the doorbell rings. I come out of the kitchen and see Ella jump to her feet. She throws her arms around Bob's neck and it breaks my already shattered heart.

'Bob, can I have a word?' I ask.

He hands Ella his car key. 'Put your stuff in the car, love.' Bob follows me into the living room.

'Please don't take her.'

'I'm not taking her, Grace. She wants to live with us for a while, and frankly I think it's the most sensible decision. You need help.'

'I'm not going to drink anymore.'

He looks at me askance and his expression is one of disbelief.

'And the phone call? Was that a figment of your imagination?'

'No!' I grit my teeth before taking a deep breath. 'Someone

tried to drive their car into me whilst I was walking home along Begonia Avenue.'

He frowns but doesn't say anything. I know Bob well enough to read his thoughts. He thinks I'm delusional.

'I know you don't believe me, but someone is out to get me, and it's because I want to find out the truth about Abi.'

'The truth about Abi is that she was murdered by a druggie in South Africa, and nothing will bring her back. I saw her, Grace. I saw her in that morgue and it's something I can never unsee. Get some therapy, take a holiday, but for heaven's sake, let all of this go. Our responsibility is to care for Ella, and if you can't, I will.'

We are both startled when my mobile phone rings, and stand there glowering at each other. But then Bob turns.

'You'd better answer that.' He opens the front door and lets himself out. The phone stops ringing.

But five minutes later, it rings again. And when I don't answer for the second time, it immediately rings for the third time. I turn the phone onto silent. The number is withheld. But then I panic. What if it's the police? Their numbers are withheld. What if Linda Hornby has something urgent to tell me? So when it rings five minutes later, for the fourth time, I answer it.

'Are you taking note of what I said, Grace?' I can't control my gasp as I recognise the robotic voice. 'Let Abi rest in peace, and you and Ella will be safe for ever. If you carry on digging, you will both die. Ella first. And if you go to the police, Ella will be tortured. I know where she is, who she hangs out with. I didn't hurt you last night, but next time I will. You need to listen.'

'Who are you?' I scream. But all I hear is a click and then silence. I am alone on the line.

Alone in life.

After checking that all the doors are locked and the

windows are secured, I walk into the kitchen. Of course I want a drink, but thanks to Ella pouring it all away, I don't have any. Instead I take out a tub of chocolate ice cream from the freezer and carry it into the living room. I sit on the sofa, wrapping myself in my peacock-coloured blanket, and spoon the ice cream into my mouth until I feel nauseous. I try to process everything that is happening. Someone is scared of me investigating Abi's life, and possibly her death. How do they know what I'm doing? The only people who know are my close friends and family, the two sugar daddies and the private investigator. But when I mentally list all of those people, and perhaps people that they've told, it's quite a large number. Besides, why should I be scared off doing what I know is right? Perhaps I should tell the police. What with the hit-and-run and these threatening calls, they could put me and Ella in a safe house. I immediately discount that. The only evidence the police have is my word. I suppose they have ways to track a withheld number, but would they really do that? Based on my conversations with Linda Hornby and Pete Fairisle, I doubt it. No. This is down to me, and I am going to have to decide what to do next.

17

For the next couple of days, I lie low. I go to the salon and do a mediocre job of cutting, colouring and styling my clients' hair. From the number of concerned glances she throws my way, it's obvious that Helena is concerned about my lacklustre engagement with customers, but I'm not doing anything wrong. I'm just distracted, and if she really knew what was going on in my life, she would understand.

Natasha has invited Ella and me for Sunday lunch. It's the last thing I feel like doing, but it appears I have no choice. She announced that she would come and collect me herself if we weren't on her doorstep at twelve thirty. What I haven't done is admit to my friends that Ella is no longer living with me. How can I explain to them that I have pushed away my remaining daughter, that she would rather be anywhere except with me? And so, the day before, I send Natasha an apologetic text saying that Ella had promised to spend the day with Bob.

The weather is glorious, the sky a deep cerulean blue, a colour I associate more with the Mediterranean than England.

I dig out a floaty maxi dress in pastel florals, a whimsical buy a couple of years ago and nothing like my normal no-nonsense block-colour practical clothes. I put on a pair of dangling earrings and a couple of bangles. I haven't drunk any alcohol for three days, but I haven't quit the smoking. I shove a packet of cigarettes and a lighter in my bag, hiding them inside a zipped compartment. I'll need something to get through the day. Perhaps it's the weather or the prospect of a Sunday roast with my best friends, but I feel a glimmer of lightness and positivity, the first time since Abi's death. Perhaps I'm turning a corner. Perhaps these few days without digging into Abi's past have laid the foundations for moving on. Is it possible to move on without forgetting?

It's colder outside than I had anticipated, so I shiver as I get in the car, wrapping a pale blue cardigan around my shoulders. I stop off at Waitrose on the way and buy a bouquet of pink flowers and two luxury bars of soap, one each for Natasha and Ruth. We don't normally bring each other gifts when visiting for a meal, but I have some apologies to make, and I am truly grateful for the steadfastness of my friends.

As I pull up into Natasha and Justin's drive, I see that Ruth's car is already here. I climb out of my Kia and tread carefully in my wedge espadrilles up to the front door. Natasha swings it open before I can ring the doorbell.

'Wow, you look gorgeous!' she says. I smile as I hand her the flowers and a soap.

'No need for these, but thank you.' She stands back to let me in. I walk through the large hall into the grand kitchen, where I hear voices.

'Look what Grace has brought me,' she says, placing the flowers on the island unit. She sidles up to Justin and snakes an arm around his waist.

'There's a little soap for you too,' I say to Ruth, handing her the floral-paper-covered bar. 'Just to say thank you for everything.'

Ruth gives me a quick kiss on the cheek. I say my hellos to Justin and Alan. The two men have always got on well, probably because they both play golf, whereas Bob, who can't abide the game, was never quite one of the gang. I think he felt a little inferior, perhaps because as a self-employed electrician, he is essentially a tradesman. Bob didn't go to a fancy university and never had any grand career aspirations. And it probably didn't help that Bob knew that Justin and I had a mini-fling when we were at school together. I'm fairly sure that Bob hasn't met up with either of them since our divorce. That's what happens – neatly divided groups of friends.

After the initial hellos, Ruth, Natasha and I congregate around the island. Natasha checks her roast potatoes in the oven, and Ruth chops up some courgettes.

'Can I help?'

'No, I think it's under control. There's a bottle of elderflower juice in the fridge for you. Besides, it's Justin who should be helping me out, not my guests.' She casts a coquettish look over her shoulder towards her husband. 'Shouldn't you, darling?'

He looks up. 'Shouldn't I what?' He strides towards her and she reaches out and squeezes his buttock. I am surprised. Justin and Natasha have never been overtly sexual.

'Can you pour Grace an elderflower?'

I notice that the others are all holding glasses of wine. It irks me that I don't get offered one. Ruth and I shift towards the patio doors, which are open wide, leading onto a patio and a small but pristine lawn beyond. The laid table looks stunning, with a white linen tablecloth and lime green napkins. Little porcelain jugs of white and lemon flowers are placed down the centre of the table. She's gone to a lot of effort for a Sunday lunch.

'You look tired,' I say to Ruth. 'Are you ok?'

She nods, but her smile is tight and her gaze flickers towards Alan and back again. If Natasha hadn't told me, I might have missed it. 'I've had to take on some extra shifts at work because too many people are taking holidays all at the same time. It's the same every year. Heaven knows why they can't sort out the rotas properly. Anyway, how has your week been?'

I don't get a chance to answer as Natasha announces that lunch is ready.

'Ruth, can you sit next to Justin, and I'll sit on the other side of my gorgeous husband. Grace, you go next to Ruth, and Alan, you're next to me.'

It's a strange set-up, different to how we're normally seated, where Justin and Natasha sit at opposite ends of the table. I don't say anything, but I notice that Ruth has clocked it. Justin carves the roast beef, which looks and smells delicious. As they serve up the food and then sit down, Natasha and Justin seem particularly high-spirited; I keep on waiting for some big announcement. Perhaps they have won the lottery, or has Justin been offered a bigger and better job at a prestigious boarding school on the other side of the country? But nothing is forthcoming. Rather, they are acting as if they are new lovers, holding each other's gazes for a little too long, brushing hands, giggling at double entendres and making awkward sexual innuendos. The contrast between the two couples couldn't be more marked. Alan and Ruth barely glance at each other.

'We've just booked a mega holiday,' Natasha announces. I hold my breath. Is this the announcement? 'We're going to the Maldives for two weeks during the October half-term. It's been so long that we've done something that is just for us, isn't it, Justin? In fact, I can't remember the last time we spent a night together in a hotel.' He nods and takes a large sip of wine.

'Lucky you,' Alan says wistfully. 'Ruth just wants to stay at home.'

'If you're flying around the globe as much as I do, home is

the place of luxury. I fancy a week at home, followed by a week on a canal barge, preferably in England, but at a push in France.' She turns towards Alan and speaks through gritted teeth. 'It would be nice if for once you understood.'

There is an awkward silence.

I note that no one asks me what my holiday plans are.

'Darling, can you get another bottle out of the fridge?' Natasha asks Justin, her voice unusually saccharine. When he returns with the bottle and stands over her to fill up her empty wine glass, she reaches up and kisses him on the cheek with a big smooching sound. I don't know what has got into Natasha, but it's thoroughly distasteful, particularly when one could cut the atmosphere between Ruth and Alan with a knife.

The conversation shifts to the men talking about golf and us women chatting about a recent aromatherapy training course Natasha has attended. By the time we have finished our chocolate soufflés, I am desperate for a cigarette.

For a moment I wonder if I should make an excuse, but then realise it would be futile. They'll smell the smoke on me. Better to own it.

'Just going to pop outside for a ciggy,' I say. I grab my box of cigarettes and lighter and step outside. The garden is small relative to the size of the house, and just a few paces takes me to the flower beds at the far end. I sit on a small bench underneath a puny cherry tree. It's a relief to be alone. I wonder if my friends realise just how difficult it is for me to watch them all drinking, or what hurt it brings me when I look at them and their happy, intact families. Even Alan and Ruth, who are clearly having marital difficulties, have a solid foundation.

I can see Alan and Justin walk together into the living room and slump down in front of Justin's massive television screen. Ruth and Natasha are standing close together, their backs to me. I saunter up the lawn, my espadrilles soundless as I walk along the patio, just a metre from the open sliding doors.

'I've never been so worried,' Ruth says. 'I think she's on the verge of a nervous breakdown. Not surprising, really. Drinking and chain-smoking.'

'At least she wasn't drinking today,' Natasha says.

'What about the water bottle she's been carrying around? She never used to have one in her bag.'

'What do you mean? Goodness, you don't think it's vodka or gin in there rather than water, do you?'

'It could be.'

I hold my breath.

'She needs to stop digging into Abi's death. Why can't she accept what the South African police say? They've got their killer; surely that's enough?' Natasha says.

'I quite agree. It's not doing Grace any good, and heaven knows what it's doing to poor Ella,' Ruth agrees.

'At least Ella isn't a little tart like Abi was. I know it's a horrible thing to say, but she probably brought it upon herself. I count my blessings that Becky is going out with Ethan and never slept around like Abi. Can you imagine having a child that prostitutes herself as a sugar baby? It's just too disgusting for words.'

'I know, I–'

I let out a gasp and Ruth spins around. When she sees me, her face is one of shock, her eyes wide and comically circular.

'Grace!' she exclaims, rushing towards me. But I dart right around Ruth and Natasha. I grab my handbag and run through the kitchen, into the hallway.

There are footsteps behind me. 'Wait, Grace. I'm sorry. We didn't mean it!' Natasha shouts. 'We would never want to hurt you!'

But it's too bloody late for that.

I rush out of the front door and slam it behind me. I run to the car, climb in and start the engine. It isn't until I've turned out onto the main road that I let out a sob. I blink hard to be able to see through my tears. After a few more seconds of driving just a little too fast, out of the corner of my eye, I see a white car pulling into the road, directly into my path.

And then I realise.

I'm not wearing my seatbelt.

18

They say everything happens in slow motion, and it's true. I can account for every millisecond. I see the small white car pulling out into my lane of traffic, oblivious to me. The calm knowledge that our cars are going to collide, that I am not wearing my seat belt, that I am driving too quickly in a thirty-mile-an-hour zone, that if I die, at least I will be joining Abi, that Bob is a good father and he will care for Ella. Tyres screech as I slam on my brakes. I wait for the crunch of metal on metal, but now I'm spinning. Still the crunch doesn't come. I feel no pain and no fear. I wait to be thrown through the front windscreen. But then my car has stopped, facing the opposite direction to which I was driving, and I am sitting here, my fingers gripped so tightly around the steering wheel, I can't loosen them. My heart is pounding in my ears, my breathing shallow and rapid. My head is shaking and I don't know how long I sit there.

There is a knock on the window. A man in his seventies, his face sallow and his eyes rheumy, leans towards me.

'Are you alright?'

I peel my fingers off the steering wheel and rest back in my seat, glancing to the other side of the road to see if the white car that was about to hit me is still there. It is parked up on the side of the road, the passenger door open. I lower my window.

'That car pulled straight out onto the road. It nearly hit me,' I say.

He nods. 'It was my wife. She got distracted. I am so sorry, love. Are you alright?'

'Amazingly, I think I am.'

I glance in my rear mirror and a white van has come up behind me. The driver sounds his horn, not surprising, as it looks like I've stopped my car in the middle of the road for a chat. 'I'll pull over,' I tell the man.

A few seconds later, I have parked my Kia in front of a couple of cottages, the passenger-side tyres up on the pavement. The man hurries towards me. 'Do you want to call the police?' He looks terrified.

'If neither of us are hurt and there was no damage to the cars, it won't be necessary.' I am relieved he hasn't noticed my lack of seat belt.

And then I hear the slamming of more car doors and running footsteps.

'Grace!' Natasha shouts. 'Grace, are you alright?' She pushes the man to one side and leans in to talk to me, her cheeks scarlet. Ruth appears next to her.

'What are you two doing here?' I narrow my eyes at them.

'We're so sorry,' Ruth says. 'For what we said.'

'I told Ruth we couldn't let you go, and because I've drunk more than she has, Ruth drove, and we were three cars behind you and saw you spin across the road. Fuck, Grace. We thought you were going to die!' Natasha speaks breathlessly.

'I'm fine,' I say curtly. 'Can you let me finish my conversation with this gentleman.' The man still looks as if he's going to faint. My supposed friends stand back.

'If you and your wife are ok, I think we can part company,' I say.

'You don't need her driving licence and details?'

'No damage done.'

He throws me a gummy smile laden with relief, and I watch as he hurries back across the road. He changes places with his wife, and then he indicates for at least ten long seconds before pulling out and driving off at a snail's pace.

My two friends are standing on the pavement, both seemingly lost for words. Natasha has her arms wrapped around herself, and she looks skinny and her face is flushed. Ruth hops from foot to foot.

'I'm going home now,' I say. 'Thanks for the lunch, Natasha. I'll be in touch.'

'But, Grace,' Ruth says. I wind up my window and cut her off.

I HAVEN'T BEEN SO relieved to be home and alone in a long time. I can't work out what has shaken me more: the near-miss car accident, or those horrendous words uttered by the two women I thought were my closest friends. They called Abi a tart, a prostitute. Is that really how they see her? Do they think she deserved to die? I drive straight to the off-licence and buy vodka, tonic and six bottles of wine that are on special offer. The credit card shakes in my hand as I try to insert it into the card reader. I am still trembling when I'm back home, and I spill vodka as I pour it into my glass. I take the vodka tonic and go into the living room, curling my feet up underneath me.

It's obvious to me that Abi became a sugar baby because we didn't have any money to give her. I recall how Becky always had the latest it-toys and the designer gear, and when she turned eighteen, she was given the keys to her first car. In contrast, Abi's clothes came from Tesco or Topshop. Zara was reserved for special treats. We couldn't afford to give her driving lessons, let alone buy her a car. So Abi worked in her holidays, and I was proud of her. I never thought she was jealous of her friends, but perhaps she felt the only way she could do the things they did was to earn quickly. I hate to admit it and it still disgusts me, but I understand why she might have been attracted to becoming a sugar baby. My mobile phone rings, but I set it to silent. I have no desire to listen to Natasha's and Ruth's hollow apologies.

I watch an old film on television; with the vodka in my veins and getting lost in a black-and-white movie set in the French riviera, I begin to feel calmer. And then the doorbell rings.

I ignore it.

It rings again. Sighing, I haul myself up and walk over to the door. I peer through the peephole, expecting to see either Ruth or Natasha. It's neither of them.

It's Dr William Jennings. What the hell is he doing here?

I attach the chain and open the door just slightly until it catches.

'Mrs Woods, I'm sorry to turn up unannounced, but you are not answering your phone.'

'How do you know where I live?'

'My private detective.' Dr William Jennings gives me a slightly embarrassed smile. 'I've got some more information I would like to share with you.'

'I'm not sure,' I say, glancing down at my bare feet.

'Of course not,' he says. 'I quite understand you don't want to let me in. I am a doctor, and as a psychiatrist, the last thing I would expect my clients to do is to let in a stranger. But would you be prepared to meet me for a drink? Is there a pub local to here or a coffee shop?'

I think for a moment, remembering what Ruth and Natasha had said, how perhaps Dr Jennings was involving himself in order to deflect from his guilt. Perhaps I am staring at my daughter's murderer. But then I look at him again. I checked him out on the internet. He has all the letters after his name; he has a practice on Harley Street; his photograph on his online biographies matches the face of the man standing in front of me. I thought I could rely upon and trust my friends, but they've just proven themselves unworthy, so what harm is there going into a public place with this man?

'I'll meet you at the Three Pheasants. It's a decent pub on Malate Way, five minutes' walk from here. Give me fifteen minutes.'

He nods. 'I'll get the drinks in.'

I wonder what he would say if he knew about my relationship with alcohol.

AFTER TWO GLASSES OF WATER, a quick brush of my hair, I apply some lipstick as a futile armour. The short walk to the pub does me good and allows me to shake off that lethargic tipsy feeling. The Three Pheasants is surprisingly busy for an early Sunday evening, but I quickly spot Dr Jennings sitting at a small table towards the rear, near the doors that open up onto a courtyard filled with hanging baskets trailing bright pink petunias and blue lobelia.

'I wasn't sure what your tipple is, so I've ordered you a white wine. Very happy to get you something else if it would suit better.'

'That's fine, thank you.' I sit down and look at him quizzically.

'How are you, Grace? If I may call you that.'

I shrug.

'I have rung you a few times, and as you never answered, I came down from London to check up on you.'

I recall receiving a few calls from unknown numbers, but

under the current circumstances, there is no way that I am going to answer calls from anyone I don't know.

'I was concerned about you; how you're coping with grief.'

Is he here to give me a complimentary therapy session? I narrow my eyes and don't answer.

'Grief is a complex process. It's often illustrated as a cycle, starting off with denial and then transitioning to anger. Typically, the bargaining stage comes next followed by the recriminations of 'if only that had happened 'or 'what if I hadn't done x, y, z'. Some people sink into depression, and then eventually we reach acceptance.'

'Thanks for the psychology lesson, but–'

'Goodness, I didn't mean to be patronising. Forgive me!'

'It's fine,' I say, sighing and reflecting on what he said. 'I'm not very far through the process, actually. I think I'm still at the anger stage, wanting to find out who the hell did this to my daughter and bring the bastard to justice.'

'That's quite understandable. You're still not convinced the South African was rightly accused?'

'No.'

We both take sips from our drinks. I think he's drinking sparkling water, although it could be gin.

'Abi was so worried about you and Ella. She felt that you had a raw deal in the divorce, and it was unfair how many hours you had to work to get by, whereas her dad spent everything on his new wife and baby son.'

I'm surprised to hear that. I didn't realise Abi had resentment towards Bob. 'That's not strictly fair,' I say, wondering for a moment why I'm standing up for Bob. 'He paid child support as long as he was required to do so, but of course once Abi hit eighteen, we couldn't demand any more money from him. He was generous to her though, giving her money for Christmas and birthdays and buying bits and pieces for when she moved to university.'

William runs the fingers of his left hand over his left bushy eyebrow.

'Abi told me she wanted to use the money she earned from Sweetner.net to buy you and Ella a holiday, as you haven't had one in years.'

I blink hard to stop the tears from spilling down my cheeks. 'That wasn't her responsibility,' I murmur.

'No, but she loved you and she wanted to help.'

'Are you sure you're not just telling me this to make me feel better?'

William sits up straighter on his chair. He looks affronted.

'I'm sure if I were in your position, I would think the worst,' he says, glancing away. 'A dirty old man like me, a professional indeed who should know better, befriending a girl young enough to be his daughter. But please believe me, Grace, I came to care for Abi deeply, as if she were indeed a stepdaughter or a niece. She shared her hopes and dreams with me, as I did with her. We had lovely chats over dinners. I was able to show her a world she didn't normally experience, and I got such pleasure from seeing her delight. I said it before and I'll say it again: I never laid a finger on Abi. I promise.'

'I believe you,' I say softly. And I do believe him. He could have just disappeared as Jared B did, but it seems he wants to do something right. 'So why are you here?'

He inhales deeply. 'My private investigator has tracked down the phone number that Abi rang on a regular basis. The number was allocated to a burner phone.'

'A burner phone?' I ask.

'A cheap phone with a pay-as-you-go number that couldn't be traced.'

'So there is no way of tracing it?'

'No. But we have been able to work out in which area the phone was predominantly used. I don't know how he does it, but it's something to do with mobile phone masts.'

I lean forwards eagerly.

'It was used in this area, in and around Horsham.'

'What?' I exclaim. That doesn't make any sense. Abi was at university in Durham, and her sugar daddies were located all over the country. Why would she be having illicit conversations with someone from her home town? Did she have a boyfriend, perhaps from when she was at school, someone she was keeping hidden away?

Or is one of her sugar daddies located right here, right under my nose?

19

NYA'S BLOG FROM THE SUGAR BOWL

FEBRUARY 21ST

I HAVEN'T WRITTEN for a while because I've been super busy. I didn't give up on life in the bowl (the sugar-baby world in case you're not keeping up with the lingo!), and it's just as well. I'm at uni in the north of England, but it's clear that most of the whales (generous sugar daddies) live in the south or in London. There are a few good whales in Manchester apparently, but I haven't found them yet. So I expanded my reach to cover London and, wowser, I got lucky! W lives and works in London. He seemed like quite a nice old-ish man. He doesn't like writing texts or emails, so we spoke on the phone quite a few times, and he speaks like the British newsreaders used to talk in the olden days. Anyway, he said he'd pay for my train ticket to London and back, so I arranged to meet another POT too. And then I got in touch with my actual true love, and he booked a hotel for us to spend the night together. That makes me sound like a slag, doesn't it? But really it's not like that.

I met W first. He was wearing a tweed jacket and a red bow tie. Honestly he looks like a bit of a tosser, but he was very polite. He insisted on taking me out for lunch at a posh restaurant on Marylebone High Street, with white linen napkins and silver cutlery and little dishes in between the main courses. He told me a bit about what he does (it's something medical) and asked me lots of questions about myself. I told him about my fascination for the 1920s and the interwar years, and we swapped book titles. He promised to take me to the Churchill War Rooms on our next date.

When the coffee came, he got all serious. 'You do know that most men will expect you to have physical relations with them even if you start out by saying that's not what you want, don't you?' I asked if that's what he wanted. He said yes, initially he thought that he did want that, but even though I'm beautiful, I am young enough to be his daughter and he could never take advantage of me. He asked if I was willing to have an arrangement with him, where I accompanied him to the theatre and concerts and the occasional convention, and he would introduce me as his niece. He has offered me one thousand pounds a month plus a dress allowance, and he'll pay for my travel to London. Obviously it's an offer I couldn't turn down! When I left the restaurant, he gave me a kiss on the cheek. It was a bit prickly, but he smells nice, and I think it's going to be ok. He also handed me a little envelope and told me to put it into my handbag

I hotfooted it to Miss Selfridge's, and when I was in the changing rooms, I had a look inside the envelope. Two hundred quid in cash! I bought two new dresses and a pair of high heels. I'll have to learn to walk in them!

And then I had to go to John Lewis on Oxford Street, as I was meeting my next guy there at 5 p.m. in one of the coffee shops. I got there first and grabbed a cup of tea and a piece of chocolate cake. Perhaps I shouldn't be eating that sort of thing anymore if I need to stay slim and sexy. Anyway, L is really, really old. I mean old enough to be my grandfather or great-grandfather even. He walks with a stick and has white fluffy hair. To be honest, I was a bit shocked when he turned up. I told him that I wanted to be a lawyer and his face lit up. Turns out that he was a judge!!!! OMG, just what I need. So we talked for a while, and then he asked me if I would do something special for him when we meet up. I got a bit worried. He said he doesn't get intimate with women anymore, but would I be prepared to sit and talk to him in his house dressed only in my underwear. I was about to say no bloody way when he said he'd pay me £500 per session, just for looking at me. Holy shit! It's a bit pervy, but if we're just gonna sit there and talk with me in my undies and I'm going to get half a grand a time for it, what's not to like?

By the time I met up with my boyfriend, I was buzzing!

20

It's Tuesday morning and I'm running late for my first client at 9.30 a.m. When the doorbell rings, I assume it's the postman. It is a delivery, but it is not post. A woman holds out a massive bunch of flowers, summery blooms in pinks and purples, hand-tied with a sumptuous velvet ribbon.

'Mrs Woods?' she asks.

I nod and accept the bouquet.

'Have a great day.'

I remove the miniature envelope and slide the notecard out.

Dearest Grace, Ruth and I can't apologise enough for what we said on Sunday. The last thing we want is to cause you more pain than you're already suffering. We loved Abi like one of our own children, and we should never have said, let alone thought, the things we did. Please forgive us. Your oldest friends, Ruth & Natasha.

I sigh as I lay the flowers on the table. I'm not sure I have a vase big enough to hold them. For a moment I think how I might have reacted should it be Becky who had been a sugar baby, and I have no doubt I would have been equally judgemental. I can't afford to lose my two friends, so I will have to be magnanimous and accept their apologies.

I didn't sleep well last night and resorted to taking a sleeping pill at 4 a.m. I can't stop thinking about who from Horsham was calling Abi on a regular basis. The one person who is likely to know is Becky. I message Natasha, thanking her for the flowers and asking if I could stop by their house later on. I get an immediate response back. *Yes.*

WHEN I ARRIVE at the small car park to the rear of the salon, I reverse into a space with the speed of a snail. Helena's car is parked two cars over, and I notice that she has already had the damage fixed. I hurry inside, putting my bag on a shelf in the staffroom and grabbing my water bottle. I am trying to reduce the amount of vodka in the bottle each day, conscious that now I'm driving to work every day, it's essential I keep below the drink-drive limit. I take a quick sip and hurry on through into the salon to my station next to the big window that looks out onto the high street.

My noon client is new. She is, at a guess, in her late thirties, with long, straggly hair. From the roots, I can see that her hair is a mousey colour, but it has been dyed red. It doesn't suit her complexion, and I'm quite sure it wasn't done here at HHH. Her hair feels dry as I run my fingers through it.

'What can I do for you today?' I ask, smiling at her in the mirror.

'I'd like to go blonde. What do you recommend?'

After establishing that she popped in for a colour test forty-eight hours ago, I fetch the colour chart and point out the three shades that I think will best suit her colouring. I explain that I will need to use a bleach-based hair dye to achieve what she's looking for. We agree on the colour. I nip back to the staffroom, take a quick swig from my 'water' bottle, pull on my gloves and apron and mix up the dyes.

I get the colour onto her head, fetch her a pile of magazines and tidy up my trolley. I don't like having to twiddle my thumbs, and normally ask the girls to book me in a quick haircut whilst I'm waiting for the first client's colour to work, but today I have no one. So I return to the staffroom and flick through a magazine, but I'm barely registering the pictures let alone reading the words. All I can think of is my meeting with William and who Abi might have been calling here in Horsham. After twenty minutes, I walk back into the salon to check my client's hair. It is progressing as expected, but could do with another couple of minutes, so I turn and glance out of the window. And that's when I see him.

Ethan is shuffling along the high street, looking gangly and giraffe-like, his trousers hanging low on his hips, a baseball cap worn back-to-front on his head. He is exactly the person I need to see.

Without thinking, I dash out of the salon, barging past a customer who is entering, and run out onto the street. It's drizzling and I'm not wearing my anorak, but I haven't got time to worry about such niceties. Where the hell is he? He was walking in the direction of Waterstones, but he seems to have disappeared. I run along the pedestrianised street, darting between shoppers, straining to see him. He can't have vanished. But now he could be anywhere. Straight ahead, left or right. I lean forwards, panting heavily, my hands on my knees. And as I'm straightening up, resigned to my wild goose chase, I spot him. Ethan is strolling out of a sportswear shop.

'Ethan!' I shout. A few people turn around and stare at me. When Ethan catches my eye, it's obvious he would rather be anywhere else except here.

'Ethan, I'm so glad I ran into you.'

He looks dubious and shuffles to the side of the street.

'I need to ask you a couple of questions. Did Abi have a boyfriend here in Horsham?'

He shrugs. I wish those green eyes would hold my gaze like they used to. 'No, I don't think so.'

'But she was speaking to someone right here on a regular basis. Who was it?'

'Sorry, I don't know.'

I grab his arm. 'Please, Ethan. Look at me.' Ethan looks everywhere except at my face. I remove my hand and take a step backwards. 'You've got to help me out here. Who could it have been?'

'I'm sorry, Mrs Woods, but I really don't know. Abi and I didn't have much to do with each other the last couple of years.'

'But hasn't Becky said anything to you? She must have done. You spend all your time together.' I know my voice is rising in pitch, but surely Ethan must know something.

He shrugs his shoulders again. 'I need to go now.'

'Where are you going?'

He throws me a confused glance. Of course I shouldn't be questioning Ethan. He's not my son.

'Sorry,' I say. 'It's tough at the moment. I'm finding out all this stuff about Abi... And well, never mind. I just thought you'd know something.'

'I wish I did. Really I do.'

Those green eyes hold mine for a moment. I wish I could hug this young man whom I've known since he was born.

'Sorry to have accosted you, Ethan.'

'It's fine. No worries.'

I watch as he lopes off. I shiver and wrap my arms around myself. It's cold and my hair is going to be a damp frizz. Not a good look for a hairdresser.

Then I remember. My client's hair.

I let out a yelp and sprint back towards the salon. I throw the door open, but I can see from Amy's face that all is not well.

'Grace, Grace! Where have you been?' She speaks in a loud, urgent whisper. 'Your client said her scalp was hurting, so I tried to wash off the colour, but her hair is, like, melting. Proper kind of falling to pieces. And it's yellow. She's crying. Helena is with her now.'

I glance at my watch. I've been away too long. It's not surprising her head is burning and her hair is disintegrating. No one should have bleach left in their hair for that length of time. I grip the back of a chair to keep myself steady. I can't believe I have made such a rookie mistake, that I got distracted like that.

'Grace!' Helena's voice has a strident edge to it at the best of times, and now it reverberates through my head as if it's going to split my brain in half. 'Come with me, now.'

I follow her into the staffroom like a naughty child who has run out of excuses.

'What the hell happened? Where were you?' She glares at me.

'I'm so sorry. I wasn't feeling very well,' I murmur.

She takes a step towards me.

'You just ran out of the salon without the slightest thought for your client. It's unbelievable.' She then leans so closely towards me, I can feel her breath on my face. 'You're bloody drunk, aren't you? Drunk at work!'

'I'm not!' I retort.

'One of the girls said she thought she smelled booze on your breath last week, but I didn't say anything because you appeared to be working ok.' She strides towards the shelf where I store my bag. Before I can stop her, she grasps the small bottle of water and removes the top. She sniffs it.

'Get out, Grace. I know you've had a rough time, but if you think you can get away with drinking in my salon, and ruining a client's hair, you can think again.' She turns on her heel and strides out to the salon. Amy stands in the doorway staring at me, her mouth agog.

'I wasn't drinking,' I mutter. 'It was a genuine mistake. I had to leave for an emergency.'

But when I look up again, Amy has gone and I'm talking to myself.

I COLLECT my bag and jacket and race out of the salon, my head down. It's a relief to be in the car and alone. But I'm angry with myself. I could have avoided that screw-up. I should have done, and now I have put my job in jeopardy. I thump the steering wheel in frustration and then start the car. Initially, I intend to go straight home, but as I drive out of Horsham, I decide it would make sense to stop off at the Bellovers' so I can talk to Becky, rather than having to make a special journey later on.

Justin answers the door and calls out for Natasha, who comes hurrying towards me. It's obvious by her reaction that she thinks all has been forgotten and forgiven. But I can't help being frosty towards her.

'It's been a really crap morning and I need to get home, but could I have a quick word with Becky?'

She looks surprised but doesn't question me. Instead, she shouts upstairs for her daughter.

'Would you like a drink?' Natasha asks as we hover in the kitchen. 'A glass of water or a tea,' she adds. I am perfectly aware she isn't referring to an alcoholic drink, and if I were feeling stronger, I might have made a sarcastic retort. Instead, I place my bag on the end of the island unit.

'A glass of water, please.'

Becky appears in the kitchen, looking nervous, as she always does these days. I wonder if Ethan has already told her about our futile chat in town. Becky's face is pale; the tan from her few months abroad has faded despite the decent Sussex weather we've been having. She looks painfully thin, and I wonder if the bulimia has taken hold again. I pray not.

'Becky, you're not to blame for anything,' I start. Natasha spins around and frowns at me. Becky's eyes open wide.

'Sorry,' I backtrack. 'What I meant to say was if there was something you didn't tell me before, I won't be angry. It's just that it's come to my attention that Abi might have had a boyfriend who lives here in Horsham.'

'Really?' Natasha interrupts, passing me a cup of tea.

'Did she have a boyfriend here, or at least someone she was seeing on a regular basis? Maybe someone you or some of her other friends were covering for?' I look Becky straight in the eyes, and for the first time, she doesn't flinch, but holds my gaze.

'I was away for most of this year and I hardly saw Abi. She seemed happy, but she definitely didn't say she had a boyfriend. I'd have known, I'm sure of it.'

'Could she have had a sugar daddy in Horsham?'

Becky shrugs her shoulders. 'I don't know. I'm sorry.'

'You've got nothing to be sorry for,' I say, squeezing Becky's bony shoulder.

When she has left the room, I turn to Natasha. 'She's very thin again,' I say quietly. I hope Natasha isn't going to bite my head off for interfering, but to my surprise she just nods.

'I know. Justin thinks we should go back to the doctor.'

'He's right.'

She twirls her wedding ring around and around her finger, and I realise that she is looking very thin as well even though her hair is lustrous. And then I think of the looks of horror on everyone's faces in the salon, and I flinch at the thought.

Natasha peers at me with concern. 'Are you alright, Grace?'

'Not really. I totally screwed up a new client's hair. Helena told me to get out of the salon.'

'Oh goodness,' she says, her hand over her mouth.

'The woman's hair came out bright yellow, and it was starting to melt.'

Natasha starts giggling. Initially, I start laughing too, but then my laughter morphs into tears and I can't stop crying; my whole body is trembling, and it feels as if the sobs will never stop.

It takes Natasha a moment to realise what's happening, but when she does, she wraps her arms around me and once again says that she's sorry.

21

H elena sends me an email that arrives the next day.

Dear Grace,
I know you are going through a very rough time at the moment, but
I'm afraid I can't have stylists working in my salon in the state you
were in yesterday or making such drastic mistakes. Due to your poor
standard of work and behaviour, unfortunately I have no choice but
to suspend your chair. I have every right to terminate our agreement,
but have decided I will hold it open for now. I would like you to take
time out for the next two months, and if, at that time, you have quit
drinking alcohol, I will invite you back.
Regards, Helena

SHIT, shit, shit. If I can't work at the salon, that's seventy-five
percent of my monthly salary gone. It is the first real screw-up
I've made on a customer since I was a trainee. I understand that
Helena thinks she has no choice, and I suppose if it were my

salon, I'd do the same. It was totally unacceptable of me to run out of the salon. But what the hell am I going to do for the next two months? For the first time, I am glad that Ella is staying with Bob. At least I can cut back on food shopping.

I FEEL UTTERLY DEFLATED.

Ruth calls. I don't answer. But when she calls for the second time, wearily, I pick up the phone.

'I'm so sorry,' she says. 'I can't forgive myself for that conversation and I wanted to check you're ok.'

I don't answer.

'Grace?'

'I'm not ok. I've just been fired from the salon and my life has disintegrated.'

'Oh, honey, I'm so sorry. Is there anything I can do?'

'No.'

'I was flying yesterday, short haul. I popped over to your house on Sunday evening to check up on you, but you weren't there. Or if you were, you didn't answer the door.'

'I was out. I had a drink with William.'

'William? The sugar daddy?'

'He's employing a private investigator to help look into Abi's life.'

'Are you sure you trust him?' Ruth asks.

'Yes, I do.'

'Is there anything I can do for you?'

'Conjure up some new clients?'

'I wish I could,' Ruth says. 'I'm away again for the next three days. Alan is home, and then he's back to Kenya at the weekend.'

'Thanks for calling,' I say.

'Take care, Grace.'

As I put the phone down, it hits me. Why the hell haven't I

thought about this before? Alan goes to Africa for work regularly. Alan has been having an affair. Was he a sugar daddy?
Did he have anything to do with my Abi? I shudder at the
thought of it. Surely not. But it could make sense. He lives in
Horsham. He could have nipped from Kenya to Cape Town,
although at over three thousand miles away, it's hardly a nip
across. It's a possibility though. But Alan, a killer?

I think of him and his slightly gauche demeanour, the way
he shoves his thick rimmed glasses up his nose whenever he's
pondering a question, his receding hairline and paunch of a
stomach. I've always thought Alan was a bit wet, if anything. I
shudder. Surely not?

But right now, I haven't got time to think about him. I need
to get to one of the few clients I have left.

YVONNE IS in her late seventies, and having broken her hip last
year, she's not very mobile. Her husband died six years ago, and
now she lives alone in a big farmhouse with a low, sloping tiled
roof and lead-paned windows, up a long track near Billing-
shurst. She tells me that her son visits every weekend, often
accompanied by her grandchildren, but her only constant
companion is her little Norfolk terrier called Leo. I visit Yvonne
every fortnight, and her appointments are frequently the highlights of my month. I take a quick sip from my 'water bottle'
before grabbing my box of hairdressing tools and walking up to
the front door. I place my belongings on the ground before
ringing the doorbell.

'Hello, my dear,' she says. 'Come in.'

Yvonne leans on a stick and smiles at me. She always
dresses elegantly; today she is wearing one of her many twin-
sets, a pale yellow jumper and cardigan with pearls as buttons,
matched with navy trousers. Although her face is heavily lined
and her jaws are flaccid, I have no doubt that Yvonne was a

beauty in her youth. I follow her through the dark hall and into her cloakroom. The room is about ten feet square with full-height cupboards lining one wall, a small mahogany chest of drawers under the window, and a sink on the wall opposite the cupboards. The toilet is in a box room through another door.

I place my handbag on the floor, but carry on holding my box of hairdressing paraphernalia.

'Oh, goodness, I'm getting so forgetful these days.' She taps her forehead with pale pink polished nails. 'I quite forgot to bring the trolley in for all your bits and pieces.'

'Don't worry,' I say. I am worried that she flinches every time she moves, and don't want her to have to walk unnecessarily. She is the sort of woman who would never complain, but the pain is etched into the lines between her eyes. 'I'll just pop everything here on the floor. It's not a problem.' Normally, Yvonne wheels in a white plastic trolley for me to use whilst colouring and cutting her hair.

She smiles at me. 'I didn't forget your tea and cookies though,' she says, beaming. Sure enough, there is a blue Denby teapot, two matching cups and saucers, and a plate of home-made ginger biscuits on a tray on the chest of drawers.

Yvonne eases herself onto a stool in front of the sink.

I smile at her in the mirror. 'How would you like me to do your hair today?'

'The normal, please.'

Leo, her little terrier, waddles into the room. He looks even chubbier than normal. He gives me a feeble woof and then, recognising me as his friend, tries to jump up on Yvonne's lap.

'Not now,' she chastises him, stroking his little head.

I lean down on the floor to sort out the hair dyes, brushes, scissors, bowls and everything else. A few moments later, I have mixed up her colour, put a plastic cape and a towel around her neck, and started painting on the dye.

'How are you coping, my dear?' she asks.

'It hasn't been the best week,' I admit. I take a step backwards and accidentally knock my handbag. My water bottle topples out of the bag and liquid puddles onto the stone floor. I clearly didn't screw on the lid properly.

'Oh, I'm sorry,' I say, trying to juggle everything without anywhere to put my stuff.

'It's only water. Forget it,' Yvonne says. But as Leo walks towards the puddle, I realise with horror what is about to happen.

My neat vodka has spilled on the floor, and Yvonne's cherished dog is about to lap it up. Is alcohol toxic to animals?

'Stop worrying,' she says, her smile wide and innocent as I stand staring at the dog.

'It's vodka!' I exclaim. 'Leo, Leo. Come here, boy.' I bend down to try to grab the terrier and in doing so manage to get a dollop of hair dye on his coat. This is turning into a total farce. When I glance up, I see the disappointment in Yvonne's eyes. I grab a towel from my box and use it to soak up the clear liquid. It's obvious what it is. It stinks of neat alcohol. At least I've saved her dog from coming to any harm. Next I wet another towel and wipe Leo's coat. I hope I have removed all of the hair colour.

'I thought I smelled something on you, but I couldn't put my finger on it. Alcohol. I'm sorry for what you're going through, Grace, but I'd like you to wash the colour off my hair.' Yvonne's expression is steely.

'But I haven't finished, and it needs to stay on for forty-five minutes.'

'I'm aware of that. Were you planning on driving whilst under the influence?'

'No, of course not,' I say, flustered. 'The water bottle filled with vodka is my safety net. I've barely drunk any, which is why it's full. I know I shouldn't drink, and I'm trying really hard to give up. But what with everything that's happened–'

'I'm an old woman, Grace. What you will not know is that twenty-four years ago my eldest son was killed by a drunk driver. I am generally a tolerant person, but when it comes to alcohol and drugs, I have no sympathy. Rinse my hair out and I will call you a taxi. You can collect your car tomorrow when you are sober.'

'But I'm not drunk!' I exclaim. 'I haven't had any today.' And it's true. I haven't had a single sip.

EVENTUALLY I PERSUADE Yvonne that I am not drunk, so she allows me to leave in my own car. I feel like a naughty child, slapped on the wrists, sent packing, but it's so much worse than that. I am genuinely fond of Yvonne, and more than losing another client, it's as if I've lost a caring aunt. But what caused me the most distress was the disappointment in her eyes; it cut through me.

As I pull out of her lane, I think of Abi, and my thoughts are drawn to Alan. I can either turn right and go back towards Horsham, where no doubt I will ease my misery by drinking, or I could turn left and drive to the coast, where Alan's business is based. A car comes up behind me and hoots.

I turn left.

I drive steadily towards Pulborough and then cross the small humped-back bridge over the River Arun – where too often the river bursts its banks and spills across the whole plain – I take the road towards Bury and Arundel. It is beautiful here, with the south Downs rising in front of me, the sun gleaming on the snaking river, and as my car chugs up the steep hillside to the summit of the Downs, I glance briefly to the left, with the beautiful green English countryside falling away and, in front of me, the glint of the sea in the distance. All I know is that Alan works somewhere near Arundel, so as soon as I see a lay-by at the side of the road, I pull in and switch off the engine.

Mobile reception is not great, but it is just strong enough to input Alan's name and Broekias Brothers, the greenhouse manufacturer he works for. I get the spelling of the name wrong, but fortunately the address is listed: a trading estate just outside Arundel.

I don't give myself the chance to think about what I'm going to say to Alan or how he might react towards me. Worse still is how Ruth will feel. All I hope is that he will actually be there.

The trading estate is a mile outside the beautiful town, so I have no view of Arundel's spectacular castle. In fact, I could be anywhere. I am surprised that Broeikas Brothers is housed in a single-storey office block. I had assumed that being a greenhouse manufacturer, they might be surrounded by greenhouses, but instead there are uniform warehouses – a business park that could be anywhere in England. I park my little red car in the single space allocated for Broeikas Brothers' visitors, and glance at my face in the mirror. Tired. My hair looks dry and frizzy, and my skin is blotchy. Should I do this? Should I confront the husband of one of my oldest friends and accuse him of something truly hideous? And if I do, will we ever be able to come back from this?

I can't do it. I am angry with myself for coming here. It's a ridiculous thought: Alan having an affair with Abi. I am about to start the engine when there is a rap at my window.

'Hello, Grace. What are you doing here?'

Alan is standing next to my car, his briefcase in his hand, his jacket over his arm.

There is no way out.

I would never just pass by somewhere like this.

Shit.

I open the car door and get out. He leans in to give me a kiss on the cheek, but I freeze. I can't help it.

'What's the matter?' he asks, placing his briefcase on the ground.

What the hell should I say?

'Is there somewhere we can go for a quick walk?' I ask.

He frowns. 'Of course. Let me put my things in my car. I've got a meeting in Chichester in an hour, but there's no hurry for me to leave.'

I lock my car and wait for him. A couple of moments later he is back. 'There's a path around the side of the buildings that leads to a public footpath. I sometimes take myself there at lunchtime to let off steam. It's lovely to see you, but what are you doing here?'

I put myself in his shoes and realise that my reaction would be so very different to his. I would automatically assume something was wrong, that something terrible had happened to a member of my family, and my best friend had gone to notify my husband. Clearly nothing of the sort has gone through Alan's mind. He is just open and curious.

'It's about Abi,' I say. 'She was pregnant and having an affair with someone from Horsham.'

'Goodness.' He rubs his chin. It's obvious from his surprise that Ruth hasn't told him. 'You don't think it was Ethan, do you?'

'No. Ethan was abroad for most of this year. Actually, I was wondering if it might be you.'

Alan stops walking. His lower jaw falls open, and he shakes his head as if he is trying but failing to assimilate what I have just said. 'Me?'

I nod.

He then takes a step towards me and holds both my shoulders. I want to run away. I'm scared and I'm humiliated because from the look of utter disgust on Alan's face, I know for certain it isn't him. I cannot meet his gaze.

'Grace, I can't begin to imagine the suffering you and Bob are going through, but this quest to find out who killed Abi is destroying you. Look at you. You look terrible; Ruth told me about the drinking, and she said there's a man behind bars for Abi's murder.'

'Are you on Sweetner?'

'What's Sweetner?'

His gaze doesn't waver from my face; his breath doesn't catch; the firmness of his grip doesn't alter. This man hasn't got a clue what Sweetner is.

'I just want to find out what really happened. I want to find out who was the father of my daughter's unborn child,' I whisper, my shoulders dropping underneath his hands.

He pulls me into a hug then. Rotund, warm-hearted, gentle Alan who probably doesn't even know what a sugar baby is. I hope he and Ruth work it out, whatever their marital problems might be. When he releases me, I step backwards. 'Sweetner is a sugar-baby website. Abi was a sugar baby.'

'Bloody hell,' he murmurs as his jaw drops.

'I don't suppose you know anyone who might be a sugar daddy, do you?'

'I can't imagine there are many of those at the golf club.' And he's not being ironic. 'They're generally a bunch of mean buggers who will do anything they can to duck out of a round at the bar, let alone pay for the upkeep of a woman.'

It makes me wonder why he and Justin seem to spend so much of their free time at the golf club.

'I'll have a word with Justin and some of the others.'

'You promise to do it discreetly?'

He takes my hand and squeezes it. Then he looks me straight in the eyes. 'I promise, Grace. But you've got to promise me something too.'

'Ok,' I say hesitantly.

'Cut out the booze. Please. My cousin was an alcoholic, and he died of it. We're all too fond of you, and Ella needs her mum. Get help. There's plenty of it out there.'

I nod, give him a weak smile and stride back to my car.

22

I wonder if I've done the right thing in confiding so much to Alan; I am unsure about him mentioning the sugar-baby websites to his mates at the golf club. So long as Abi's name is never mentioned, perhaps it'll throw up some more leads.

Back at home, the answer machine is flashing.

'Grace. William Jennings here. Please, can you give me a call?'

When I dial his number, the phone is answered by a receptionist. 'Dr Jenning's practice. How can I help you?'

'My name is Grace Woods. Dr Jennings asked me to give him a call.'

'Are you a patient?'

'Um, no. It's a personal matter.'

'Please hold the line and I'll see if he's available.'

A couple of minutes later William is on the phone.

'Perfect timing, Grace. I'm just between patients. My investigator has uncovered some interesting things. I've got a very busy week and was wondering if you could pop up to London to meet me. I've found out where Sweetner.net's offices are and thought we could pay them a visit. I've also got some other information to share with you. What do you think?'

'Um, yes. I can come to London.'

'Tomorrow, let's say 1 p.m. Does that suit you?'

As I have no hairdressing clients, there is absolutely nothing keeping me from going anywhere.

'Yes.'

'Right. I've got to be at the Royal Marsden Hospital at 2 p.m. for a research project I'm involved in, so let's meet at South Kensington Tube. Everything is within walking distance. If you're coming from Victoria, you'll be on the District and Circle line platform. I'll meet you on the platform underneath the tube map.'

'Can you tell me why–' I want to know what he has uncovered now, not have to wait until tomorrow.

'Sorry, Grace. My next client is here. I must dash. See you tomorrow.'

I HAVE ABSOLUTELY nothing to do. No work and neither of my girls to care for. I call Ella, but her phone goes to voicemail. I leave a quick message saying that I love her and hope she'll be coming home soon. So I pace around my small garden, staring at my beloved plants. I need to do some weeding and dead-heading, but I'm just not in the mood.

After pacing futilely for a while, I grab my heavy wrought-iron chair and once again place it in the middle of the lawn, sitting there with my bare feet in the grass. My garden is enclosed on three sides by high fencing panels, and I can see the tops of my neighbours' houses. I suppose they can see straight into my garden, and up until now, I was proud of how pretty my little patch looked. I want a drink, but I think of Yvonne and Ella, and I know I must dispel that urge. I close my eyes and lean my head backwards, feeling the hot sun on my cheeks. But all I can think about is drinking. Furious with myself, I get up and pace back into the kitchen. I grab my cigarettes and lighter from my bag and take them back out to the garden. There are three cigarettes left in the packet.

I smoke them, one after the other, and then, disgusted with myself, I grab the empty box and crumple it up in my palm. That's it. I'm finished with artificial ways to make myself feel better. I am going to sort myself out. I am going to be a good mother to Ella, and I will get the answers I need about Abi's life and death. Before I can change my mind, I stride back into the house and grab every bottle of booze I have. Three full bottles of wine. A half-drunk bottle of vodka. A full bottle of brandy. One by one, I pour all the contents down the kitchen sink. Knowing that distraction is of utmost importance, I make myself a proper supper. I marinade a chicken breast in lemon and herbs, dice some potatoes and create a stir-fry of the rather lank and minimal selection of vegetables remaining in the fridge. And then, feeling right in the flow, I bake a chocolate sponge cake.

By the time I sit down to eat it, I'm knackered. It's so much more fun cooking for others. Nevertheless, I'm resolute. After locking up downstairs, I go up to the bathroom and run a bubble bath. Following a good soak, I follow my nightly ritual: going into Abi's room, using the feather duster that I keep behind the door to gently remove any dust or cobwebs, checking that everything is just so, and finally lying on her bed, my face in her pillow. For the first time, my tears don't flow. Perhaps it's because I'm feeling an iota of hope that William may really be able to find out what happened to Abi. Twenty minutes later, I return to my own bed.

Something wakes me. A crackle. I sit bolt upright and grab my alarm clock. Pressing the illumination button, I see that it's 1.08 a.m. I flick on the bedside lamp, but nothing happens. And then I cough. My sense of smell has never been great, but there is no disputing it. Something is burning.

I have always been terrified of fire. I am one of those ultra-cautious people who dislikes burning candles, just in case I forget to blow them out. I fumble around for my phone, but I can't find it, so keeping the light button pressed on my alarm clock, I hop out of bed and rush to my bedroom door. I fling it open.

A terrible mistake.

Heavy, acrid smoke is curling up the stairs, gushing into my lungs, making me cough and splutter, scalding my eyes, blurring everything. Flames are dancing downstairs and now they're racing up the carpet, up towards me, with a terrifying whoosh. *No!*

I scream and run back into my bedroom, slamming the door behind me. Coughing and spluttering, I race to the window, jamming the curtains back. Thank God I live on a residential road with street lamps. I swing open the window and scream, 'Help!'

I can hear the fire now. The roar as it takes hold of downstairs. And my sheer terror. Is this how I'm going to die? Should I jump now or wait a bit? How many feet down is it? There is only pavement beneath, no grass or bushes to soften my fall. I scream again, 'Help! Fire! Help!' Surely someone must hear me?

And then running footsteps on the road outside. A man wearing a high-vis jacket.

'I've called the fire brigade. They're on their way!' he shouts. 'Stay there! I'm going to get my ladder.'

'Don't go!' I say, but I'm choking now and he disappears around the corner. I shout again, but my voice cracks.

'Please don't let me die,' I beg. Is this how Abi felt? Knowing that her life was about to be wrenched away from her? How will Ella survive without both her mother and her sister? Surely life can't be so cruel?

Something crashes downstairs and I can feel the heat now, rising up through the floor. Is the floor going to give way underneath me and I'll crash and burn below? I grab the sweatshirt that I discarded on my bedroom chair last night and pull it on. Then I haul myself up onto the window ledge, my bare legs dangling out of the window. All I'm wearing is a skimpy cotton T-shirt that reaches to my mid thighs.

And then I hear the siren. *Hurry, please hurry.*

The man in the high-vis jacket is back, carrying a ladder, but he stops in the middle of the road, his eyes wide. I can see the flames downstairs reflected in his face, bouncing lights off his ladder. The sirens are getting louder, deafening now. Two fire engines speed up on our road, brakes slamming on. Blue lights spinning around and around.

'Stay there. We're coming to rescue you!' a fireman yells.

And then strong arms are around me, carrying me down a ladder. I shut my eyes.

SOME TIME LATER, I don't know how long, I am sitting in the back of an ambulance wrapped in one of those metallic blankets. They stopped me from looking, from seeing how my house was destroyed from bottom up. I couldn't care about the house itself. It's insured. But the contents: Abi's bedroom, all of her things, the sacred space I had made into a shrine for my daughter – it's all gone. I have absolutely nothing that belonged to my daughter. It's as if her life has been destroyed without any trace of her ever having existed.

I can't stop crying.

'Grace.' The ambulance woman squats in front of me. 'We would like to take you to the hospital to get you properly checked out.'

I shake my head. 'No. There's nothing wrong with me.'

'You have suffered smoke inhalation.'

'I'm fine. It's all over.'

'What's all over, Grace?'

'My life, everything to do with Abi.'

'Your life isn't over. Your house is destroyed, but the most important thing is that you are safe and no one got hurt.'

And then a policeman is standing in front of me. Not one of the ones I recognise. A young man with crooked teeth and a long, beaked nose.

'Grace, we're going to need to investigate what happened here tonight, and will be working alongside our colleagues in the fire brigade. In the meantime, I'm afraid you won't be allowed back into your house for quite some time. Who can we call to come and support you?'

I shrug my shoulders. I am sitting here with nothing. No clothes, no belongings, no phone, no money. Lost in the deep fog of what has happened, I can't even remember anyone's phone numbers.

'You can call Bob,' I say. But then I change my mind. I don't want Ella to be awakened in the middle of the night to be told her house has burned down. We need to protect her for as long as we can, so instead I say, 'Call Natasha Bellover or Ruth Newton. They're my best friends, and both live just outside Horsham.'

23

N atasha and Justin arrive together. I am still seated in the back of the ambulance, but Natasha jumps up into it and flings her arms around me, squeezing me so tightly, I start to splutter. I must look absolutely frightful. No makeup, hair on end, red eyes, snot running down my face, and my bare legs with varicose veins on show. If Justin notices, he is polite enough not to stare. He leans into the ambulance and says, 'I'm so sorry, Grace. As if enough bad things haven't already happened to you.'

'I've brought you some clothes,' Natasha says, producing a plastic bag and pulling out a pair of jogging bottoms, some trainers, socks and a thick jumper that feels so soft, it must be spun from cashmere.

Justin walks away, ostensibly to speak to a fireman.

'Why don't you get dressed, Grace, and then once everything is okayed with the police, you can go back to your friend's house,' the ambulance woman says.

Natasha hops down from the ambulance, and the door is pulled shut to give me some privacy. I really don't know how I find the strength to get dressed, to process what is happening.

Perhaps I don't, because I am aware that people are talking to me, but I have no idea what they are saying. The ambulance door is reopened, and I am helped down. I am standing behind it; there are lots of people talking, mostly dressed in uniform.

'It's shock,' I hear someone tell Natasha.

A policeman turns to me and I am forced to look at him. 'You can go home now,' he says.

I know he means well, but it is a truly insensitive thing to say. I burst into sniveling sobs yet again. 'To your friend's house,' he backtracks, but it's too late.

Natasha and Justin support me on either side. I stop walking, trying to turn around to glance at my shell of a home, but Justin is quite forceful.

'Don't look,' he says, steering me forwards. And I let him. We walk past small groups of people, mostly wearing dressing gowns, their arms wrapped around themselves as if to give themselves some artificial protection, standing on their doorsteps, their eyes wide with horror as they assimilate what has happened on their street. Most of them glance away as we walk past. Natasha opens the front passenger door to Justin's black Range Rover, and somehow I get myself inside. Despite the warmth of the night and the thick jumper, I am shivering uncontrollably. Justin jumps in and starts the engine, turning the heaters up to full blast, directing them at me.

'Thank you,' I murmur. We drive in silence.

When we arrive back at their home, Natasha takes control. 'Justin, make Grace a hot chocolate, and I'll go upstairs and put sheets on the bed in the spare room.'

I sit at the kitchen table whilst Justin spoons some Green & Black's chocolate powder into a mug, pours in milk and heats it in the microwave. When it pings, he takes the mug out and hands it to me. He hovers awkwardly.

'I really am sorry,' Justin says. I glance up at him and think I see pity in his eyes, but then he looks away. I wonder whether he ever imagines what it would be like to be married to me rather than Natasha. Very occasionally, I feel a rush of envy towards Natasha, for her easy life, her successful and dashing husband and her beautiful home. But perhaps Justin's easy-going and sympathetic manner is his social façade. I suppose if I'm living here for a while, I'll find out what he's really like.

And then I have to stifle a sob. I don't want to be here in the middle of the night in the Bellovers' luxury, modern house, beholden to them; I want to be back in my own home, surrounded by my things, and be able to lie down in Abi's bed.

Natasha pads in, making us both jump. She's removed her shoes and is walking barefoot.

'Are you ready to go to bed?' she asks, barely concealing a yawn.

'I know it's late, but can I have a shower?'

'Of course you can. I've laid out some clothes for you, night-wear and things for you to wear tomorrow. We'll have to take you off shopping. At least one good thing will come out of this, you'll get a whole new wardrobe.'

I don't share Natasha's sentiment. I think of my clothes and Ella's. They're cheap and functional, but they're mine, and I've collected them over many years. And then, there are all of those designer dresses of Abi's that I still hadn't unpacked. I was planning on taking them to a charity shop. Thank goodness that Ella had taken most of her favourite belongings to Bob's house.

I follow Natasha upstairs and into her spare bedroom suite. She has pulled the cream linen curtains; large beige and cream tassels hang limply on either side. The centrepiece of the room is an enormous bed with a plump beige head-board. Cushions are piled high on top of the pillows. Small bedside tables stand on either side, both with neutral-coloured table lamps. The wall to the left of the bed houses a full-width built-in wardrobe, and on the opposite side is a door leading into the en-suite bathroom. I pick up the cream-

coloured, fluffy towels that she has left me on the end of
the bed.

'Thank you, Natasha. Thank you for having me to stay.'

'I was hardly going to leave you on the street, was I? We're
all here for you, honey.'

As I stand under the shower, trying in vain to rinse away
the remnants of the fire, I can't help but see those flickering
flames and hear the roars and crashes as they swept through
my home. I want to block it all out, push the horrors away,
but how can I empty my brain? I turn the heat in the shower
up so high, every drop feels as if it is scorching my skin. I
never thought I was masochistic, but perhaps I am. I wash my
hair using Natasha's sweet-smelling shampoo. What I would
do for a drink right now. It's so ironic, isn't it, that less than
twelve hours ago, I swore I would follow a more virtuous
path.

Natasha is waiting for me, perched on the end of the bed,
when I emerge from the bathroom.

'I'm sorry you've had to stay up all night for me,' I murmur
as I glance at the clock. It must be getting light outside already.

'You need to take this,' Natasha says, holding out a glass of
water and a pill. 'It's a sleeping pill. I don't normally agree with
taking drugs, but in this instance, you need it.'

I nod and accept the pill.

WHEN I AWAKE, I struggle to work out where I am. And then it
hits me. My house burned down. I have nothing. As the fog
from the sleeping pill starts to clear, I ease myself up in bed. A
fire doesn't just start spontaneously. I think back to yesterday.
Did I leave any appliances on? I'm sure I didn't. I haven't done
any washing in a few days; with just me in the house, I don't
bother with the dishwasher. I used the oven and the hob to
make my supper yesterday, but both are electric. The fire

clearly started downstairs, so my only conclusion is that it must have been an electrical fault. From what, I've no idea.

I can hear clattering downstairs, so I make my way to the en-suite, have a quick wash and put on Natasha's clean clothes. She's taller and slimmer than me, but has left me a skirt with an elasticated waist, a loose-fitting T-shirt and a cardigan. I slip my feet back into the trainers she loaned me last night. I walk along the hallway, past paintings of flowers, and pause at the top of the stairs. I can hear whispering, so I pause for a moment, straining to hear what is being said. It sounds distinctly like Justin and Natasha arguing, but over what, I can't make out. I carry on walking downstairs and into the kitchen.

They pull away from each other when they see me.

'Hey,' Natasha says. 'Did you sleep?'

I nod.

'Justin and I have been talking, and we'd like you to stay here for as long as you need. Weeks or months, it really doesn't matter.'

I glance at Justin, who looks distinctly displeased about the offer. I don't blame him. Although their house is large, I can't imagine any man being over the moon about having one of his wife's best friends staying indefinitely.

'That's really kind of you, but I'm sure once the insurance money comes through, I'll be able to rent somewhere.'

'Our home is yours,' Natasha says. 'I've already spoken to Ruth and she extends the same offer, although obviously their house is smaller, so it's a bit more awkward. We have all of this space just for the three of us, and most of the time, Becky isn't even here.'

'It's very kind of you,' I say. Thank goodness for Ruth and Natasha; otherwise I might have ended up having to beg Bob and Sue to stay with them. That really would have been awkward. I literally have nothing now. No money, no income, no home, no possessions.

'We've already had a phone call from a fire investigator. He'll be here in about an hour.'

'Why?' I ask, but then I realise it must be standard practice. They'll need to work out if it was an accident or arson.

'Not sure. I guess there are procedures that need to be followed in circumstances such as this. I've made bacon and eggs. Would you like some?'

The smell makes my stomach curdle. I shake my head and instead accept a strong coffee and a piece of toast with marmalade. Justin has retreated to his study, and Becky has spent the night with Ethan, so it's just Natasha and me. I'm relieved.

'Are you fully insured?'

I nod, recalling how shocked I was by the enormous bill I received for my renewal last year. I hate to think what it will be this year. But without my phone or computer, I've no idea how I am going to access all the information I am going to need.

When the doorbell rings, I jump. It feels as if my nerves are totally strung out, as if the slightest little thing will set off a chain of violent pings that ultimately might stop my heart from beating. I take in a few deep breaths, but I can still taste the embers, and my throat feels sore.

Natasha leads in an exceptionally tall man with the complexion of dark tea. He has a thin moustache and a little tuft of hair sprouts from the cleft of his chin.

'Mrs Woods, I am Simon Ahmad and I am overseeing the investigation into your house fire.'

I shake his hand.

'Why don't you both go into the living room,' Natasha suggests. We follow her through. I sit on the edge of the large white sofa, and Mr Ahmad settles down opposite me. He is wearing a navy suit and carrying a briefcase that he puts at his feet.

Natasha disappears.

'My condolences for the loss of your house,' he says. His hazel eyes are piercing, and his lips narrow. I imagine that little gets past this man. 'We have started our preliminary investigations, and I would like you to talk me through what happened last night.' He leans forwards and flicks open his briefcase, removing a small lined pad of paper and a biro.

'It doesn't make any sense to me,' I say. 'No appliances were on. I never burn candles. The boiler was checked a few months ago.' My voice peters out. Has the person who is threatening me upped their game? Was it arson?

'I understand that you were alone last night.'

'Yes.'

'When was the last time anyone else visited the house?'

I try to remember. Ella popped home for some things a couple of days ago, but even Bob hasn't been around recently.

'My daughter two days ago. No one since.'

'Do you smoke, Mrs Woods?'

I catch Natasha's eye and I can tell what she's thinking. I probably got pissed, fell asleep and dropped a lit cigarette. But that is absolutely not what happened.

'Yes, but I smoked my last cigarette yesterday early evening.'

Mr Ahmad's eyebrows rise.

'Last night, I resolved to give up everything, cigarettes and alcohol, and concentrate on finding out about my daughter.'

'Your daughter?'

'My eldest daughter was murdered in South Africa. I want to know more about her life.'

'I am sorry to hear that.'

And then I shiver. It must be arson. Did someone set fire to my house intentionally? And if so, did they want Ella and me to die?

'You say you stopped smoking last night. At what time?'

I wrap my arms around myself and try to stop my right leg from bouncing up and down. I need to concentrate. If it was arson, I must remember every detail of what happened to help him work out who did it.

'It must have been around 6 p.m. I was smoking in the garden. I finished the packet and threw it away, straight into the big bin outside, because it was the green bin collection day today. Then I made myself supper, had a bath and went to bed.'

'How do you explain the remnants of cigarette butts and the vodka bottles found amongst the rubble of your kitchen?'

'I can't!' I exclaim. 'That's crazy! It wasn't me. I didn't even smoke in the house. What are you saying?'

'From the pattern of the fire, we believe that it was ignited via lit cigarette ends and quite possibly the vodka was the accelerant. Obviously, we are at the very early stages of the investigation, so once we have fully assessed the burn path, we will know more.'

'It's got to be arson!' I jump up from the sofa. Both Natasha and Mr Ahmad frown at me as I pace around the room, my feet sinking into the extra-long shaggy white carpet. 'I smoked my last cigarette seven hours before my house caught fire. It wasn't me!'

From the way he slowly closes his notebook and raises one eyebrow at me, I can tell that Mr Ahmad thinks I'm crazy. But I'm not. It sure as hell wasn't me. And if someone else did that, it is obvious they wanted me to die.

I shiver.

Natasha sees Mr Ahmed to the door while I remain pacing her living room, trying to banish the vision of flames licking my stairs. This must be all related to Abi's death and my probing. Why else would someone want to destroy my home and kill me?

I become vaguely aware of car doors slamming and the chattering of voices. When Natasha returns, Ruth is with her. She is wearing her air stewardess uniform. Justin hovers in the doorway.

'I cannot believe so much shit is happening to you,' Ruth says, shaking her head as she hugs me. 'How are you, or is that a stupid question?'

I try to smile.

'It's all been a terrible shock, hasn't it, Grace? Ruth has come here straight from the airport.' Natasha sits down next to me and plumps up the cushion that Mr Ahmed was sitting on.

'Thanks, Ruth. But you didn't need to come over.'

'Natasha messaged me last night, and of course I had to come straight here. Don't worry about me. I'm not even that tired.'

'Would any of you ladies like a cup of coffee?' Justin asks.

Natasha and I decline. Ruth requests a black coffee. When Justin has left the room, Ruth slumps into the armchair opposite Natasha and me. 'What did the fire investigator say?' she asks. 'Was there an electrical fault?'

Natasha speaks before I can answer. 'He says the fire was started by cigarette butts.'

There is a pause and then Ruth says, 'Oh, Grace.' Her voice is laden with disappointment.

'It wasn't me!' I exclaim, but my two best friends glance at each other, and I catch the expression that passes between them. They don't believe me. After one of those painfully prolonged moments that probably only lasts a second, Natasha stands up and claps her hands together.

'There's no point in hanging around here feeling glum. I think you, me and Ruth – if you're up to it, Ruth – should go shopping. My clothes aren't exactly flattering on you, Grace. You'll need some basics, makeup, stuff like that. I'll lend you as much money as you need until your insurance cheque comes through.'

I sigh. 'I don't feel like it, Natasha. Besides, I've got to be in London for noon.' I remember now how I agreed to meet William. 'Can I borrow your phone a moment?'

She hands it to me, and I pull up a map of London and type in directions to see how I can get from Victoria station to South Kensington. It's too far to walk, so I'll have to take the tube.

Justin appears with the mug of coffee for Ruth. She darts him a quick smile and mutters thanks. 'Did you say London?' Ruth asks. 'You can't go to London, not with everything that's just happened!'

'I have to.'

'What's so urgent?' Natasha questions.

'I'm meeting Dr Jennings, the Harley Street psychiatrist, the decent man from the sugar-baby site. He has some information for me, and we're going to Sweetner's head office. I know neither of you understand, but I have to do this.'

Both my friends speak at the same time, and I can't make out what they're saying. I put my hands over my ears and shout, 'Stop!'

They stare at me, their faces comical with shock. 'I'm sorry, I know you both mean well, but I am going to London. Natasha, can I borrow some more clothes, a bit more formal than these?' I gesture towards the jogging bottoms.

'Okay.'

'Where are you meeting him? Is it somewhere safe, in a public area?' Ruth asks.

I sigh. 'Yes. I'm meeting at a tube station. You don't need to worry. I'm not going to his home. And it won't be for long, because he's got to go to a meeting at the Royal Marsden Hospital.'

'Just so long as you stay safe,' Natasha says, squeezing my arm.

24

NYA'S BLOG FROM THE SUGAR BOWL

MARCH 14TH

I NOW HAVE two sugar daddies (SD) and I've learned loads in the past fortnight. Here's my list:

1. *Don't ever let on that you have more than one SD. And never let on that you have a boyfriend. These men are in serious need of ego stroking, and they want to think they're special.*

2. *Agree how long you're going to be with them. It got a bit awkward last week with L. There I was sitting in his living room in my new black lacy underwear (think it's going to take me a while to get used to that!) and it was getting later and later. I had a train to catch. Eventually*

I stood up and said I needed to go. I actually thought he was going to bail out of paying me because he looked so disappointed, so I had to promise to make up more time the following week.

3. *Don't look shocked if your SD tells you he's married.*
4. *Trust your instincts.*

I MET up with M. He's much younger than the other SDs – only thirty. He says he's on Sweetner because he hasn't got time for regular dating. He works in the city and earns a fortune. On his profile picture he looks like he could be a male model, so I was quite excited prior to meeting him. And I have to say that he was as gorgeous in the flesh as in his picture. Because he's a workaholic, he said he can't commit to a regular day or time, so he offered to pay me per meeting – one thousand pounds!!! He looked at me with his big blue eyes and asked if I would be willing to meet him that night. I explained I had a train booked back to uni, but he said he'd rebook it for me the next morning, first class. Three hours later (having been shopping to buy a new, sexy outfit) I met him in a fancy hotel. He bought a bottle of champagne and told me all about himself. And then he said he'd booked dinner to be delivered to his room. I was uneasy about that, but also a bit tipsy. The hotel room was seriously plush and there was a table laid up for two. But then he grabbed me, hands and tongue everywhere they shouldn't be, and I got really scared. I told him that I didn't do benefits, and he said that's what all the girls say, but they don't mean it. I lied and told him I was a virgin because I thought that might make him think twice, but it got him even more excited. I swear to God he was going to rape me, but then there was a loud knock on the door, and a waiter announced that he had brought our dinner, so M had to step away from me, and as soon as the waiter opened the door, I ran out past him, into the corridor, down the stairs, and I hotfooted it out of the hotel.

M has been messaging me non-stop. First of all, he apologised for any misunderstanding and asked for another date. When I didn't answer, he got more aggressive. And then he called me a whore. I blocked his number, but I have to say I'm a bit scared. Actually, incredibly scared.

APRIL 10TH

THINGS ARE GOING PRETTY WELL with my sugar daddies. I have three regulars. I already mentioned W and L, and then I hooked up with a third called J. He's younger and better looking than the other two and he travels quite a bit for his work. That's where I come in. He gets lonely when he's away from home, so he pays for me to join him. Normally it's a night over in Leeds or London, but he also flew me to Paris. It was so romantic, and I had to remember that this wasn't a date and he wasn't my lover. Sometimes when you fancy your SD, it's hard to remember the rules that you set yourself (if you get me). Ok, I'll admit it. I was a naughty girl. But hey, it was Paris and you're only young once, and he bought me a pair of Louboutins and a dress by Chloé.

I TOLD one of my uni friends that I am a sugar baby and she totally freaked out. She said she never took me for a tart and how could I sell my body for money. I told her that I didn't, I was just selling my time, but she didn't get it. So I decided I wouldn't tell anyone, not even my housemates. They want to know how come I've got so many expensive clothes and why I'm away so much. I had to lie and say that my dad came into lots of money (ha, I wish!) and that I'm going to London regularly to see my boyfriend. That's kind of true. But it's hard work having to lie.

SOMETIMES THOUGH *I feel really bad. I mean seriously bleurgh. If it ever got out that I was doing this sugar-baby stuff, it would break my mum's heart. It might even make her take up drinking again and that would be the worst. So you do need to think about that. But soon I'm going to have enough money to take my mum and sister on holiday. A proper holiday like to the Caribbean, not just to Centre Parcs. The problem is, I'm going to have to explain how I earned so much money. She's going to know that I could never earn that much working as a barista (which is what I told her). I'm going to have to come up with another lie. More lies. And I can't even talk to my boyfriend about all of this, because he thinks he's the one and only. Grr...*

25

B oth Natasha and Ruth fuss over me. I know they think I'm still in shock, and undoubtedly I am, but I need to see William. At least doing this will take my mind off the horrors of last night. Natasha offers to drive me to the station, whilst Ruth says she needs to go home and get changed.

'Ring me and I'll come and collect you,' Natasha says as she lets her car idle in the drop-off bay at Horsham station. 'And please take care. I'm really not happy about you meeting this man again.'

'It'll be fine,' I say as I undo my seat belt. 'Thanks for everything, and see you later.'

Natasha has loaned me a navy skirt that must hang loosely on her because it is too tight around my hips. If I didn't have more important things to think about, I would be concerned that the seams might split when I sit down. I'm wearing a pretty pale-pink blouse and a long-length navy cardigan that hides some of the bulges in the skirt. Her only shoes that fit me are the trainers, so I'm still wearing those. She also loaned me a handbag, £100 cash and an old mobile

phone to which she added twenty pounds credit. It makes me
feel terrible to accept so much from her, but what else can
I do?

After paying for my ticket to London Victoria via the self-
service ticket machine, I walk up and down the stairs to the
platform. Frustratingly, it's a long twenty-five minutes' wait for
the next train. I wonder about the sanity of doing this, going to
London. As I haven't even told Bob and Ella that the house has
burned down, I ring Bob. When I explain what happened, it's
as if his brain can't compute what I'm saying.

'What?' he asks several times. 'Holy shit, Grace, that's terrible. What do the police say?'

I don't tell him about the cigarette butts, not yet. I don't
want to give him any more ammunition for keeping Ella away
from me, although that's a bit ironic now, as she doesn't have
another home to go back to.

'Don't tell Ella yet,' I say. 'I would like us to tell her together.
She'll be really upset.'

Fortunately, Bob agrees.

'Where are you now?' he asks.

'I'm at Horsham station about to go to London.'

'Why?'

'It doesn't matter. Look, I'll be staying with Justin and
Natasha. You can get hold of me there. Perhaps bring Ella over
tonight.'

'Ok. I'll have a word with Natasha. Take care, Grace.'

THE TRAIN CARRIAGE is surprisingly busy for mid-morning on a
weekday. I settle into a window seat. There is so much I am
going to need to do. Cancel bills, notify utility companies, but
most importantly, I need to contact my insurers. It takes me a
while to remember their name, but when I do, I search for their
telephone number and call them, but just when I'm about to be

connected to an advisor, I lose reception and the call is cut off. Sighing, I give up and slip the phone back into Natasha's bag.

As I'm sitting there, watching the countryside pass by, I begin to feel uneasy. It's as if someone is watching me. I try to rationalise the feeling. Of course I'm feeling uptight and scared. I have suffered horrendous traumas. If my theory of arson is correct, then whoever set my house on fire last night wants me dead. I resolve to speak to DI Fairisle and hope that he will believe me. With everything that has happened, it is evident that someone is trying to shut me up. The police will have to offer me some protection, won't they? Surely now they will investigate properly.

But if I really am in danger, should I even be on this train? Perhaps Natasha was right. It's not too late. I could get off at the next station and take the next train to Horsham. As the train pulls into Three Bridges, I decide against it. If I don't go to see William, all I will be doing is delaying something that needs to happen. Besides, William can't even contact me now, as my mobile phone was lost in the fire.

I try to be discreet as I glance at the other passengers. No one is looking at me. They're all reading or busy with their phones or gazing out of the window. But still, I feel a disquiet, as if the hairs were standing up on the back of my neck. What I would do for a drink right now...

When the train chugs over the Thames, passing by what was Battersea Power Station but is now a gargantuan edifice of upmarket residential apartments, my heart rate quickens. I decide to hold back and be one of the last off the train. I wait as everyone else stands up and makes their way slowly along the carriage to the open doors. And then, when the last elderly lady has shuffled off the carriage, I leave. I glance behind me. There is no one there. Ahead there are hordes of people, mostly striding with a sense of purpose. I follow them, passing through the security gates and then on through the vast open space of the station. From time to time, I throw a glance over my shoulder, expecting to see Jared B, but he isn't there, and if someone is indeed following me, I can't work out who it is.

The crowd of people sweeps me into a narrowing corridor, down the steps into the underground station. Here I have to queue for a ticket. After buying my ticket, I walk towards the escalators, swept up once again in a large melee of people. But suddenly, I feel as if I can't breathe. My heart is racing, pumping wildly in my ears. I need to get out of here. Now.

I bend over, trying to inhale slowly. One, two, three, four. People jostle me, so I move towards the wall.

Someone touches me on the back and I jump. 'Are you alright, dear?' It's an old woman leaning on a walking stick.

'Thank you, I'm fine,' I say, feeling guilty that she is asking me how I am when clearly she is the one in poor health.

I turn to face the wall and count my breaths. In, out. In, out. I lose track of how much time passes, but eventually my heart rate settles and I feel a bit better. To my left is a large tube map. When I study it, I realise it's a mere two stops on the District and Circle line to South Kensington. No distance. Waiting for a gap in the crowd, I feed my ticket into the automatic gate and am swept forwards, onto the escalators that descend deep underground. As I'm walking through the passageway to the platform, there is a roar and a huge swish of hot air. The tube has arrived. I hurry forwards and jump onto the train just before the beep sounds, signaling the closing of the doors. There are no empty seats, but I don't mind. I lean my back against the glass partition and, to distract myself, study the advertisements plastered on the inside of the carriage.

After just a couple of minutes, the train slows down and eventually shudders to a stop. My heart starts pumping a bit faster once again, but I try to reassure myself. This happens all the time on the tube. The lights are on; nothing has flickered. There is nothing to worry about. So long as I am in a public place, surrounded by other people, I am safe. I glance at the other passengers, and no one looks in the slightest bit perturbed.

But the train still doesn't move. I fish Natasha's phone out of her handbag to double-check the time. I have time. I won't be late. After a further long five minutes, other passengers begin to get impatient. Some stare at their watches in the forlorn hope that by studying the time it will force the train to restart. Others are shifting in their seats, and one man, dressed in a pin-striped suit, attempts to make a phone call, garnering disapproving stares from his neighbours.

Another five minutes pass. There must be something wrong. This is just what I don't need. William has no way of contacting me. I suppose I could reach him via his receptionist at his Harley Street clinic, but I don't have any mobile reception down here underground. The whole trip will be a waste of time if I'm stuck in this tunnel. And then the train conductor's disembodied voice comes through the speakers.

'Due to a trespasser on the track, I regret that this train will terminate at Sloane Square. I repeat, this train will terminate at Sloane Square.'

There are lots of sighs and tuts, but eventually the train starts up again and chugs forwards very slowly. After another few long minutes, we pull into the station.

'All out, please. This train terminates here at Sloane Square. All out.'

I, along with everyone else, get off the tube train and am swept up with the crowd onto the escalator that rises up to street level. I find myself standing outside the station in front of Sloane Square, wondering which way I need to go to get to South Kensington tube station. I gave myself forty-five minutes to get from London Victoria to South Kensington, and I'm glad I did; otherwise I would have been very late. As it is, I have just under fifteen minutes to get to the station. Hopefully, that will be quite long enough.

I am feeling hot and flustered, darting between lingering shoppers. But once I start walking along Sloane Avenue, I am the only person striding along the pavement. It is a longer walk than I anticipated, past large apartment blocks and small local shops, a garage, and then, eventually, the Conran Shop on my left. At the Fulham Road, I stop a man to ask for further directions, and he points that I need to go straight ahead. I cross the road, race past fancy designer boutiques, and then, eventually, on my right up ahead, I see South Kensington station. I have just a minute to spare.

There is a large crowd of people milling at the entrance to the tube station. I ease my way through them, muttering, 'Excuse me,' repeatedly. And then I realise. The station is closed.

How am I going to meet William?

I use Natasha's phone to search for William's practice phone number.

'Hello. I'm meant to be meeting Dr Jennings at South Kensington tube station right now, but unfortunately the station is closed. Is it possible for you to give me his mobile number, please?'

After confirming who I am and double-checking in the diary, the receptionist gives me his mobile number.

I try calling it, but it rings for a few seconds and then goes to voicemail. Damn, he must still be stuck on a train underground. I try again every couple of minutes, but still no one answers. Now I'm not sure what to do. I call his receptionist once more and explain the situation. I give her the new telephone number from Natasha's phone, explaining how William won't be able to reach me on my old number.

The crowd is even bigger now, and then suddenly people start rushing forwards. They must have reopened the station. I follow them through and down the steps. A tube official is standing there shouting: 'Circle and District line is closed in both directions. Do not attempt to get onto the Circle and District line.'

I sigh and start walking back up the steps. I wait outside, adjacent to the most wonderful flower stall brimming with sumptuous multicoloured blooms grouped into buckets. If William doesn't turn up, perhaps I should see if I can visit Sweetner's offices alone, although I recall my failure to locate their physical address. It's now nearly one thirty. I blow out air in frustration and try William's phone yet again.

'Hello.' A woman answers and I'm confused. Has his phone been redirected back to his office, or did I dial the wrong number?

'Hello, is anyone there?' she asks.

'Um, yes, sorry. I'm looking to speak to Dr William Jennings. Is this the right number?'

'Who am I speaking to?'

'My name is Grace Woods. I was due to meet Dr Jennings at 1 p.m.'

'Ms Woods. My name is Police Constable Brown. Where are you at present?'

'Just outside South Kensington tube station. Why?'

'I'm very sorry to tell you, Ms Woods, but Dr Jennings has suffered a fatal accident.'

26

'He's dead?' I ask. I want to scream. This can't be possible. William cannot be dead!

'I am walking out of the station,' the policewoman says. 'Where are you?'

'Next to the flower stall.' But I don't want to stay here. I don't want to talk to a policewoman, not again. I am so tempted to run. She doesn't know who I am or what I'm doing here.

'Please stay on the line,' she says.

But I can't run. This phone number will be logged, and although it's Natasha's phone, it will be linked right back to me. Besides, I haven't done anything wrong. And then, whilst my thoughts are still a maelstrom, and I feel as if I simply can't take any more shocks, a young policewoman dressed in uniform strides towards me. I remove the phone from my ear and end the call.

'Ms Woods?'

I nod.

'PC Brown. May I ask you a few questions, please?'

'Yes.'

'What is your relationship to Dr Jennings?'

'Um, none. Not really. He was a friend, I suppose, just helping me out with a few things. I didn't know him well; in fact, I only met him twice. What happened to him?'

'He fell in front of a train.'

I gasp. The trespasser on the line wasn't a trespasser at all. I want to ask if he was pushed, but I realise that will sound too suspicious, so instead I ask, 'Was it an accident?'

'We are not sure at this moment in time. We will be investigating,' PC Brown says. 'Could you tell me, please, what sort of doctor was William Jennings?'

'A psychiatrist.'

'And were you a patient?'

'No, absolutely not.'

'Why were you meeting him?'

'He was helping me with regard to some information about my daughter. We had a meeting planned at a local business.' I know that is a stretch of the truth, but how else can I explain why we were meeting?

'And you were due to meet him where and when?'

'At 1 p.m. on the District and Circle line platform in South Kensington station.'

'Could you please give me your name and contact details.'

I have to scroll through the phone to find out the mobile number. She looks at me quizzically.

'It's not my phone,' I mutter. 'I've just borrowed it from a friend for a couple of days.'

'Thank you. We will be in touch.'

I WATCH her as she returns to the station, and I notice other people staring at me. I need to go. Now. Several bright red double-decker buses pass by, but I am too shaken to attempt to work out which one goes in the direction of Victoria station, so I start walking briskly the way that I came. And then I see a black London taxi with its light illuminated. I stick out my arm. The taxi pulls over and I clamber in.

'Where to, love?'

'Victoria station, please.'

I sink into the black leather seat. I can't believe William is dead. Was it an accident, or was he pushed? It can't have been suicide; that makes no sense. This was a man full of vitality on a mission to help me, and then he was on his way to the Royal Marsden Hospital for a research project meeting. I know little about suicide, but I feel sure that this could only have been an accident at best; murder at worst.

My god. Was he killed because he was about to reveal something to me? Has whoever killed Abi and whoever burned down my house struck again? Or is this just a horrible coincidence?

The taxi pulls up in front of Victoria station, and I really don't want to get out. I feel safe inside this car. Could someone have followed me? I count out the money that Natasha loaned me, and pay for the ride. Reluctantly, I walk into the station, constantly looking over my shoulder, glancing around me. Who even knew that I was going to meet him? My best friends, their husbands and possibly my ex-husband, assuming he spoke to Natasha or Justin. That is ridiculous. These are people I've known for the majority of my life. But has Jared B been behind everything? Perhaps he has been watching me, waiting, ready to strike when no one is looking. I have to trust someone. I have to trust the people I've known the longest.

I get lucky with the train, and five minutes later, it is chugging out of Victoria station back to Sussex.

I send Natasha a text message. I can't face talking to her right now.

'On way home. Will get into Horsham in an hour. Can you pick me up, please?'

I get an immediate response. 'Sure. How did it go?'

I don't answer.

The carriage is empty with the exception of a youth who is wearing large headphones. The heavy beat he is listening to thumps over the sound of the train.

I simply can't think straight, and spend the hour-long journey chewing my nails, so that by the time the train pulls into Horsham, the sides of my fingers are red and raw. I am desperate for a drink to dull the fear, but unfortunately, Southern trains from London to Horsham don't have food or drinks trolleys.

When the doors open, I rush out, running up the stairs, and when I'm at the top, I glance behind me. There are only three of four people walking up the steps at a sensible pace, and I don't recognise any of them. I then run down the steps, and after shoving my ticket into the automatic barrier, I race to the doors. Natasha's car is idling in exactly the same spot she dropped me off.

When she spots me, she jumps out of the car.

'How did it go?' Her face is bright.

'Terrible.' I get in the car and she follows suit.

'He's dead,' I splutter and burst into tears.

'What? Who's dead?'

'William Jennings. He died under a train.'

Natasha shakes her head and narrows her eyes. 'Dead? Bloody hell.'

'And it's all my fault, because it wouldn't have happened if he hadn't been coming to meet me.'

'Hey, that's a ridiculous thought.' Natasha strokes my arm. 'People die all the time on the tube. You know how easy it is to fall onto the line if there are too many people on the platform. You mustn't beat yourself up about this. You know nothing about this man. He may have committed suicide, for all you know.'

I wipe my tears with the back of my hand and sniff.

'Shall we go home?' Natasha asks.

I nod.

But I am still gently sobbing when we get back to Natasha's house. She puts her arm around me as she guides me inside.

'Have a seat. I'm going to make you a hot chocolate. You really have had a terrible time,' Natasha says as she stirs cocoa powder into milk.

'It's all related. Abi's death. The threats to me. My house. William's death.'

Natasha tips her head to one side, and her golden hair catches the light. 'Come on, sweetie. That is really silly. I know you're scared, and who the hell wouldn't be after everything you've been through? But trying to connect all of those, that doesn't make sense. Why would someone kill William? Why not kill you?'

I shudder. I have had exactly the same thought.

'Don't bite my head off for suggesting this, but you have been drinking and smoking a lot. Could this have made things worse?'

I don't answer for a long while. Eventually I say, 'I've got a headache. I'm going to lie down for a bit.'

Natasha lets me go.

I SURPRISE myself and fall asleep, but when I awake, it is with a start. My mouth feels dry, my head is pounding and my heart racing. I drag myself up into a seated position, and as I come to, I remember. My house has burned down and William is dead. I remember the threats from the person who rang me on my birthday whilst I was at the spa and again at home, and how someone tried to drive into me, and my heart lurches as I think of Ella. Whoever burned my home down might have assumed she was living there, too. The thought of her being there terrifies me. I need to speak to her now.

'Hi, Mum. Why are you calling from someone else's phone?'

'I've lost mine and had to borrow Natasha's,' I lie. It's been nearly twenty-four hours and I still haven't told Ella what's happened. 'Where are you?'

'At Dad's. I'm babysitting Tom.'

'You're alone?' The panic makes my voice sound hoarse.

'It's fine.'

'Can you make sure all the windows and doors are closed and locked.'

'For God's sake, Mother. Not this again. I'll speak to you later.' She hangs up on me.

I know I didn't handle that well, and I realise I'm driving Ella further and further away, but she needs to understand that she might be in danger. I contemplate calling Bob, but then there's a knock on my door.

'Come in.'

Natasha puts her head around the door. 'I thought I heard you speaking. Ruth is here and I've made a pot of tea. Are you up to joining us?'

'Sure.'

But when I'm in Natasha's luxurious marble-lined bathroom, I can't stop thinking about what William was going to tell me. If only I knew the name of his private investigator, I would be able to make direct contact. I consider speaking to his receptionist, but discount that. The chance that the receptionist knows anything about William and the private investigator is about zero. So now what? I close my eyes, but this time the flames appear right in front of me, and I have to open my eyes and clutch the cool marble sink to stop myself from hyperventilating.

Eventually I feel able to go downstairs. Ruth and Natasha

are sitting at the kitchen table, their heads close together, a large pot of tea between them.

'Hey,' Ruth says as she sees me. 'I bought your favourite, Battenberg cake.'

My smile feels false as I acknowledge the bright yellow cake standing on a white plate on the table. What I really want is a glass of vodka, not cake. But there is no off-licence within easy walking distance of the Bellovers' house. I need to get my car. Perhaps I could ask Natasha to take me home so I can pick up my car, but then I remember that my car keys will have been destroyed along with everything else. Fat lot of good that would be. My best option is to sneak into Justin's booze cupboard and take a swig from a bottle of vodka or gin.

'Grace!' Ruth interrupts my thoughts.

'Sorry,' I say. 'I can't seem to think straight at the moment.'

'That's exactly what I was saying to Natasha. You've had so many shocks, and combine that with the excess booze, how on earth can you be expected to think straight? Did the doctor give you any antidepressants?'

'No,' I say.

'It might be worth a trip to the doctor to get some,' Ruth says.

'I'll nip to the health-food store to buy you some natural sleeping remedies,' Natasha says. 'I gave you my last sleeping pill last night.'

We are interrupted by my phone ringing. We all look at it with surprise. It's a withheld number again, and my heart lurches. Eventually, I pick it up.

'Hello.'

'Mrs Woods, this is DI Pete Fairisle. I've had a call from the Metropolitan Police with regard to the death of a Dr William Jennings. One of my colleagues will be coming to Crawley Police Station tomorrow morning. We would like you to come in for an interview to discuss your involvement with Dr William Jennings.'

'What!' I exclaim. 'But why do you want to interview me? Shouldn't you be concentrating on finding out what happened to Dr Jennings and why someone set fire to my house and why someone is stalking me and scaring me?'

'Please, Grace. There is no need to get excited. We simply want to talk to you.'

This incenses me further. 'I assume you knew that my house burned down last night? Just last night. And it wasn't me who set it alight. Someone is trying to hurt me, kill me even. Perhaps you'll take it seriously when I'm dead!' I hope I haven't said too much to him. I remember too late how my unknown assailant was threatening Ella and me with death should I reveal anything to the police.

Natasha and Ruth glance at each other. Ruth frowns. I turn away from them.

'Rest assured that everything is being investigated by the relevant departments, Mrs Woods. Come and have a chat with us in the morning. In the meantime, I understand that you are staying with your friends–' There is a pause whilst he rustles some papers. 'Mr and Mrs Bellover.'

'Yes, that's correct.'

'Will 10.30 a.m. be convenient for you?'

'I'VE GOT to be interviewed by the police. He's asked me to go into Crawley Police Station tomorrow morning.' I chuck the phone on the table, and it skids across the smooth wooden surface. Ruth catches it just in time.

'Why?' Natasha asks.

'About William's death, because I was the person he was meeting, I suppose.'

'Bloody hell, Grace. You're the victim here,' Ruth says.

'Ruth is right. They should be looking out for you, trying to get to the bottom of everything that's been going on, not hauling you in for questioning.' Natasha looks as exasperated as I feel.

'I need a bloody drink,' I say.

Ruth and Natasha look at each other, yet again. I know they mean well, but I'm fed up with their nannying. I stand up and stomp off to my bedroom.

Just as I'm sinking onto the bed, the phone rings again. It's Ella and she's hysterical.

'Is it true, Mum? Has our house burned down?'

Shit. I had wanted to protect her, to tell her myself.

'Mum?' she screams at me down the line.

'Yes. I'm sorry, darling, it's true. It burned down last night, and everything has gone. Thank goodness you were staying at Dad's.' All I want to do is fling my arms around her and hold her tight. I will ask Natasha to drive me to Bob's house. 'How did you find out?'

'Rachel told me, and I asked Dad if it was true. How could you have not told me? Why did I have to hear about this from my friend?'

The line cuts off.

I bury my face in my hands. I should have told her this morning. Why wasn't I thinking straight? And now she's heard through her friends, when all I wanted to do was protect her. I call Bob's mobile, but it goes to voicemail. And then I ring their landline. Eventually Sue answers.

'Can I speak to Ella, please.'

'Bob is comforting her. I don't think it's a good time, Grace.'

I grit my teeth. I bet she loves saying that. She's always been holier than thou, thinking herself the superior wife, the one who has managed to hold onto her husband.

'She's my daughter, Sue, and I would like to speak to her.'

Sue sighs, but I can hear her footsteps as she walks through the house. There is some whispering, and then Bob speaks. 'Ella doesn't want to talk to you. Best if you call again tomorrow.'

'But–'

'We'll call you in the morning.'

27

T his is the first time I have ever been into a police station. Crawley Police Station is a large imposing red-brick building with double-height pillars either side of the front door. All of the doors and window frames are constructed from blue metal, which just adds to the strangeness of the place. I really don't want to be here. Just by entering the building, I feel in some way diminished, as if I have been judged and found wanting without being given the chance to defend myself. I wonder if I should be accompanied by a solicitor. Too late now. I don't know any, and I have five minutes to spare until the meeting.

Linda Hornby is in the reception area when I walk in, and her look of pity does nothing to ease my nerves.

'I heard about your house fire,' she says as we walk along a carpeted corridor. 'Just so relieved no one was hurt.'

I nod. William's death has overshadowed the fire, but just the mentioning of it causes my chest to constrict with fear. I start coughing, dry, pathetic coughs. Linda ushers me into a small room with a window that looks out onto the car park.

'Stay here. I'll get you some water.'

She is back just a couple of moments later holding a plastic cup. I gulp the water down. And then DI Fairisle arrives, accompanied by another policeman who introduces himself as DC Stuart Conner from the Metropolitan Police. After shaking hands, the two men sit down at the table opposite me.

'Give me a call if you need anything,' Linda says as she leaves. The door closes silently behind her.

I want to ask her to stay; it feels like I'm being fed to the wolves.

'Mrs Woods, thank you for coming in to see us this morning. You are not under arrest and you are free to leave at any time. You have agreed to be here to give a voluntary interview, and you are entitled to legal advice,' DI Fairisle says.

'Legal advice?' I interrupt. 'Do I need a solicitor?'

'No, you don't, but you have the right to have one present should you wish.'

And now I don't know what to do. Should I ask for one, or will that make them think I'm guilty, or should we just get this over and done with? They said it was an informal chat, and I can always leave if I don't like their questions. They are both staring at me, waiting for an answer. But I didn't do anything wrong, so of course I don't need a solicitor.

'It's ok, we can continue,' I say eventually.

'Please let us know if you need any refreshments or want to use the facilities.'

I nod.

DC Connor takes over. 'As you know, we're investigating the death of Dr William Jennings, who was killed by a tube train at South Kensington station. As Dr Jennings was on his way to meet you, we would be grateful if you could explain the nature of your meeting.'

And now I realise how very unprepared I am. Should I say 'no comment'? But that would be really suspicious. I take a deep breath and the words tumble out. I'm a bloody awful liar anyway.

'Dr Jennings was helping me find out about my daughter Abi's life and death. We were going to go to the offices of Sweetner.net.'

'The sugar-daddy website?' DC Connor scrunches his forehead.

'Yes.'

'How did you get to know Dr Jennings?'

'I went through my daughter's emails and discovered she was on that website. Dr Jennings was one of her clients.'

Both men sit up straighter. The atmosphere in the small room changes; it gets colder. I shiver.

'We believe that Dr Jennings was pushed in front of the train,' DC Connor says.

I gasp. My hand rushes to cover my mouth.

'Did you push him, Ms Woods?' DC Connor asks.

'No!' I want to jump out of my chair.

'How did you feel about him taking advantage of your daughter?'

I stare at DI Fairisle. Why is he letting DC Connor ask all of these accusatory questions? Fairisle doesn't meet my eyes.

'You've got it all wrong. He didn't take advantage of Abi. He became a friend to her, like a godfather. He never had sex with her.'

'How do you know that?' DI Fairisle asks, gazing at me now through those black-framed glasses.

'He promised me he didn't, and I believe him.' The long, heavy pause suggests their disbelief.

'What were you going to do at Sweetner's offices?' DC Connor asks.

'William said he had uncovered some more information he was going to share with me; I think we were going to try to find out the identities of the other sugar daddies.'

'You think?'

'I'm not sure exactly. William had worked out what we needed to do. Look, none of this would have happened if you had investigated Abi's death properly.' I jab my finger at DI Fairisle. I know that antagonising him won't do anything to support my cause, but the more I think about it, the more he is to blame. 'I told you that someone has been threatening me, and all you said was that Abi's killer is behind bars in Cape Town. But someone is trying to stop me from digging into Abi's life, and if you'd done anything to help me, William might still be alive and I'd have a house to live in and–' I stifle a sob. I glance away, through the louvred blinds and out to the car park. I wish I were there.

'The problem we have, Grace, is that we have CCTV footage.' DI Fairisle leans across the desk and switches on a computer. He turns the monitor so that we can all see it. It flickers to life.

'We can see you getting on the train at Horsham station. You then got off the train at Victoria station.'

This is horrific. I watch myself walking head bowed as I stroll through the open concourse towards the tube station. I lose myself for a moment in between the crowds, but there I am again, waiting in line to buy a ticket.

'As you can see, you purchase your ticket. You then will have descended the escalators towards the District and Circle line. The timing is such that you would have arrived into South Kensington station sufficiently early to be on the platform at the time that Dr Jennings was pushed.'

'No, that's not possible!' I say. 'You've got that all wrong.'

'We already know that you had plenty of time to meet Dr Jennings. The platform was exceptionally crowded that lunchtime, with people packed in like sardines, due to the opening of the dinosaur exhibition at the National History

Museum and another popular exhibition at the Victoria and Albert Museum. It was school holidays, a busy time.'

'But I didn't take the tube to South Kensington, I got off at Sloane Square!'

'That was convenient, wasn't it, Ms Woods?' PC Connor asks, his tone drawling and sarcastic.

I throw him a filthy look, but I expect that the terror I am feeling inside is evident on my face.

'I had a panic attack just before I was due to get on the tube at Victoria station, so I was delayed for a few minutes. And then my train stopped at Sloane Square, and we were all turfed off it. Don't you have the CCTV for that?'

DI Fairisle glances at his colleague.

'So you are saying that you never set foot on the District and Circle platform at South Kensington?'

'That's exactly what I'm saying.'

'You do realise, Ms Woods, that we will be able to verify all of this when we get hold of the relevant CCTV footage? I strongly advise you to consider your answers carefully.'

'I didn't go inside South Kensington station. I never saw William. Anyway, how do you know he was pushed? Could it have been an accident?'

'According to eyewitnesses, no.'

'If people saw the person who pushed him, then why am I here? You must have been able to identify the culprit.'

'Unfortunately not. The individual was wearing a baseball cap and was lost in the crowd. Eyewitnesses are notoriously poor at providing accurate representations of what happened. The witnesses were, understandably, in deep shock. Unfortunately, the platform was exceptionally packed, so the CCTV on the platform did not capture the event. Naturally, we have requisitioned further camera footage, but we are working on the premise that either Dr Jennings was subjected to a spontaneous attack or it was premeditated.'

The explanation is like a kick in my stomach.

'Grace.' DI Fairisle leans forwards towards me, pushing his rectangular-framed glasses up his nose. 'I appreciate it's been a very difficult time for you. Grief plays out in a myriad of ways and–'

'You're not taking me seriously, are you? Someone tried to burn my house down along with me inside it. Someone did manage to kill William, most probably because he was helping me find out who killed my daughter. If I die or someone else close to me dies, it will be on your heads!'

They both sit there in silence, arms crossed, staring at me.

'Get the CCTV from Sloane Square and you'll see that I got off the tube there.' My hands are trembling so much, I have to sit on them.

'Thank you, Ms Woods. You are free to go now, but we will want to talk to you again. I will also liaise with the fire investigator with regard to the fire at your house.' DI Fairisle pushes his chair back and stands up. I do the same. DC Connor remains seated at the table, scribbling notes on a pad.

DI Fairisle holds the door open for me, and DC Connor nods at me as I leave. I hope I never have to see DC Connor again.

28

W hen I leave the police station, I feel as if I have been through several cycles in the washing machine. My legs are so weak they can hardly keep me upright, and I just want to wail until my eyes run dry.

Ruth is sitting in the driver's seat of her Tiguan, reading a book. I open the passenger door and get in.

'How did it go?'

I can't keep my emotions in check in front of my lovely friend and I burst into tears. She tugs me towards herself and strokes my hair as if I were her child. Eventually, I pull away and blow my nose on a manky tissue retrieved from the depths of my bag.

'They think I pushed William.'

'You? Bloody hell, Grace.' She runs her hands around the steering wheel.

'I'm the victim here, but I'm being made to look like the evil person or the mad person. I tried to tell them that William was my friend. Besides, I wasn't even at South Kensington station.' I think of William and what a lovely man he was. His patients will miss him, but I wonder who else will.

'They haven't charged you with anything, have they?'

'No, thank goodness. But if this carries on, I'll need a solicitor. As if I haven't got enough things to worry about. I'm going to have to get the house insurance sorted and speak to the bank, get a new car key, talk to the utility companies. And I just don't have the energy.' I lean my head back against the headrest. Ruth starts the car.

'I'm free for the rest of the day. I can help you.'

'Thanks, Ruth. I don't know what I'd do without you and Natasha.'

'Natasha has clients, but she said we can go back to her house. I've picked up some food from M&S for lunch. If you don't mind, it would be easier to have lunch and make the phone calls at Natasha's. Alan is working from home today, so he'll be hogging our phone.'

I nod, squirming inside as she mentions Alan. I assume that he has been good to his word and hasn't mentioned my accusation. During the drive back to Horsham, I think about everything that I need to do, and it is overwhelming. I have lost absolutely everything, from my hairdressing tools to my clothes, to every photograph, every book, the jewelry left to me by my mother. I bite my lip to stop myself from crying again. All the mementos of Abi: they have all been destroyed. The only things left are the memories in my head and the paltry number of photographs that Bob took with him when he moved away.

RUTH and I spend the afternoon on the phone. She helps me make a list of everyone that I need to contact, and we work through it one by one. Most people can't be more helpful. The mechanic from the garage says he will source replacement car keys and will drop them around to Natasha's house at the end of today. That is such a relief. At least I won't be so dependent on my friends when I can drive. The bank promises to send out new cards, and the mortgage provider is giving me a three months' holiday.

But the kindness of everyone is dampened by the insurance company. The woman explains it could be weeks until they can make a payout to me. They need to appoint an assessor, and if there is a police investigation, well then, she has no idea how long it will take. What the hell am I meant to do in the meantime? I can't live at Natasha's forever.

When Ruth leaves shortly before 5 p.m., I retreat to my bedroom. I try calling Ella, but both her and Bob's phones ring out, and I'm damned if I'm going to beg Sue again. I'll go over to Bob's house tomorrow to see Ella in person. In the meantime, I send her a long text message telling her I love her.

The need for a drink is becoming overwhelming. I want to dampen all the horrors that play over and over in my brain. Death. Destruction. Fear. I decide it's ridiculous that Natasha is stopping me from drinking. I'm an adult. I can control myself; it's just sometimes I choose not to. I decide to sneak into their living room and help myself to one of the many bottles they keep in their drinks cabinet. I decide I don't care if they catch me; I'm an adult and can do what I like. I'll just brazen out their judgements.

I walk out onto the landing to the top of the stairs. I can hear raised voices. Justin and Natasha are fighting again. I try to make out what they are saying, but without getting nearer, I can't. I suppose it's over me; Justin not wanting me to stay in their house. Maybe it would be better if I move to a hotel. I can't afford it, but I'll suggest it anyway. Tomorrow perhaps, when Justin is out of the house.

I tiptoe to the bottom of the stairs and then jump, letting out a squeal.

'Mum asked me to come and get you. Supper is ready,' Becky says as she emerges from the living room.

'Is everything alright?' I ask, nodding towards the kitchen.

Natasha and Justin are still hissing at each other in inaudible whispers.

Becky shrugs her shoulders and sighs. 'It's normal,' she says, her lips pursed. It surprises me. I never imagined Natasha and Justin would argue so much.

I follow Becky into the kitchen. Natasha is sitting at her place and Justin is serving up what looks like a chicken casserole.

'My turn to cook tonight,' Justin says chirpily, as if nothing were the matter.

'Can I help?' I ask.

'Come and sit down. Keep me company.' Natasha indicates the chair next to her. Becky helps Justin carry the plates to the table.

'This looks delicious,' I say, for the first time in days, if not weeks, feeling properly hungry. 'I didn't know you were a whizz in the kitchen, Justin.'

'I have a limited but successful repertoire. It's just that *someone* likes to keep me out of the kitchen.'

'You mean you normally expect your dinner on the table and only want to pretend you help out when guests are around. When was the last time you actually made a meal?' Natasha narrows her eyes at Justin's back.

There is a stony silence. Becky sits down opposite Natasha and keeps her eyes firmly on her plate of food. I notice that her portion is about a quarter the size of mine. There is a bottle of wine on the table. Natasha pours herself and Justin a glass, but there is no wine glass in front of my place.

'Could I have a glass of wine too, please?' I ask.

Becky looks up. 'Sorry, Grace,' she says, standing up. 'Mum said you didn't drink.'

'I would love a glass tonight.' I smile at Becky, who walks over to the cupboard and extracts a wine glass. I can feel Natasha's eyes on me, but refuse to catch her glance.

'How did you get on at the police station?' Justin asks.

I tell them everything and how I was made to feel guilty even though I haven't done anything.

'Did they really have no description of the person who pushed your doctor?' Justin asks. He looks tired, which surprises me, as it's the summer holidays now and he rarely goes into work. Perhaps all that golf is a strain.

'If they do, they didn't tell me.'

'I don't understand why they think it's murder. Couldn't it have just been an accident, or a suicide even?' Natasha suggests.

I shrug. 'The police think not. And now William has died, I've got no idea what he wanted to tell me. Perhaps I'll try to visit Sweetner's offices by myself next week, but what I really want to do is find out the name of the private investigator William had hired. Perhaps his secretary will know.'

I can't fail but notice the strange glance that passes between Justin and Natasha. They may have been arguing a few moments ago, but now they seem united by some secret language only they understand.

'What is it?'

'We both think the time has come to drop all of this,' Justin says. He lays his knife and fork neatly on the side of his plate, even though he hasn't finished eating. He wipes his mouth with his blue linen napkin. 'You need to grieve, get on with your life. I know all these terrible things have happened to you, but it's as if you're courting disaster.'

The glare on my face makes him backtrack.

'Look, we all loved Abi, but it's time to make peace. You need to get yourself sorted out, get Ella back living with you, and we're all here to support you to do that.'

'End of sermon by Justin the headmaster,' I say. I can't help the sarcasm, and regret it as soon as the words leave my lips.

Becky lets her cutlery fall onto her plate. She pushes back

her chair and the legs screech on the floor. She rushes from the room.

'Becky!' I shout after her. 'I didn't mean that.'

Natasha lets out a loud sigh. 'She's not upset with you.'

'What is it? Is she still finding it hard to come to terms with Abi's death?'

'Something like that,' Natasha says. I wonder if Natasha is going to follow her daughter upstairs, as I would do if one of mine had stormed out, but she doesn't. She carries on eating her food. We all continue, in silence.

IT TAKES a long time for me to fall asleep, and when I awake after just three or four hours, morning light seeps through the sides of the curtains and I realise my phone is ringing. With a pounding heart, I grab it. Once again, the number is withheld.

'Grace, it's DI Fairisle. I'm calling to say that you are no longer a person of interest with regard to Dr William Jennings's death. We obtained the CCTV footage from Sloane Square station and can see that you got off the tube there and walked towards South Kensington. Dr Jennings met his death some minutes earlier.'

I close my eyes and sink back onto the pillows. At least that is one relief: I am no longer a police suspect.

'Do you think it could have been an accident?' I ask.

'We still believe it is homicide and will continue our investigations. I will, of course, keep you updated. Also, I am waiting for the report from the fire investigation team regarding your house. I will let you know what the outcome is there, too.'

A FEW MINUTES LATER, I have emerged from a quick shower and am dressed in yet another ill-fitting outfit loaned to me by Natasha. I really must go shopping. I am about to go downstairs when once again I hear loud whispering. Then the front door slams.

I hurry downstairs and almost collide with Natasha, who is walking out of the kitchen.

'Is everything alright?' I ask. 'Would you rather I move out?'

'Absolutely not,' Natasha says. I notice that she is looking particularly smart today, wearing a cream linen trouser suit and high-heeled tan shoes.

'Justin seems a bit uptight, if you don't mind me saying.'

'Justin is always uptight, and never more so than before a governor's meeting. I'm sorry about his sanctimonious speech last night.'

'It's fine. I know he means well.'

'He struggles with removing his headmaster's hat when he's home,' Natasha says. 'Anyway, once today is over and the meeting is out of the way, hopefully he'll calm down. I'm also out today, going to a neurolinguistic programming convention in Brighton, but I've organised for Ruth to pop over and take you out shopping.'

'I don't need babysitting,' I say as I rummage in the cupboard for a bowl.

'It's not babysitting, it's making sure that you're ok. It's horrid what you've been through, and both Ruth and I want to be there for you.'

'I appreciate it, but—'

'It's organised,' Natasha says. 'I'll be home about 6 p.m., and Becky is spending the day with Ethan.' She hands me a white envelope. 'There's three hundred pounds in there. It won't buy you much, but hopefully just a bit of a starter wardrobe. Oh, and the man from the garage dropped off your car key. I've left it on the console table in the hall.'

'Thank you, Natasha,' I say. I don't try to argue this time.

'Right, I must dash. Have a good day.'

'Thanks, and you too.'

.   .   .

When I hear Natasha's car speeding out of the drive, I telephone Ruth.

'I know you've been seconded to take me shopping, but I've got a migraine, and if you don't mind, I'm going to go back to bed.'

'Oh no. Do you need any painkillers?'

'It's fine. I've got everything I need.'

And so my little lie gives me a whole day all to myself. A day when I can delve into William's life, see if I can find out the name of the private investigator, and indulge in a bit of solitude. As much as I love my friends, I am craving time alone.

My sleeping pills were lost in the fire and I'm missing them, so my next call is to the doctor's surgery. When I explain my situation, I am surprised and relieved that I am offered an appointment for 11 a.m. I need to hurry, because first I intend to pick up my car.

I call a taxi and fifteen minutes later I am in the back of a cab, speeding towards home.

'Did you hear about the house fire?' the taxi driver asks. 'Nasty, it was.'

I nod. I don't want to get into conversation. I get him to drop me at the end of the road and I walk slowly towards my house. The pavement in front of my house has been cordoned off with blue-and-white police tape, and after throwing it one quick glance, I can't look again. I don't want to see the blackened remains of our home; I don't want to remember the terror. Instead, I hurry to my car, open the door and hop inside. I drive to the doctor's surgery and park in an adjacent road.

Dr Sarah Perbody is the doctor who prescribed me sleeping pills straight after Abi was killed. She is wearing a red sleeveless dress that compliments her brown shoulder-length hair, and she gives me a wide smile when I enter her room.

'How are you, Grace?'

'Things haven't got any easier. My house burned down.'

She looks horrified.

'I would like some sleeping pills, please. The ones you prescribed me were destroyed.'

She nods. 'And how are you coping?'

I shrug. I try to be nonchalant, but tears spring to my eyes. I bite the inside of my cheek.

'It's very normal when you have terrible shocks,' Dr Perbody says. 'I'm thinking that it might make sense for you to have a short dose of antidepressants. How do you feel about that?'

I nod.

'Come back to see me in a week's time, and we can have another chat.'

Gripping the prescription, I stop off at the pharmacy and, with a box of antidepressants and a box of sleeping pills, I feel as if I'm properly armed for battle.

I RETURN to Natasha's house and make myself a sandwich for lunch, using an opened pack of smoked salmon and an avocado. Justin and Natasha's extra-wide fridge is packed full of organic food from Waitrose. It isn't until I'm sitting at the kitchen table, nibbling my lunch, that I realise I haven't told either of my friends about the police exonerating me from the investigation. Some good news to share with them, later.

I clear up in the kitchen and wander back to my bedroom, ready to start investigating Sweetner's address. The old phone that Natasha has loaned me doesn't lend itself to easily searching the internet. I know that Justin has a computer in his study, and I wonder if he'd mind if I use it. I also want to try another reverse image search on Jared B. I walk back downstairs and stride along the corridor to the back of the house. I've only been into Justin's study once or twice, and that was some years ago, shortly after they moved into the house.

It is a small dark room, made somewhat claustrophobic with walls painted in a dark olive green. A bookshelf lines one wall, with a set of Wisden cricket books taking up the top shelf. I know nothing about cricket, but am aware that these are highly collectable. Pictures line the short wall opposite the door. There are at least ten of those long, narrow school photos ranging in date from when we were at school to the present day. In the recent ones, Justin is seated in the centre of the photos, beaming proudly. I peer at the very top photograph and find Natasha, Ruth and I standing next to each other, aged about sixteen. We look so young and naive, with big frizzy hair and those ridiculous school ties that never hung correctly. Natasha appears to be sniggering, while I look surprisingly contemplative, probably worrying about my future, wondering how I'll get a job with three O levels with lowly grades in art, biology and geography. Ruth is grinning like a Cheshire cat. Of the three of us, despite all of that travel, she is the least changed. It takes a while to find Justin. He is standing in the back row, his arms crossed, looking serious. I wonder if he was dreaming of becoming headmaster even back then.

His wooden desk is positioned underneath the small window that looks out onto their garden. Silver cups are lined up on the window ledge – golfing trophies. A large monitor and keyboard sit on the desk, along with a large pile of papers in an in-tray and a pile of books. His pens are lined up neatly. I hesitate, but then I sit down at Justin's desk and turn on his computer. I suppose I shouldn't be surprised that it is password-protected; I have absolutely no idea what password he might use, so I switch it back off again.

I pick up the book on the top of the pile. It's *The Good Schools' Guide* and I wonder if Justin's school is in it. But it's the book underneath that, that catches my eye. It is a copy of

Shakespeare's play *The Tempest.* The cover is black fading into dark blue; I remember this book so well. Abi studied it for her English A level exam. She got an A, much to my surprise and her delight. I think of all of those quotes now, the ones I learned as well as she did, even if I didn't really understand them. It's strange how readily they come back to me. "We are such stuff as dreams are made on, and our little life is rounded with a sleep."

My eyes well up with tears, but nevertheless, I run my fingers over the well-worn pages. What did that quote mean? Was it something to do with finding the meaning of life in sleep? Has my beautiful daughter found the meaning of life in her eternal sleep? I flick the pages open, and as I stare at one page after the next, a familiarity nudges at my brain. Those scribbled notes written in faded pencil are so familiar. The roundedness of the script, the occasional dot of an *I* shaped into a heart, the little interlocking circles that she scribbled when she was bored.

Those notes are in Abi's handwriting.

I flick back to the front of the book and there is her name, slightly faded but written in her distinctive script: *Abigail Woods, L6th*

Why has Justin got Abi's copy of *The Tempest?*

Justin teaches geography, not English, and he barely gets to do any teaching these days. He is forever complaining how the job of headmaster means he has to sacrifice teaching.

I drop the book.

Have I've got it all wrong? Was Abi having an affair with Justin? Was Justin a sugar daddy after all?

29

I am standing in Justin's study shaking from head to toe. I can think of no reason for Justin to have Abi's book. She might have left it in Becky's room, I suppose, but Becky didn't do English A level, and if Abi had left something at the Bellovers' house, they would have returned it to her. I recall how some years ago, Natasha turned up at our house one evening with Abi's gym kit, which Abi had left in the boot of Natasha's car.

Leaning down, I pick up the book and flick through it, page by page. On the final page, an A5 piece of paper flutters to the floor. I bend down and pick it up. It is a receipt from a London hotel for a double room with breakfast for two on April 17 this year, costing £245; the receipt says payment was taken in cash. But what takes my breath away is the handwritten word *Thanks,* followed by an *x.* There are only seven letters, but that script is Abi's. I am sure of it.

But surely not? Justin is a headmaster; he takes such pride in his position of authority, forever proclaiming about what is right and what is wrong. Surely he would never have had an affair with a student, and especially Abi, who not only was twenty years his junior, but also a child he has known since birth. Perhaps Natasha and Justin stayed there together, but when she mentioned their planned holiday to the Maldives, I remember her saying that she couldn't recall the last time she stayed in a hotel with Justin. Is it really Abi's writing? I run my index finger over the text.

Could Justin have been Abi's sugar daddy? Perhaps not through Sweetner, but he could have paid her money, perhaps even bribing her to keep silent about their affair. I groan at the horrific thought. I wonder if Loaded-Len could, in fact, be Justin, but if William's private investigator was right, that wouldn't be possible. Justin is twenty years too young, and I am positive that if Justin had had a vasectomy, Natasha would have mentioned it. Besides, they struggled to conceive, so it seems rather unlikely. I really can't see Justin being a sugar daddy. The risk is simply too great. What if one of his ex-pupils spotted him? His beloved career would come tumbling down. The only possibility is that Justin had been having an affair with Abi. But just because he has her book, and just because there is a receipt for a hotel room inside it, doesn't mean they were having an affair.

I pace around and around his small study as I try to think straight. Did Abi just turn to Justin to share her secrets with him? Was he helping her? If so, that would explain all the calls from a Horsham number, but why use a burner phone? None of this makes any sense.

I run my fingers through my hair. Am I making much too much of Justin having Abi's textbook? Probably. And that receipt could be anyone's; perhaps Abi stayed there with one of her other sugar daddies. I go around and around in circles; none of it makes sense. What I need to do is find out if Justin went to Cape Town during the few days that Abi was there, but how the hell am I going to do that?

I flick through the papers on his desk. They are mostly

outstanding bills, a letter from the local council about a neighbour's planning application, a letter from an ex-student telling Justin how grateful he was for the good references Justin provided. There is absolutely nothing linking Justin to Abi. What I need is proof that he flew to Cape Town at the same time as her, or if I can't find that proof, I need to show that he wasn't where he said he was.

I switch on his computer, and as I expected, it is password-protected. I try some obvious passwords, such as *Becky* and *Natasha*, but nothing works. Eventually, I switch the machine off. I pull open the drawers in his desk. There is another pile of bills. He has scribbled the word *paid* on most of them. And then I find his mobile phone bill. I sit down at his chair to study it. There are no calls to numbers I recognise, but I'm most interested to see if he has any international charges, or whether he made any suspicious calls during the week Abi was away. I groan. Yes, he made local calls that week, and no, it doesn't suggest he was abroad. But it isn't conclusive. Natasha could have used his phone, and he could have taken the burner phone with him.

I stand up and try to open the filing cabinet underneath the window. The drawers are locked. Are his credit card bills there? Would they show the purchase of a ticket to Cape Town? I grit my teeth and sigh. There is nothing left in here for me to find.

I walk back through the house and upstairs. Natasha and Justin's bedroom is to the left of the staircase. I ease open the door, feeling guilt running through my veins. I hate that I'm snooping, but I need to be sure that I haven't missed anything. It's obvious who sleeps on which side of the bed. On Natasha's bedside table there is a photograph of Becky, an alarm clock, a tube of hand cream and a vial of homeopathic pills. On Justin's side is an autobiography of a man I've never heard of and a pair of reading glasses. I feel sick as I pull open the drawer of his bedside table. The top drawer is full of bits and pieces: coins, tissues, a mini padlock, a strip of painkillers, an unopened pack of condoms and a Valentine's card from Natasha.

I shove the drawer shut and open the second drawer. Inside, there is a stack of golf scorecards. They mean absolutely nothing to me, so I close the drawer again. There are two doors facing the bed. One leads into a sumptuous en-suite with double sinks, a roll-top bath and a separate walk-in shower with a massive rain head. The second door leads into a walk-in wardrobe. Natasha's clothes hang on two of the three walls. On the third wall are drawers and shelves housing shoes. I am taken aback by how many clothes she has. And then I notice the safe. It is a large grey box with a big handle. I stare at it, knowing that I will never see inside. I switch off the light, close the door and walk out. On the wall by the door is a photograph of Justin holding a large gold cup, the winning trophy from some big golfing tournament.

As I walk slowly back downstairs, I wonder if the golf club might hold the key to Justin's movements at the end of June. Natasha said that he entered every competition there was, that he is a golf fanatic. If there was a golf tournament when Abi died...

I take my phone out of my pocket and sit at the kitchen table. I search for the name of his golf club and look at their schedule of events. There was a competition the day that Abi died. But how can I find out if Justin played in it? I see a link to the golf club's Facebook page and click through. Nothing.

I plug Justin's name into Facebook. We're friends, but neither he nor I have posted anything in the past six months. Just as I'm about to give up, I have a look through his Facebook friends. I click on each smiling face. Most of them have updated their privacy settings so I can't see much about them, but there is one man called Andrew Jones who clearly has no idea about privacy. His feed is open for everyone to view, and he is evidently as big a golfing aficionado as Justin, perhaps even greater. Andrew Jones posts a picture almost every other day of himself or his buddies out on the golf course. Doesn't he work? He looks too young to have retired. I scroll back through his feed and find a photograph of him with his arm around Justin. This is looking promising. And then, bingo, I see it.

Andrew Jones is holding a silver cup up above his head. Justin is standing to his left and another man to his right. The date is 29 June. The day that Abi was murdered. But if Justin was in Horsham, playing golf on that day, then evidently he wasn't in Cape Town killing my daughter. Or could the photograph have been taken a couple of days beforehand and only posted on 29 June?

I click the page away and shut my eyes. None of this makes sense. I should be happy that Justin had nothing to do with Abi, and yes, of course I'm relieved, but I still don't understand why he has her copy of *The Tempest* and that hotel receipt. And I struggle to imagine Justin threatening me, trying to burn my house down, pushing William into an oncoming train. Justin is a good man, someone who cares about people. So why the hell am I making a big deal of him having a copy of Abi's book, and why am I trying to pin this on him?

I pace around and around the house and eventually find myself in the living room, standing in front of Justin and Natasha's drinks cabinet. I open the door. Both shelves are packed with spirit bottles. I turn away from the cupboard. Booze is not going to help me solve any of the conundrums around Abi. I walk towards the living room door, but it is as if those bottles are magnets, tugging me back towards them. If I don't obliterate the confusion and terror that is churning my brain, I might go mad. At least alcohol will numb that, will help me get through the next few hours. I walk back to the cabinet. Just one glass. I will have just one glass. I choose a bottle of vodka from the back of the cupboard, one the Bellovers hopefully won't miss. It's full. I return to the kitchen, help myself to a glass tumbler from their Welsh dresser, take a large bottle of tonic from Natasha's magnificent larder, and return to my bedroom.

But I lied to myself.

I drink.

And I drink.

One glass after another.

I know it's irresponsible. I acknowledge how weak I am. I know I will feel terrible later or tomorrow. But for now it stops all of that whirring in my head, the questioning of the people who love me, the loss of my daughter, the concern that my other daughter may no longer love me, and the fear that something terrible is going to happen to me and the people I love.

Eventually, I drop off to sleep.

I AM in that horrible disoriented state that exists between sleep and full wakefulness, where I know I need to come to, but sleep is tugging me backwards. I want to wake up. I need to wake up, but something is pinning me into sleep. Footsteps and voices get louder, and then, with a gasp, I'm awake. I scrunch my eyes closed, and when I open them, I blink several times. The curtains are wide open, but the light outside is fading. My mouth is parched and a headache pounds behind my eyes.

There's a knock on my door. 'Grace, are you in there?'

I sit up and see the almost-empty vodka bottle standing on my bedside table along with the empty glass. I grab both of them and shove them under the duvet.

'Yes. I fell asleep.'

Natasha opens the door.

'Are you alright?' She switches the light on, and I have to pretend that it doesn't feel like I have daggers in my eyes.

'Yes.' I yawn, trying to pretend I don't have a thumping

hangover. 'Actually, I had good news. I'm no longer a suspect in William's murder.'

'That's marvelous,' Natasha says a little too casually, as if she really doesn't care. 'Just wondered if you wanted any supper? Becky is staying the night with Ethan, so it's just us adults.'

I can't think of anything worse than pretending to have a normal conversation with Justin and Natasha this evening. 'That's kind of you, but I'm not really hungry. I've got a headache and might try to sleep.'

I think I see her nose wrinkle, perhaps from the fug of alcohol fumes that undoubtedly fill the bedroom, or maybe I imagined it.

'Sleep well,' she says as she closes the door.

30

NYA'S BLOG FROM THE SUGAR BOWL

JUNE 6TH

SO much has happened, I just haven't had the time to write this blog. But the most important thing is that I'm going to stop being a sugar baby. And that's because I'm going to be having a real baby! Yes, I know I'm young, I know my mum will be gutted, but it feels so right. I'm in love and he loves me too. We're going away together in a fortnight, and when we come home, I'm going to officially quit the sugar bowl. It's time for me to start a new life with my new family. I'm going to have to quit uni too, but I'm not giving up on my dream of being a lawyer. I will do online courses and hopefully transfer to a uni nearby where we're going to live.

IT'S BEEN a blast being a sugar baby, and I'm going to say byee with a few last thoughts:

1. *It's your life; it's your body; it's your time. Don't take no shit from anyone else. If they don't like what you're doing, it's their problem. So long as you and no one else gets hurt, then there's nothing to worry about.*
2. *Set your boundaries at the beginning and stick to them. If you want to sleep with your SDs or do the kinky stuff, that's up to you. I chose not to (except for my little transgressions with J!). Do what you're comfortable with and get the hell out of there if your gut is telling you something is off.*
3. *My life has changed so much from having been in the bowl. I've been to some amazing places, had some amazing experiences (theatre, music, ballet, museums – who knew I'd end up being so cultured!) and met some amazing people. Yeah, it's risky. But I reckon it's worth it.*

Kisses to ya all! Axxx

31

As I lie back down in bed, everything aches. I wonder if I'm going down with the flu or whether it's simply the effects of too much vodka combined with fear and heartache. I unearth the bottle and glass from under my duvet and pour myself one more shot, but just a single sip makes me feel queasy, so I lie back down and sleep.

The next time I awake, it is dark outside and the house is quiet. I reach for the alarm clock. It's nearly 11.30 p.m. I switch the light on and swing my legs out of bed. I am in desperate need of a large glass of water and something to eat: a banana or a piece of toast perhaps. I'm also disgusted at myself. I collapsed into bed in my underwear and I feel dirty, not having had my nightly shower. I pull on Natasha's joggers and a jumper and tiptoe out of my room. The lights are off in the house, so I use the torch on my phone to light up the stairs. Clenching my jaw and walking on tiptoes, I try to avoid the places in the upstairs hallway that creak. I don't want to wake anyone. I make it downstairs in silence and then pad through the hall and into the kitchen. Natasha's fancy kitchen appliances give the room a spooky blue glow, just enough light to see what I'm doing. I am reaching up to a shelf to grab a tumbler when I yelp.

There is a person sitting at the kitchen table in the dark.

'What the hell!' I exclaim.

Justin turns around and stares at me.

'Hello, Grace,' he says, his voice deadpan.

'Goodness! Sorry, you gave me a fright. What are you doing here sitting in the dark?'

'Drinking a whiskey, thinking about my life.'

I notice the crystal tumbler on the table and the golden bottle standing next to it.

'I'm sorry to disturb you. I just needed some water and to eat something.'

'You're not disturbing me. You're welcome in our home.'

'Okay,' I say hesitantly.

'Why don't you join me?' Justin holds up the whiskey bottle.

I grimace. The last thing I feel like is more alcohol. I stand by the sink for a moment and think. Now is my time. When else am I likely to have the opportunity to talk to Justin without Natasha overhearing?

'Can I switch the light on?' I ask.

'If you wish. But turn the dimmer down so the lights are low.'

I do as instructed and then stand leaning my back to the sink.

'There's something I need to ask you, Justin.'

He raises an eyebrow.

'I was bored earlier today and was looking for something to read. Forgive me, but I went into your study and I noticed that you have Abi's copy of *The Tempest*. Why?'

He frowns and tugs at his left earlobe. He turns his head away from me and appears to gaze out of the window.

'I'm a headmaster. I have books from all students, past and present.' He looks back towards me, his face creased with confusion, his voice hesitant. He is clutching his glass so tightly his knuckles look sharp in the low light.

'The thing is, you complain that you hardly teach anymore. Besides, you are a geography teacher, not an English teacher. I just find it curious that you should have a book belonging to my daughter.'

'I'm not sure what you're getting at, Grace.'

I inhale deeply. If I don't ask him outright, I am never going to have the courage to do so. I dig my bitten fingernails into my palms. 'Did you have an affair with Abi?'

He coughs and splutters, spraying his whiskey across the table. It seems to me that he is making a great show of this, perhaps buying himself time. 'Are you crazy?' he asks, after several long moments, but the tone of his voice doesn't match the question.

'Please don't lie to me, Justin. Did you kill Abi when you found out she was having your baby?'

He stands up now and shifts from foot to foot. My heart pounds. Justin must be at least six feet two inches and he towers over me.

'How could you even begin to think such a thing?' There is an edge of panic to his voice. I don't think Justin is a good liar.

'I just want to know what happened to my daughter,' I say quietly. 'Surely you must understand that, Justin? If you had a relationship with Abi, you need to tell me.'

He turns away from me now, and I hold my breath for several long seconds. When he turns back again, to my utter dismay, I see tears in his eyes and anguish in his face.

'What?' I whisper. I try to take a step backwards, but my back is already up against the sink and the counter. There is nowhere to go. They say a mother's intuition is always right, but how I wish I were wrong.

He takes a pace towards me and I hold my breath. His feet are bare and his shirt is hanging out. But then he stops still.

'I loved her, Grace. I loved you first, and then I loved Abi.'

I shake my head vigorously. 'No!' No!' My voice is a scream now. 'No! How could you do that to her? It's disgusting! You're like a father figure. A married man. A headmaster!'

'Grace, you don't understand.' He runs his fingers through his short hair. 'I would never hurt Abi. I loved her. She loved me. It's just that circumstances didn't work out. I'm married; she was too young, too beautiful, too naive, too everything for me. I never deserved her.'

I think I'm going to be sick. I edge sideways and then turn so my back is facing the door to the corridor. I take a step backwards and then another one. He stands there like a pathetic giant, his shoulders shaking. I cannot look at this man for a moment longer, let alone speak with him. I need to get out of his house now. I turn and run, along the corridor, up the stairs, into my bedroom. I grab my handbag and the long cardigan and shove my feet into Natasha's trainers, and then I race down the stairs. Justin is standing in the doorway to the kitchen, his face contorted with misery.

'I didn't kill her,' he says quietly. 'You must believe me! I didn't kill her!'

I throw him a look of disdain. Then I turn the key in the front door and tug the door open, racing through it and letting it slam behind me. The floodlights at the front of the house come on, throwing light and shadows into the quiet night. I race to my car, rummage for my car key and fling the driver's door open. I chuck my bag onto the passenger seat and pull the door shut, immediately pressing the central locking button on so that no one can get in. I let out a sob. My hand is shaking too much to insert the key into the lock, and then I burst into tears.

I have been living with the man who killed my daughter. One of my closest and oldest friends. A man with whom I had a fleeting relationship all those years ago. The man who the whole community thinks is so virtuous, so successful. No wonder he didn't come to her funeral; no wonder he paid to have her body repatriated. The bastard. What should I do now? Should I drive straight to the police station or call 999? I have nowhere to go. No home. No money. The thoughts flood through my brain. I try to insert the key again, and then there is a rap on my window.

I let out a squeal and drop the key into the footwell. I turn my head slowly towards my window. Justin is a big, strong man who could easily break the glass in the car window if he chose to. But it isn't Justin. It's Natasha.

She looks frightful. Her hair is messy and her eyes are red and raw, tears staining her pale make-up-free face. She is wearing a thin white nightdress that is almost see-through and she is standing shivering next to the car. She knocks on the window again.

'Please let me in, Grace.'

I lower the window.

Natasha sobs.

'Hey,' I say, unlocking the doors. 'Get in the car.'

She walks around the front of the car and climbs into the passenger seat. I lock the doors again. We stare at each other, but she speaks first.

'I heard everything,' she says, her voice catching. 'It was Justin, wasn't it?'

I nod and reach over to squeeze her hand. She is trembling, in a much worse state than me.

'I want to come with you.'

'What?' I say.

'Wherever you're going, I want to come with you. I can't bear to look at my disgusting husband for a moment longer. He repulses me. I thought I knew that man. I thought I knew everything about him. How could he do that? How could I have got it so wrong?' She turns away from me and stares into the darkness. The exterior lights have gone off now, and there is just a faint glow of light illuminating one of the downstairs windows.

'It shouldn't be you who leaves, Natasha. You must get Justin to leave the marital home. Don't you remember, when I split up with Bob, what the divorce lawyer said?'

She shakes her head. 'No. No. I can't look at him. I need to come with you.'

'I don't know where I'm going. I haven't got a house, remember?'

I can't believe how our roles have reversed in such a short space of time. How I'm having to be the strong one now.

'I need to clear my head. To be apart from Justin for a few days. There is one thing having an affair, but another sleeping with a girl the same age as his daughter. And was Abi's baby Justin's? All that time we tried to get pregnant, those failed IVF rounds, and wham, bang, he impregnates a twenty-one-year-old!'

We sit in silence for a while, but I have to ask her.

'Do you think he killed her?'

She shrugs her shoulders. 'I don't know anything anymore,' she whispers. And then her voice becomes stronger and more resolute. 'Please, Grace. Will you wait for me? I'm going to go back into the house and get changed and pack an overnight bag. I'll be as quick as I possibly can.'

I nod and squeeze her hand.

32

I watch Natasha tiptoe back into the house. It must hurt walking over the gravel with bare feet. When the flood-lights come on, her body is illuminated through her white nightdress and I notice how thin she is, just like Becky. She opens the door and Justin stands there towering over her. I am terrified for my friend now. Is he going to hurt her?

There are raised voices, insults being hurled, but then they both disappear into the body of the house and I can no longer hear or see them. Is Natasha at risk? I drum my fingers on the steering wheel, totally unsure what to do. Should I call the police? Natasha would hate that. I remember how she told me once that she would never 'air her dirty laundry in public'. This would be the ultimate humiliation. I can just see the headlines in the local newspaper: *Police called to headmaster's home to break up marital spat.* She would hate me forever. But this is her safety at stake, and quite probably mine, too. But it's possible that Justin might have already killed two people and burned my house down.

I rummage in my bag for my phone and have just pressed the first 9 when Natasha raps on the passenger window.

'Open up!' she says.

I unlock the door. She chucks a large holdall onto the back seat and climbs into the passenger seat. I marvel at how quickly she got dressed and ready.

'Lock the doors,' she says.

I am still holding my phone.

'What are you waiting for? Lock the doors and let's go. We need to get out of here, now!'

I put the phone down in the central console, nod and start the car. As I reverse, I look in my rear mirror, expecting to see Justin standing in the doorway, but the front door is shut and no one is there.

'Please go fast, Grace.'

I put my foot on the accelerator and my tyres make the little stones on the driveway fly up and clatter against the metal sides of the car.

'Where to?' I ask as we reach the main road.

'Let's go to the twenty-four-hour Tesco. I need a bloody drink, and then we can find a hotel.'

'Shouldn't we be going to the police station?' I ask.

'Oh God!' Natasha moans. 'This is my husband we're talking about. Other than being a bloody cheat, we don't know if he's done anything wrong.'

I realise how hard this must be for Natasha. All the evidence suggests that her husband is a murderer. I try to imagine if it were me in her position, if Bob had done what Justin did, but it's simply impossible to conjure that up.

'Can you go a bit faster, Grace?' Natasha asks.

As I put my foot down further on the accelerator, keeping to a steady ten miles per hour above the speed limit, I realise that I must be over the alcohol limit. I drank the best part of a bottle of vodka. It was several hours ago, but even so, I definitely should not be driving. I wonder if I should say anything to

Natasha, but decide not to for now. At least it's nighttime and no one else is on the road.

It takes less than five minutes to reach the big Tesco. I drive in and park near the entrance. I have never seen the car park so empty, but then again, I have never been shopping at this time of night.

'Take this,' Natasha says, handing me a fifty-pound note. 'Can you buy some booze? I look a mess.' She pulls down the passenger seat visor to look in the mirror. I'm surprised that she's bothered by what she looks like at a time like this, but nevertheless I accept the money. She must be in shock. I think of all the shocks I've had over the past few weeks, and I certainly didn't act rationally after them.

'What do you want me to buy?' I ask.

'Don't care. The stronger the better.'

As I stride quickly into the supermarket, I feel safe. Here I am in a public place, with strangers all around and security cameras. And securely locked inside my car, Natasha should be safe, too. I put my hand into my bag just to double-check I have my car keys, and am relieved when my fingers curl around them.

I grab the first large bottle of vodka that I see on the shelf, along with two bottles of lemonade, then I dash to the check-outs. I am glad that the young male cashier doesn't catch my eye. I race back to the car.

'Good choice,' Natasha says, eyeing the bottles. I don't know the brand, but then I'm hardly a discerning drinker. I place the bottles carefully on the back seat.

'Where to now?' I ask, relieved that Natasha appears much calmer.

'We'll have to go to a hotel.'

'We could ring Ruth and see if we could stay at hers?'

Natasha looks horrified at the suggestion, so I quickly backtrack. 'Okay, which hotel? I think there's one of those cheap chain hotels near the station. How about that?'

She nods.

We are just a few hundred metres away from the hotel when Natasha gasps. I turn briefly to look at her.

'Have you got any of your bank cards yet?' she asks.

'No. I lost them all in the fire. You know what the banks are like. They say it'll take at least five to seven working days until they're sent to me. Why?'

'I'm worried that Justin might cancel my credit and debit cards, and then we'll have no money.'

'Bloody hell, Natasha. Do you really think he'd do that?' I glance towards her, but she's looking out of the passenger window, so I can't see her face.

'I don't know,' she replies quietly.

'Has he ever hurt you?' The words catch at the back of my throat. I think then of how that estate agent raped me when I was a young woman and how I've kept that secret from my friends for all of these years. I wonder if Natasha has been keeping secrets too.

'No.'

'But do you think he's capable of hurting you? Capable of murder?'

She buries her face in her hands. 'I don't know, Grace. I simply don't know. All I do know is that I'm not prepared to find out.'

I steer the car into the hotel car park.

'Pull up over there so your car can't be seen from the road.'

I do as she suggests. As we're getting out, Natasha rubs her forehead with the palm of her hand. 'I'm going to get the maximum amount of cash out of the cashpoint, just in case the accounts get frozen. Can you check in and I'll join you in the room when I'm done?'

'But I've got no ID or credit cards.'

Natasha digs into her handbag, removes her wallet and hands me a black credit card. 'The pin is 7864. Use it to check in with.'

'But it's in your name.'

'Pretend you're me. Look, I'll be with you in ten minutes. There's a cashpoint just a hundred metres or so down the road, and I really need to get cash out before it's too late.' She turns and walks briskly towards the road.

After a moment's hesitation, I take our meagre bags out of the car and walk into the reception area of this anodyne chain hotel that could be anywhere in the world. The young, bearded man on reception looks up with surprise. I don't suppose they get that many new visitors checking in well after midnight.

'Can I have a room, please?' I ask.

He taps into his keyboard. 'We have one twin-bedded room available on the third floor or a queen bedroom on the fourth floor, but that's the executive floor, so it's more expensive.'

'The one on the third floor will be fine,' I say.

'Can I have your credit card, please.' I hand over Natasha's card. He glances at it.

'Thank you, Mrs Bellover.'

I bite my lip.

'Could you fill in this form, please?' He passes the piece of paper and a blue biro across the counter. I complete it using Natasha's name and my address, because I can't remember what number her house is.

Five minutes later, I am upstairs in a spacious twin-bedded room with a shower en-suite. The furniture is all in a dark wood; there are lime green curtains and lime green cushions on top of the white duvet covers. It looks clean, but the bright green hurts my eyes. And then my phone rings. It's Natasha.

'Which room are you in?'

'315 on the third floor.'

'I'll be with you in a couple of minutes.'

As soon as Natasha arrives, she finds two glasses in the bathroom and pours us each vast measures of vodka. She sits in the single chair, and I perch on the end of one of the beds.

'I thought I'm not meant to be drinking,' I say, trying to make light of the situation.

'Not tonight. You and I are going to get totally pissed.'

I'm not going to argue with that.

'I need to know, Natasha. Do you think Justin could have killed Abi?'

She shakes her head. 'Anything is possible. I'm as confused as you are right now.'

'But did he go to Cape Town?'

'No, but he could have hired someone to kill her on his behalf. And for all I know he might have followed you to London when he said he was playing golf, and pushed that doctor of yours onto the tube tracks.'

I shiver. It must be truly terrible for Natasha to be thinking her husband could be a murderer.

'Did you know he was having an affair with Abi?' I ask. I take a sip from my drink. It is way too strong, even for me, and I have to control myself from spluttering.

'Of course I didn't bloody know. I'd have chucked him out of the house immediately. Grace, I just want to drink. Let's not talk, let's just get pissed.'

I nod. I can't remember Natasha ever wanting to get drunk for the sake of it, even when we were youngsters. But then these are not exactly normal times.

We sit there in silence, listening to the low thrum from the air conditioning, and I try not to think of Justin with Abi. What a terrible abuse of power. I realise how a young girl might be flattered by the attention of her headmaster, but even so, it's a stretch.

'Just drink,' she replies. 'I need to work out what the hell we're going to do, and I need to protect Becky. Just think what this is going to do to Becky.'

33

Having already drunk way too much in the past twenty-four hours, I simply don't feel like drinking any more. I wonder if this is me turning a corner regarding my relationship with alcohol. But I do need to go for a pee.

I lock the bathroom door behind me, and as I'm sitting there, I cogitate over the events of the past hour. It beggars belief that Justin seduced my Abi, and it seems even more unlikely that he is a murderer. But how much do we really know about our friends? I suppose we only know the facade that they choose to show us. One thing is certain, whether she likes it or not, either Natasha or I will have to tell the police. Once DI Fairisle knows that Justin had an affair with Abi, surely he will reopen the investigation into her murder, with Justin as their prime suspect. I understand why Natasha wants to bury her head under the carpet, but we need to talk about it.

I wash my hands and walk out of the bathroom.

Natasha is facing away from me, but her shoulders are juddering and I can tell that she is sobbing silently.

I put my arm around her and try to give her a squeeze, but she gently pushes me away.

'I'll be okay,' she says, sniffing. 'I'm not sure I could ever forgive myself if it turns out that Justin was responsible for Abi's death. She was my goddaughter.' Her voice cracks.

She is about to pour some more vodka into my glass, even though my glass is half full. I cover it with my hand.

'Come on,' she says. 'You're the alkie boozer and you're slacking.' I try not to flinch at her description of me. 'I don't want to drink alone, Grace.'

I remove my hand from my glass and she tips in a further generous slug of vodka, topping it up with minimal lemonade.

'I thought Alan was having an affair with Abi. I even confronted him about it,' I admit.

'You what! Oh my God, that's hilarious!' Her laugh sounds manic, as if she can't decide whether it's funny, tragic or both.

And then there is a knock. Neither of us move. I'm not sure if it was on our door or one of our neighbours'.

But it comes again. A much louder knock, very definitely on our door.

We freeze.

And once again.

'Shit,' Natasha says quietly. She stands up. I try to do the same, but I'm suddenly incredibly woozy, as if I'm drunk and my legs won't support me. As I move my head, the room spins. My legs feel as heavy as tree trunks, and exhaustion settles throughout my body. I stay sitting.

'Open up, Natasha! I know you're in there.' It's Justin's voice.

'Shit,' Natasha whispers. 'Shit! Shit! I forgot Find Friends is still on my phone.'

I try to focus my eyes on Natasha's face, but although she is standing stock-still, staring at the door, her lips pursed together tightly, she doesn't say any more. A terrifying shot of adrenaline courses through my veins, and for a few seconds, I am totally lucid. I stand up too, grabbing onto the edge of the table and then grasping the wardrobe handles. I watch with horror as Natasha takes steps towards the door.

'Don't open it!' I say, but my words sound strange, almost jumbled. I try again. 'Don't open the door. Call the police!' I must be so much more drunk than I thought I was, because even I realise that my words don't sound right. Natasha is ignoring me and still walking to the door. Her French-manicured nails are poised on top of the door handle. Why is she going to open it? Doesn't she realise Justin might have a knife? He is so tall and broad and strong. Once Justin comes inside, there is little she and I will be able to do to protect ourselves.

'Natasha!' I say, but the syllables come out like 'ssshh'.

Natasha doesn't turn around. I watch as she turns the door handle, as if in slow motion. She pulls the door open and steps outside into the corridor, leaving the catch down so the door closes behind her, but it's still ajar by a few centimetres. I can barely walk now, the room is spinning so much. This isn't right. I have to help her; I have to stop Justin. I ease myself along the room, my hands on the walls, grabbing onto any furniture that will help me. And then I hear him speak.

'What are you doing here?' Justin asks.

'Go home, Justin! I need time away from you.' I don't recognise the tone of Natasha's voice. She must be utterly devastated that Justin had an affair with Abi.

'Are you here with Grace?' he asks.

Natasha doesn't answer the question. Instead she hisses, 'You promised me that no one would find out. How dare you humiliate me like this! Everything I have done is for you. To clear up your mess. To save our family. I am doing this for you.'

'You've done what?' Justin asks.

And then the door closes with a gentle thud and I can't hear any more.

I stare at the closed door in absolute horror. What does

Natasha mean, that she has done this for Justin? Natasha is my friend. She's been my friend for decades. But why am I feeling so strange, so totally drunk and dizzy? I was normal less than half an hour ago. It doesn't make sense. But now isn't the time to think about me. I need to call the police. Something horrible is happening, and if my fears are right...

I lurch back across the room, trying to reach my bag, trying to get to my phone. My old M&S brown leather handbag is on the table, just behind Natasha's cream leather Gucci bag. It's her favourite one, given to her by Justin for her last birthday, worth nearly two grand apparently. As I lunge for my handbag, I knock Natasha's Gucci bag to the ground.

'Whoops!' I say out loud, and then it's me who is on the floor trying to pick up all of her belongings, stuffing them clumsily back into her Gucci bag. A box of pills has fallen underneath the table. I reach for it, about to put it back in her bag when I pause. It looks familiar. I hold the box close to my face as I try to focus on the words. And then, to my dismay, I read my name. These are my pills, the sleeping pills that Dr Sarah Perbody prescribed me just yesterday. Or was it today? Everything is jumbled in my head. I fumble to open the box and the strip falls out. Every little pill pocket is empty, yet I haven't taken a single one. What the hell?

And then it strikes me. Natasha, my friend, has drugged me. I think she put every one of those little pills into my vodka, and that's why I'm feeling so...

34

I crawl on hands and knees to the bathroom. I know how drink and drugs work. I have a short window of opportunity, and if I don't use it, maybe my life will be over, too. The bathroom floor feels cold and slippery, but I make it to the toilet. And now I need to make myself vomit. I don't know how I do it, but sticking my fingers down my throat really does work. Or perhaps it's a desperate survival instinct taking over that allows me to throw up again and again.

How much time do I have?

How quickly will I feel better?

I try so hard not to panic. If I keep a clear head, I can be alright. I will be alright. Are Justin and Natasha in this together? I try to recall what I heard Natasha say, how she was taking care of everything. Does that mean that she killed Abi and William? Are they now plotting together to get rid of me?

When I'm only bringing up bile, I wipe my mouth and crawl back into the bedroom. I need to look through her phone, find her emails. It's password-protected, but Ruth, Natasha and I know each other's phone logins. Natasha's is Becky's birthday. 1510. My fingers don't work properly, and it takes me several attempts before I can type the numbers correctly and get into her phone. I flick through to her emails, but I don't know what I'm looking for. An airline ticket perhaps? I can't see anything relevant. So then I click onto her calendar and scroll back to the date of Abi's death. And there I see it, the day before. Air France. I try to remember. Of course. Natasha was in Paris seeing her mother, and there was nothing unusual about that. She visits very regularly. Nevertheless, I click on her tickets app, and then I drop the phone. Natasha Bellover took an Air France flight from Paris to Cape Town the day before Abi died.

My friend Natasha killed my daughter.

My friend Natasha is a murderer.

And now I know for sure what she has done. She has drugged me, and I suppose I'll be next, and everyone will say, *Poor Grace, she couldn't cope after the death of her daughter. She drank herself into oblivion. She burned her house down. She was hallucinating that someone was out to get her. She took an overdose of sleeping pills.*

But no. It cannot play out like that. Ella needs me and I need Ella. I stand up, slowly and carefully, holding onto the back of the chair that my friend was sitting on only a few minutes ago. The dizziness has lessened. I drink straight from the lemonade bottle, hoping to dilute any of the drugs that may still be fizzing inside me. I know I need to get out. Now.

I grab my handbag, which I left on the end of my bed, and, clutching the room key, I peer through the peephole in the door. But I can't see much, just straight in front of the door, and there is no one there. I ease the door open, carefully and quietly, grateful that it doesn't squeak. Holding my breath, I pull it fully open and gingerly look into the corridor, left and then right. It is empty and there is total silence. I try to recall which direction we arrived from; where is the lift?

I close the door as silently as I can behind me, which, due to the clunky locking mechanism typical of hotel doors, sounds deafening in the tranquility of the hotel. I walk soundlessly along the corridor, grateful for the industrial carpet underfoot, and then I arrive at the lift. With trembling hands, I take my phone from my bag and dial 999. But I don't have time to talk.

To my horror, I see that the lift is moving. The red illuminated numbers flash up, one after the other, and the lift is on its way up. Floor one. Floor two.

I need to get out of here, now. Shoving the phone back into my bag, I turn my head, looking frantically for the fire exit signs. There must be a staircase here. My heart sounds as if it's going to beat straight out of my chest, and my breath is coming out shallow and fast. There. To the right of the lift, there is a door. I grab it and haul myself through and, just as the lift pings to announce its arrival on the third floor, the door closes. I don't think my legs are going to be able to support me. They feel so weak that I have to grab onto the stair rail just to stay upright.

But I haven't got time to waste. My legs must support me. They need to get me downstairs and away from Justin and Natasha. I hold my breath as I tiptoe down the stairs. The stairs are made from concrete, and my trainers make a squelching noise with every step. How many steps are there to the ground? I must go carefully. I can't slip. Not now.

And then I hear the opening of a door above me.

'Grace.'

I freeze.

'Grace, where are you going?'

I turn to look up at her. She is walking down the stairs towards me.

'Grace, you need to go back to the room, now. Don't go downstairs. Justin is in the lobby looking for you. It's not safe. Come back to the room with me. We can lock the door so he can't get in.'

I don't move. I know my eyes are open wide with terror. Who is this woman that I thought I knew and loved? Why did I think she had lovely pale blue eyes? They are steely, hard, and her expression is a chilling, dispassionate stare.

'Don't,' I say in a whisper.

'What?' Natasha tilts her head to one side. 'Stop being silly, Grace. You need to get back to the room. For God's sake, I've only got your best interests at heart.'

She is just a few steps above me as she extends her left hand.

'You did it, didn't you?' I say, gripping the handrail.

'Did what? Come on! If Justin finds you, he'll kill you. You need to trust me. Hurry up and go back to the room!'

'Natasha, it's you, isn't it?'

Her face hardens again. 'It's me, what?'

'You killed Abi and William and set my house on fire. And you nearly drove into me and did your damnedest to try to scare me. I know you did it all.'

'Don't be so bloody stupid.'

'Just tell me,' I say, in a desperate, hoarse voice.

And then she changes; in that split second, she morphs from the Natasha I thought I knew into a woman all-consumed by rage.

'You're a bloody fool, Grace. Is this what you really want?' She shakes her head. 'Oh, Grace.' She throws me a look of contempt, her upper lip curling in a sneer. 'You give me no choice now. Absolutely no choice.'

'So you're going to kill me, in the way you killed Abi and William. But why? Why do you want to hurt me, to kill me?'

'Because you are going to ruin my life. Why should my marriage and my life be destroyed because of your tart of a daughter? That's all she was! A whore. And then when she fell pregnant and threatened to destroy Justin's career, our marriage and everything that we have spent the last twenty years creating, how could I stand back and let that happen? You would have done the same if the shoe had been on the other foot.'

I shake my head. 'No. No. I would never have done that. Never.'

Natasha laughs a piercing, bitter laugh that sickens me. 'When I explained to Justin how much we would all lose by his sordid little affair, he understood the error of his ways and agreed not to go to Cape Town. He made one mistake, being led on by that little tart, and all I was doing was trying to make things right.'

'So you went to Cape Town instead?' I whisper, shock causing my whole body to tremble.

'I did what had to be done, Grace. I'm sorry it was your daughter, but I had no choice.'

I hear Abi's voice screaming in my head, *no, no, no!* My stomach is churning and another wave of nausea passes through me. I swallow bile.

'Did you kill William as well?'

'Ah, Dr Jennings. He was too clever by half, wasn't he? He asked for it, with his noseying around and probing into other people's business. And so disgusting, paying young girls for sex when he was a highfalutin psychiatrist. Such a hypocrite.'

'But why did you burn down my house?' I am shaking from head to toe and I have to concentrate on staying upright.

'You don't get it, do you? All you needed to do was stop that incessant investigating into Abi's life. I wanted to scare you, to get you to stop. Believe it or not, I love you, Grace. You and Ruth are the sisters I never had.' She shakes her head as if trying to dislodge her feelings. 'But you leave me no choice. What a shame. You have pushed me into a corner, so you're going to have to die too.'

And then from the step above me, she kicks out hard with her right foot, jamming her ankle boot into my left shin. The pain is excruciating, but my right hand is clutching the stair rail, limpet-like. I must not let go. My handbag slips off my left shoulder, and the bag falls to the ground, bouncing from one step to the next until it comes to a halt a few steps down.

Natasha takes a step towards me so that we are level, both standing on the same narrow concrete step. I glance over the rail and into the stairwell below. We're at least four flights up, and if I topple over the rail, there is no chance of survival.

But where is Justin? Surely he must realise what is happening? Why isn't he here to stop Natasha?

'Justin!'

'You think my husband is going to save you?' Natasha's laugh curdles inside me, bringing an acerbic realization that either she has killed him too, or he is leaving me to my fate at the hands of his murderess wife.

And then her strong, bony fingers are around my neck, squeezing tighter and tighter, and her breath is hot on my face. I try to scream, but no sound comes out. I keep hold of the stair rail with my left hand and use my right hand to try to loosen her grasp, but it's too tight. I can't breathe. I must breathe. She's surprisingly strong for such a slender woman. I bring up my right knee, catching her hard in the groin, and she grunts and releases her grip. For a split second, I think I have the upper hand and I kick her again, but she is quicker than me and darts back up one step.

We stare at each other, both of our breaths coming short and fast.

'Poor Grace, who will be found at the bottom of the stairs of a third-rate hotel. Poor Grace, who never got over the death of her daughter. Poor Grace, who is so drunk and drugged up, she has died too. No one will be in the slightest bit surprised when the hotel cleaners find you smashed up and dead on that concrete floor tomorrow morning.'

'Don't!' I say, but she ignores me. She shoves the palm of her hand into my chest, but although I stumble, my left leg slipping down one step, I am gripping the rail too tightly to fall.

I need to get away from her, to run down the stairs. I have a split second. Releasing my grip of the rail, I race down two steps, three steps. But it's no good. I am too slow; the drugs she fed me make me clumsy. She grabs the neck of my T-shirt and jumper, yanking me back towards her. I jab my right elbow backwards, and now once again, we're on the same step. Her fingers are curled up into a fist and she jams it towards my face, but I refuse to let her kill me. I pull my face away and scream, 'No!' She catches me on the side of my jaw, and my head bangs against the wall. I see stars in front of my eyes, and in that second, I realise that I'm not strong enough. There are too many drugs in my body; I am too unfit, simply too tired to go on. Natasha is so much stronger than me. I am going to die.

But as I see her fist coming towards me yet again, I hear Ella's voice in my head. 'Fight, Mum! You've got to fight for me!'

So I spit at her. It catches her in the right eye, and immediately I bring my fist up and jam it into her nose.

'Bitch!' she screams, taking a step downwards. But I have bought myself a moment. As the blood pours from her nose, she wipes her eye. I am on the step above her, so I push her hard. She stumbles down one step, but then she lurches upwards and grabs my right leg, forcing my knee to buckle, and I slip, jamming my coccyx on the sharp edge of the concrete step. I gasp. Natasha grabs my right foot and pulls me down one step, two steps. There is hatred in her blue eyes and blood dripping from her nose. I try to get up, but she is leering over me, her fist coming back down towards me. I can't let her. I just can't.

I kick out, ignoring the searing pain through my back and leg, and jam my foot into her stomach. She takes another step downwards, but she doesn't see my handbag. She stumbles and loses her footing, her knees slamming into the concrete step. She releases her grip of my foot.

It's as if it happens in slow motion. From my sitting position, I cling onto the stair rail once again and kick her as hard as I can, catching her chin so her head jars backwards, her teeth slamming together. I hear a loud, piercing scream and can't tell if it's coming from Natasha or me or perhaps our voices fuse into one terrible yell. But then we're not together. She falls, a tangle of arms and legs tumbling down several steps until she reaches the landing, at least eight steps below. Her head crashes back against the concrete step with a horrible thud. And then she is still.

For several long moments, I stay here, sitting on this cold step, staring at the immobile woman I thought was my friend. She looks like she's dead, lying there like a statue, her eyes closed, blood puddling on the narrow landing. But how do I know if she's really dead? Natasha has proven how clever she is. If I tiptoe towards her, to check for a pulse, she might spring back to life. And then it will be me who is tumbling to her death.

And so I stay there, immobile for many long minutes.

THE DOOR OPENS ABOVE ME. I hear heavy footsteps, but it is impossible for me to move.

Justin puts his arms around me. 'You're safe now, Grace. I've called the police.' But even as I stay there, shivering in his arms, I don't feel safe. This man repulses me.

'Go away,' I whisper. And he does. He releases his grip and stands up. As he looks at me, there are tears in his eyes. Then he walks down one step after another until he is level with his wife, and he crouches down, stroking her hair over and over again, tears of grief splashing on her pale cheeks.

When the police come and the ambulance men take Natasha away, I am mute. It's as if the horrors have shut down my brain. But Justin speaks so calmly as he explains everything that has happened. He tells them how Natasha found out that

Abi was having his baby; how he knew the affair was wrong, but somehow it was also so right; how Natasha was surprisingly calm when she found out, saying that she loved him and questioning why he was willing to lose everything – their family, his job, his status in society, for a young girl who didn't know her own mind. And Natasha managed to persuade Justin not to go to Cape Town to be with Abi. She said she would forgive him, but only if he walked away from Abi once and for all. So he did. He walked away from Abi, but he had no idea that Natasha had gone to Cape Town instead of him; he had no idea that his wife was capable of murder, or that Abi would die at the hands of a monster – a monster who turned out to be his wife. Justin says that he only found out what Natasha did this evening.

He turns to me and says, 'I'm so sorry, Grace.'

THE POLICE TOOK him away and questioned him for hours and hours. I presume they thought he was an accessory to murder, but ultimately there was nothing to suggest that Justin knew what Natasha had done. It seems that she acted all alone.

And the sugar daddies – well, they were a diversion.

Kungawo Nkosi, the South African man accused of Abi's murder, was exonerated and released, only to be returned to prison three days later, charged with dealing drugs.

Natasha clung on to life for several weeks in a vegetative state, but then her organs began to close down, just as her brain had done on the night she tried to kill me. They say there was a funeral for her, but no one I know attended it. Even Becky didn't go.

35

ONE YEAR LATER

'Are you coming, Mum?' Ella floats into my bedroom, looking ethereal and beautiful in a long tiered white skirt and an apricot-coloured T-shirt. I glance around this charming room, with the muslin curtains wafting in the breeze and the pillows piled high on the last bed that Abi slept in.

'I'm ready,' I say, clutching the wooden box.

Becky, Ethan and Ella are standing in Karolyn's kitchen. I watch them as they laugh at something Karolyn says. She smiles at me as I walk in. I warmed to her when we 'met' for the first time over Skype, but now I know her in the flesh, there is an undeniable connection between us. I am certain that we will be friends for life, however different our paths have been.

'Shall we go?' I ask.

The three youngsters look up at me. I know how difficult this will be for them, and I am so proud that they have coped.

Especially Becky, who only opened up to Ruth and me after her father was forced to resign from his position as headmaster and their big house was put up for sale. There we were, thinking she had a happy upbringing, surrounded by wealth and security. How wrong we were. Natasha and Justin's relationship had never been an easy one, and Becky was on the receiving end of their angst a lot of the time.

And then there was Abi's relationship with Justin. I still shudder to think of it. I doubt I will ever understand how my daughter could have fallen for a man so much older than her, a married man, too. But I suppose I haven't exactly been a model mother. I did the best I could, but perhaps it simply wasn't enough. Becky had her suspicions about Abi's relationship with her father, but she buried those suspicions. I don't blame her. And she knew about Anya's Blog. Abi sent her a link to it shortly before she flew out to Cape Town. Fortunately, there weren't any raunchy videos. Natasha made that up when she was pretending to be Abi's ghost. After Natasha died, Becky showed the blog to Ella, who showed it to me. None of this was Becky's fault. But it does explain why she acted strangely towards me.

We walk towards the front door. It is intricately carved in a rich hardwood reclaimed from India. Ella turns around. 'Are you coming with us?' she asks Karolyn.

'No, love. This is something you must do, just the four of you. I'll have dinner ready for you when you return, and some of the best South African wine is chilling in the fridge. We will raise a toast to Abi.'

Ella nods and we walk out of the door.

THERE IS a chill to the air and the beach is quiet despite it being early evening. This is winter for the people of Cape Town, and not so very different from a bad summer in Sussex – wet and

chilly. And the strange thing is, I haven't felt unsafe or threatened at any point since our arrival into Cape Town airport. Yes,
there is distressing deprivation, and the endless tin shacks of
the shanty towns can't fail but shock us privileged westerners,
but the people exude a warmth and kindness that I simply
wasn't expecting.

Today, on the anniversary of Abi's death, the temperature
has been a warm 20 degrees and the sun has shone. We all
wear parkas this evening, as there is a bite to the air now, and
Becky is wearing a pink knitted beanie given to her by Abi. The
sea is unseasonably calm, lapping against the jagged rocks. We
have to walk down a short staircase of concrete steps and
through a tunnel under the railway line in order to get to the
beach. My heart thuds and my breath quickens as it always
does when I'm faced with concrete stairs, but Ella grasps my
hand and we walk side by side.

And then we are on the beach, our feet sinking into the
sand as we try to avoid getting tangled up in the massive brown
fronds of kelp that have been washed up by the waves. The sun
is setting to our right, painting the sky with streaks of pale
yellows and gentle oranges, silhouetting the mountains. In
front of us there are candy-pink-coloured clouds, and the sea is
sparkling in silvers and the palest of blues. A seagull squawks.

We all hold hands as we face the sea. I am on the left,
holding the casket, my right hand in Ella's. Becky is between
Ella and Ethan. They are no longer dating, the stress of the past
year being too much for fledgling romance, but they are still
great friends. It wouldn't surprise me if they ended up together
one day. But for now, we are here to say goodbye to my beautiful eldest daughter.

'You go first, Mum,' Ella says.

I nod. 'My beautiful girl, I will miss you every single day. I
am sorry that the people you should have been able to trust
betrayed you so badly. Things will never be the same and the

world will never shine as brightly without you in it. So many people loved you, but no one more than your dad, your sister and me. My promise is that I will never drink or smoke again, and I will move on with my life.'

'I'll go next,' Ella says. I squeeze her hand.

'Abi, I was so lucky to have you as my big sister. You were hardworking, clever, beautiful and funny, and those are big shoes to fill. My promise is that I'll try my best. I love you, sis.' Ella's voice catches and she bites her lower lip.

We are quiet as we wait for Becky to speak.

'I don't suppose I'll ever forgive myself, and I'll never forgive my parents for what they did to you. They knew you were a sister to me, and I wish I could have protected you. Your mum asked if she could adopt me, what with my mum being dead and Dad in prison for covering up what Mum did, and I said yes. It's strange to be adopted at the age of twenty, but your mum is what a true mother should be, and I'm so grateful to be given another chance. I'm changing my surname by deed poll, so now I really am your sister. I'm Becky Woods. And I'm at college now, kind of following your footsteps. I want to be a policewoman and help make the world a better place. That's my promise, and I think you'd approve of that.'

Ella leans over and gives Becky a kiss on the cheek.

Ethan is last to speak. 'Abi, I'm speaking on behalf of all of your friends, from school, home and uni. You were a bright spark in all of our lives and you will be missed forever. I promise never to forget you. I'm at uni now, and I want to work in the charity sector. I guess we've all had to grow up really fast, but perhaps that's a good thing. Bye, Abi.'

We are all silent, gazing out to the sea. The sun has sunk behind the mountains and the air is chilly. I let go of Ella's hand.

'Shall we?' I ask.

They nod. We walk forwards towards the edge of the sea

and I open the wooden casket. I throw the contents into the air, and the particles of love that were Abi are carried by the wind into the night sky. The moon is fat and round and moving quickly upwards, behind the mountains to the left of us. A bird flies across its face, white feathers catching the light. It could be a seagull, but I like to think it's a dove.

A LETTER FROM MIRANDA

Thank you for reading The Arrangement.

A good friend asked me why I write psychological thrillers and how I come up with the ideas. I'm going to let you into a secret! It's like therapy for me; a way to confront and articulate my greatest fears. And there is nothing more terrifying than the thought of one's children coming to harm. This wasn't an easy book to write and it certainly took me on a roller-coaster of emotions.

I didn't have any knowledge of the world of Sugar Babies before starting this novel and gathered information from online sources and blogs. I'm blessed to have wonderful friends and family who I call upon to seek their expert advice. In particular, I would like to thank Penny Lines, Samantha Scott, Glen James-Miller, Stephen James-Miller and Becca Macauley. I'm so grateful for your help and of course all mistakes are mine.

I am dedicating this book to my cousin, Chris Silverston. Even though we are first cousins, Chris and I only met for the first time eleven years ago. Since then she has become like an older sister and despite the distance, she has been my greatest supporter during the ups and down of the past decade. It's thanks to her that I fell in love with South Africa. I just hope the residents of the charming coastal town of Kalk Bay will forgive me for setting a murder on their stunning beach! If you're lucky enough to visit Cape Town, go to Kalk Bay. It's full of quirky shops, an independent bookshop, outstanding restaurants, a stunning harbour with resident seals and the views are breath-taking.

This book, and my previous novels, wouldn't exist without Brian Lynch, Garret Ryan and the team at Inkubator Books. I am so lucky to be published by such a forward thinking and supportive publisher. I can't thank them enough.

Lastly but most importantly, thank *you* for reading my books. Without you and the reviews left on Amazon and GoodReads, I wouldn't be living my dream life as a full-time author. Reviews help other people discover my novels, so if you could spend a moment writing an honest review, no matter how short it is, I would be massively grateful.

My warmest wishes,

Miranda

www.mirandarijks.com

ALSO BY MIRANDA RIJKS

Published by Inkubator Books
www.inkubatorbooks.com

Copyright © 2020 by Miranda Rijks

Miranda Rijks has asserted her right to be identified as the
author of this work.

THE ARRANGEMENT is a work of fiction. People, places,
events, and situations are the product of the author's
imagination. Any resemblance to actual persons, living or dead
is entirely coincidental.

No part of this book may be reproduced, stored in any retrieval
system, or transmitted by any means without the prior written
permission of the publisher.